IN THE COMPANY OF
SHERLOCK HOLMES

STORIES INSPIRED
by the HOLMES CANON

EDITED BY LAURIE R. KING
AND LESLIE S. KLINGER

PEGASUS CRIME

NEW YORK LONDON

IN THE COMPANY OF SHERLOCK HOLMES

Pegasus Books LLC
80 Broad Street, 5th Floor
New York, NY 10004

First Pegasus Books paperback edition December 2015
First Pegasus Books cloth edition November 2014

Interior design by Maria Fernandez

Library of Congress Cataloging-in-Publication Data is available.

ISBN: 978-1-60598-917-4

10 9 8 7 6 5 4 3 2 1

Printed in the United States of America
Distributed by W. W. Norton & Company

To Sir Arthur Conan Doyle: Steel true, blade straight

CONTENTS

IN THE COMPANY OF SHERLOCK HOLMES

AN INTRODUCTION

So who is this Holmes fellow, anyway? The world's most perfect observing and reasoning machine, yet his method seems to depend heavily on nicotine-fuelled flights of imagination. A bare-knuckle and martial-arts fighter, who also claims to be the laziest thing in shoe leather. A lethargic amateur actor with a drug problem, yet a man capable of extreme physical exertions. A solitary misanthrope—who has two friends (doctor and housekeeper) so devoted they would lay down their lives for him.

A solver of mysteries, who is a mystery himself.

Holmes as an archetype—the word means "original model"—is of one of the defining images of the past 150 years, a variation on Jung's "artist-scientist" figure. The world did not know what it lacked until Conan Doyle showed us—but then, stand back, for when an archetype comes to life, he is, in the terminology of the new millennium, a *meme*.

The meme is a contagious artifact—image, idea, phrase, behavior—that spreads like a virus. And like any other virus, be it biological or computer-based, it grows, reproduces, mutates—and above all, affects its host. And as a virus holds a world of genetic information in its DNA, a viral meme can carry a lot of meaning on its narrow shoulders.

Variations on the theme of Holmes have been played ever since the man first saw print. Some have been whimsical, others deadly serious; some have even taught us something about ourselves. For Sherlock Holmes is both us, and a super-hero, armed not with greater-than-human powers, but with wits, experience, a small community of dependable friends, and the occasional singlestick or riding crop. Like the artist-scientist, Holmes takes a mass of cold, unrelated, and inert fact, shapes it between his narrow, nicotine-stained hands, and then electrifies it—and us—with a bolt of inspiration.

Come to think of it, perhaps we should envision him, not as an archetype, but as a golem, a mud figure brought to life by human need.

In any event, Sherlock Holmes shows no sign of flagging in this new era. A century and a quarter after the world was greeted by his gleeful cry at a laboratory discovery, men and women still find Holmes the ideal vessel to carry a variety of stories, aspirations, reflections.

The current volume finds another group of those restless minds, men and women who look for companionship on the road, and gleefully find themselves . . . in the company of Sherlock Holmes.

⊰◈⊱

This book took an amazing journey to end up in your hands. It began when Les was asked to assemble a panel on Sherlock Holmes (no surprise there) for Left Coast Crime, a conference held in 2010 in Los Angeles. He agreed, chose Laurie King for the panel, and then asked for Jan Burke, Lee Child, and Michael Connelly. "But those are the guests of honor!" he was told. He knew that, but he also knew that they were all fans of the Sherlock Holmes canon. Our panel was a great hit. Jan, Lee, and Michael all chimed with erudite commentary on topics Sherlockian (usually after a preface of, "Well, I don't really know much about Sherlock Holmes . . .")

From this panel sprang the idea of a book. We put it together in 2011—*A Study in Sherlock*—and were delighted at how many friends wanted to play "The Game," creating stories inspired by the canon. Others said they'd love to but had other deadlines, and so the idea of a second volume was conceived before the first was published.

During the preparation of that first volume, the Conan Doyle Estate—collateral relatives of Sir Arthur, who own the U.S. copyrights to the ten Sherlock Holmes stories published after 1922—asserted that we had to obtain their permission to use the characters of Holmes and Watson in new stories. We disagreed, but the publisher chose to simplify matters by paying for permission.

Meanwhile, the world of Sherlock Holmes got bigger. *Sherlock Holmes: A Game of Shadows* broke all box-office records for a film about Sherlock Holmes. (Les, a technical advisor, takes full credit for its success.) *Sherlock*, starring Benedict Cumberbatch and Martin Freeman, set records in England and America for viewing audiences and brought a new generation of readers into the Sherlock Holmes fold. Almost simultaneously, *Elementary*, with Johnny Lee Miller and Lucy Liu, gave its leads the distinction of having appeared on-screen as Holmes and Watson more than any other actors in history.

In 2012, as we readied this volume for publication, the Conan Doyle Estate notified the publisher that if we did not obtain a license for the use of the characters of Holmes and Watson, the Estate would block distribution of the book. At that, the long-simmering dispute came to a head.

"Leslie Klinger v. The Conan Doyle Estate, Ltd" was filed in federal courts, and the Free Sherlock movement was born, seeking definitive judgment that the characters of Holmes and Watson were no longer protected by U.S. copyright law. The argument was: since fifty of the original Doyle stories *were* in the public domain (that is, free of copyright protection), the remaining ten—although retaining their copyright to original characters and situations—did not redefine the central characters of the stories, and thus, Holmes, Watson, and the others were free to be used in new ways.

The District Court agreed, as did the Seventh Circuit court of appeals. We made history, and Sherlock Holmes is "free." (Hardly *Jarndyce v.*

Jarndyce, although the case felt like that at times—we are eternally grateful for the patience of our long-delayed contributors! For details on the case, visit www.free-sherlock.com.) At long last, we were able to proceed with this collection of amazing stories by brilliant authors and artists, all of whom (well, other than the artists in our little Company) reveal here for the first time how they were "inspired by Sherlock Holmes."

We hope you agree that it was worth the wait.

Laurie R. King & Leslie S. Klinger

THE CROOKED MAN

by Michael Connelly

The address was at the top of Doheny beyond a guardhouse and swing gate that protected a community of mansions with price tags of ten million and up. It was where the city's royalty lived. Movie moguls and captains of industry, sitting on top of the mountain and looking down on all the rest. But sometimes all the gilding and guarding wasn't enough to protect one from the inside. Harry Bosch held his badge up to the man in the gray uniform at the guardhouse door and said nothing. He was expected.

"You know which one it is?" the guard asked.

"I'll find it," Bosch said.

The guardrail opened and Bosch drove on through.

"Going to be hard to miss," said his partner, Jerry Edgar.

Bosch proceeded past estates that sprawled across the southern ridge of the Santa Monica Mountains. Vast green lawns that had never accepted a weed because they didn't have to. He had never been in the Doheny Estates but the opulence was even more than he expected. Up here even the guesthouses had guesthouses. They passed one estate with a garage that had a row of eight doors for the owner's car collection.

They knew only the basics about the call out. A man—a studio man—was dead and a wife—a much younger wife—was on the premises.

Soon they came to a house where there were three patrol cars parked outside the driveway entrance. In front of them was a van from the coroner's office and in front of that was a car that looked like it belonged in the driveway rather than the street. It was a long, sleek Mercedes coupe the color of onyx. Bosch's battered black Ford looked like a mule next to a stallion.

Edgar noticed the incongruity as well and came up with an explanation.

"My guess, Harry? She's already lawyered up."

Bosch nodded.

"That will be just perfect."

Bosch parked in front of the Mercedes and they got out and headed back to the driveway, where a patrol officer stood next to the yellow tape strung between the stone lions on either side of the gray cobblestone drive. The officer wrote their names down on a crime scene attendance log.

Another officer stood outside the set of twelve-foot-high doors that gave entrance to the house. He opened one side for them.

"The sergeant's with the coroner's team in the library room to your right," the officer said. And then, as if unable to contain himself, he added, "Can you believe this place?"

He looked at Edgar as he asked the question. Both men were black and it was as though the officer thought only a fellow black man could appreciate the over the top wealth that was on display.

"Who actually has a library in their house?" Edgar answered.

He and Bosch moved into the house, stepping into an entry hall that rivaled the square footage of Bosch's entire house. Bosch looked to his right and saw the patrol sergeant who was in charge of the scene and who would soon transfer that command to Bosch as the lead on the homicide team.

Bosch and Edgar moved through a living room so large that it had two separately designed sections of furniture, each with its own piano and fireplace. An ornate serving table separated the two sides. Displayed on it was a collection of bottles containing amber liquids of various gradations and undoubtedly too high end for Bosch to identify.

"What is this?" Edgar asked. "One side for daytime and the other for night? This place is over the top."

Bosch didn't respond. Sergeant Bob Fitzgerald was waiting by the closed double doors on the other side of the room. The so-called library, Bosch assumed.

"What do you have, Nox?" he asked.

Fitzgerald's nickname was a study in police brevity. Everything was always reduced to acronyms or the shortest terms possible in the department. That went for nicknames as well. Bob Fitzgerald had originally been branded with the sobriquet Bobnoxious after his decidedly forward personality, especially when it came to female rookies. Over time that got trimmed down to simply Nox.

"We've got a James Barclay on the floor in here," Fitzgerald said. "He's CEO of Archway Studios. I should say *was* CEO. He's not looking so good right now. He's dead. And we've got his wife, a Nancy Devoy, sitting in a study on the other side of the house with her lawyer."

"What's she say happened?"

"She's not saying shit, Harry. Her lawyer ain't letting her talk. So we don't know what the hell happened yet. That's why they pay you the big bucks, right?"

"Right," Bosch said. "When did the lawyer get here?"

"Was already here when my guys responded to the nine-one-one. The lawyer's the one who made the call. He called it an accident, by the way. It doesn't look much like an accident, you ask me."

Bosch ignored Fitzgerald's detective work. No one was asking.

"What's her lawyer's name?"

"Klinger—perfect lawyer name, you ask me. I didn't get the first."

Bosch could not remember a lawyer named Klinger that he had any previous interaction with. It was likely that he was a family lawyer. People up this high on the hill didn't usually have criminal defense experts on the payroll.

"Okay, Nox."

He turned to his partner.

"Jerry, you go over there and start with her," he said. "See if the lawyer's willing to let her talk to an investigator. I'll check out the scene first and meet you over there."

"Sounds like a plan," Edgar said.

He turned and headed back across the double living rooms. Bosch looked back at Fitzgerald.

"You going to let me go in or do we stand here all day?"

Fitzgerald shrugged, then knocked once on the door and then opened it.

"And they call *me* Nox," he said as Bosch passed by.

Bosch entered the library to find a coroner's team along with a forensic criminalist and a photographer working around the body of a man sprawled on the floor near a brick fireplace. The dead man was fully clothed in blue jeans, a golf shirt, shoes and socks. Bosch recognized the deputy coroner and was immediately pleased. Art Doyle was one of the more thorough cutters in an office beleaguered by staff cutbacks and low morale. But more important than what he did in the autopsy suite was his work in the field. The guy was a crime scene artist, so good at interpreting the physical nuances of murder that for years he had been known by one name of distinction and respect. It was a sobriquet that could not be abbreviated or reduced in any way.

Equal to Doyle's interpretive skills was his willingness to share his findings and discuss possibilities with detectives on the scene. This was indeed rare. There were many deputy coroners, fearful of being wrong or of talking out of turn or of facing the wrath of a defense attorney in court, who wouldn't dare comment on a possible cause of death at the crime scene—even when looking at a body at the bottom of a swimming pool.

Doyle was manipulating the dead man's head, turning it right and left, using both of his gloved hands to hold it securely. He then moved his hands lower and palpated the neck. Bosch heard him comment to his investigator that rigor mortis had retreated. The investigator wrote a note on his clipboard.

Before moving in toward the body, Bosch decided to survey the surroundings. All four walls of the library were lined with bookcases floor to ceiling. The dark wood cases were ten feet high and a brass railing ran along the upper shelves with a ladder on wheels that could be slid into position to access books on the upper reaches. The cases were built around two windows on one wall and a set of French doors on an adjoining wall. One of the doors was open and there was glass from the window pane next to the door handle scattered across the dark oak floor. Outside the furthest trajectory of glass was a white stone the size of a potato. It was the instrument used to break through the glass.

Careful not to step on the broken shards, Bosch stepped out through the door without touching it and moved out into another vast yard that was perfectly manicured and featured a shimmering blue pool. He realized how quiet it was up here so far above the city. It was so silent it was eerie.

After a moment's reverie Bosch turned to go back inside and noticed the white stones used to create a border between the lawn and the strip of plantings that ran along the side of the house. He saw the gap where one of the stones had been taken to be used to break the glass on the door. Whoever had broken in hadn't had a plan. Grabbing the stone was improvisational.

Bosch stepped back through the open door and looked to see if Doyle had noticed him yet. He hadn't. But Bosch knew from experience with the deputy coroner that he should ask permission to approach the body. He pulled a pair of latex gloves out of the left pocket of his suit coat and put them on, snapping the rubber loudly in an effort to draw Doyle's attention.

It didn't work. Bosch cleared his throat and spoke up.

"Sherlock?"

Doyle finished his examination of the neck and looked up at Bosch.

"Ah, Harry. Come in to our little circle here. The game is afoot."

He smiled at his own conceit. Permission granted, Bosch walked over and squatted next to the body in a baseball catcher's stance. He placed one hand down on the floor to stop himself from losing balance and lurching forward. Only then did he see the deep gash on the left side of the dead man's forehand. And what he had thought from a distance was possibly a bad toupee was actually the victim's hair stained black with dried blood from the wound.

"You came in early today," Doyle said.

Bosch nodded.

"Always do," he said. "I like the squad room when it's empty. Before everybody starts coming in."

Doyle nodded.

"Must be hard to keep that routine these days," he said. "I mean, now that you leave a woman behind in your bed."

Bosch looked up from the dead man to Doyle. He controlled the urge to ask him how the hell he knew about Hannah. He looked back down at the body.

"Okay, so what have we got here, Doc?"

"We are looking at the obvious, Detective. The decedent exhibits only the laceration on the forehead. The wound is deep and examination reveals the weapon penetrated the frontal bone, exposing the brain. Untreated immediately, this would be a fatal event."

Bosch nodded as he reached into the right side pocket of his coat for his notebook.

"I saw you checking rigor. Anything on time of death yet?"

"We've done liver temperature and rigor confirms death last evening. I estimate between ten and midnight. We can try to narrow it down further after we take Mr. Barclay to the autopsy suite."

Bosch wrote it down.

"Can you give me an idea about the weapon?" he asked.

"I can point out to you that the tool set belonging to the fireplace behind me is missing the poker," Doyle said. "This specific tool is usually a combination of spear and barb so that burning wood can be poked, prodded, hooked and pulled."

Bosch looked over Doyle's shoulder at the iron stand next to the stone fireplace. It had individual forks for holding the tools—a spade, a broom, and a two-handled vice for gripping firewood. The fourth prong held no tool.

Bosch scanned the room and didn't see the poker anywhere evident.

"Anything you can tell me that I wouldn't have found on my own?" he asked.

Doyle frowned and adjusted his own position at the head of the body, revealing his infirmity. Doyle was close to seventy and scoliosis had bent his back over time. It was as curved as the Pacific Coast Highway and required him to walk with forearm crutches to maintain balance. Bosch always thought it must pain Doyle deeply to be betrayed by the very thing he had spent his life studying.

"I can tell you a lot, Detective," Doyle said. "Only you can determine if you would have made these discoveries on your own."

"I'm ready when you are."

"Very well. Something for you to note first."

Doyle leaned forward with two gloved hands and pressed down on the victim's chest and stomach area, then continued.

"When we evacuate the decedent's air passages we emit a distinctively chalky scent of almonds and oak."

Bosch was immediately confused. Doyle had just reported that the blow to the head was the likely cause of death.

"I don't follow," he said. "The scent of almonds? Are you saying he was poisoned, too?"

"No, not at all. I am saying if you retreat to the living room you will notice a collection of cognacs and brandies atop a Louis Fourteen giltwood center table."

"I saw the bottles, yeah. I wouldn't know a Louis Fourteen from a Louis C.K."

"Yes, I know this. Anyway, on the table, look for a bottle of tear drop design displayed either in or on an oaken shrine. I believe our victim ingested a quantity of Jenssen Arcana shortly before his death."

"And Jenssen Arcana is what?"

"It's a cognac, Detective. One of the finest in the world. One of the most concentrated, too. Aged ninety-eight years in French oak. Five thousand, five hundred dollars a bottle the last I checked."

Bosch stared at Doyle for a long moment and had to give in.

"So you are saying that you can tell what kind of brandy this guy was drinking by what you just burped out of his dead body?"

"Quite so, Detective."

"You've tasted this stuff at fifty-five hundred dollars a bottle?"

"Actually, no. I am told that a taste of Jenssen Arcana is a life changing experience but to this date I have not imbibed. On a public servant's salary I have only had the occasion to sample the aroma of the great cognacs— the Arcana included."

"So you've sniffed it."

"It is said that the olfactory experience related to cognac is indispensible to the pleasure derived. I should not forget the Arcana. I do have a predilection for fine cognac and I have categorized the scent of those I have been lucky enough to both imbibe and sniff, as you say."

Bosch looked down at the body for a moment.

"Well, I'm not sure what our knowing what he was drinking gets us, but okay, I'll take it, I guess."

"It means a lot, Detective. You savor Louis Fourteen. It's for very special occasion or—"

"Look at this place, Doc," Bosch interrupted, raising his arms as if to take in the opulence far beyond the walls of the library. "I don't think five grand a bottle would bankrupt this guy. Louis Fourteen could've been the house juice, for all we know."

"That could not be the case, Detective. Quantities of the fourteen are extremely limited. You must have wealth to afford a bottle, true, but one bottle may be all you ever get in a lifetime."

Bosch grudgingly saw his point.

"Okay, so what do you think it means?"

"I think it means that before his death, something happened in this house. Something bad."

Bosch nodded, even though Doyle's conclusion did not help him. Usually something bad happens before every murder. A guy getting drunk on five-hundred-buck-a-shot cognac was indicative of nothing.

"I assume you drew blood and you'll get me an alcohol content," he said.

"You'll have it the moment we have it," Doyle said. "We'll run it as soon as we get Mr. Barclay to Mission Road."

He was referring to the location near downtown where the coroner's office was located.

"Good," Bosch said. "So then let's move on. What else you got, Doc?"

"Next, I refer you to the decedent's extremities," Doyle said. "First the left hand."

Doyle lifted the left arm and hand and presented it to Bosch. He immediately noticed a slight discoloration on the points of all four knuckles.

"Bruising?" he asked.

"Correct," Doyle said. "Ante-mortem. The impact was very close to time of death. The blood vessels are damaged and just beginning to leak blood into the tissue. But the process was almost immediately halted when the heart stopped."

"So, signs of a struggle. We're looking for a killer who might have bruises from the punch."

"Not exactly, Detective."

Doyle manipulated the hand into a fist and then took a ruler and laid it across the knuckles. Its surface met the bruise point of every knuckle.

"What are you saying?" Bosch asked.

"I am saying that the bruise pattern indicates he punched a flat surface," Doyle replied. "It is rare that you find uniformity in bruising from a physical altercation. People are not flat surfaces."

Bosch drummed his pen on his notebook. He wasn't sure what the bruising report got him.

"Don't be impatient, Harry. Let's move to the lower extremities. The underside of the right foot in particular."

Bosch crab-walked down to the lower extremities of the body and looked at the bottom of the dead man's shoe. At first he saw nothing but upon leaning down further saw a tiny twinkle of reflection. He leaned down further and looked into the shoe's treads. He saw it again.

"What is that?"

"It's glass, Detective. I believe you will be able to match it to the array of glass on the floor by the door."

Bosch looked over at the French doors and the spread of glass on the floor.

"He walked on the glass . . . ," he said.

"He did indeed."

Bosch looked at the body for a moment and then stood up. Both of his knees cracked. He took a half step back to steady himself.

Doyle signaled his assistant and was helped up into a standing position. The assistant handed him his crutches and he slipped his arms through the forearm cuffs and leaned forward on the supports. He looked at Bosch, turning his head slightly as if trying to get a better angle on something.

"What?" Bosch said.

"I would not dismiss that as a symptom of aging," Doyle said quietly.

Bosch looked back at him.

"Dismiss what?"

"BPPV—you have it, Detective."

"Really. And what is BPPV?"

"Benign Paroxysmal Positional Vertigo. You needed to balance yourself both when you squatted down and when you got back up. How long has this been going on?"

Bosch was annoyed with the intrusion.

"I don't know. Look, I'm sixty years old and my balance isn't what it—"

"I repeat. It is not a symptom of aging. More often than not it is caused by an infection in the inner ear. My guess, since you listed both times to your right, that the problem is in your right ear. Would you like me to take a look at it? I have an otoscope with me."

"What, a thing you stick in dead people's ears? Thanks, but I'll pass."

"Then you should see your own doctor and have it checked. Soon."

"Okay, okay, I'll do that. Can we get back to the case now?"

"Of course."

Doyle pointed one of his aluminum poles toward the French doors and they moved across the room. They looked down at the glass as if the pieces were like tea leaves waiting to be read.

"So . . . ," Bosch began. "You're thinking he's the guy who came through the door?"

"The bruises on the knuckles suggest impact with a flat surface," Doyle reminded.

"You're thinking he was on the outside and he tried to break the glass with his fist at first."

"Exactly. Then the rock."

Doyle pointed his right pole at the rock.

"So punching plate glass like that, not smart," Bosch said.

"If he broke through he would have torn his arm up to the elbow," Doyle said.

"He wasn't thinking clearly," Bosch said.

"He wasn't thinking at all," Doyle said.

"The cognac," Bosch said.

"He was possibly drunk," Doyle said.

"And angry—someone was in here he was angry at," Bosch said.

"Someone who had locked the doors to get away from him," Doyle said.

"He couldn't break the interior door down so he went outside," Bosch said. "He thought he could break the glass."

"Impact resistant glass," Doyle said. "He hurt his hand."

"So he picked up the rock," Bosch said.

"He broke the glass," Doyle said.

"He reached in and unlocked the door," Bosch said.

"And he came in," Doyle said.

They had spoken quickly, brainstorming and filling in the story as if joined in a single thought process.

Now Bosch moved away from the door and back toward the body. He looked down upon James Barclay. His eyes were open, frozen in surprise.

"Whoever was in here was ready for him," he said.

"Quite so," Doyle said.

"She probably had the lights out," Bosch said. "And she hit him with the poker as he moved into the room."

"She?" Doyle asked.

"Percentages," Bosch said. "Most homicides in the home are the result of domestic disputes."

"Elementary," Doyle said.

"Don't start with that shit," Bosch said.

He looked around the room. He saw nothing else suspicious.

"Now we just need to find the poker," he said. "She left him here all night. She could have driven it out to the Pacific in all of that time."

"Or it could have never left the house," Doyle said.

Bosch looked at him. He knew Doyle knew something, or had surmised something.

"What?" he said. "Give."

With a half smile on his face, Doyle slid the rubber tip of his left crutch across the floor toward the shelves until it reached a line scratched in the floor. It was a perfect quarter of a circle.

"What would make a mark like that?" Doyle asked.

Bosch moved over and looked down.

"I don't know," he said. "What?"

Doyle toyed with him for five seconds but knew not to push it further.

"A door, perhaps?" he said.

Then Bosch understood. He looked at the shelves. This section was lined with old leather-bound tomes that looked as old as Doyle. Bosch stepped closer and studied the framing of the shelves. He saw nothing of suspicion. From behind him Doyle spoke.

"Doors that are not pulled open are often pushed open."

Bosch put his hand on the vertical support of the three-foot wide section he stood in front of. He pushed on the seemingly stationary edifice and the section moved in a half inch, engaging a spring-loaded release. He let go and the entire section came out a few inches and Bosch was then able to pull it open like a foot-thick door. As it swung outward, he heard it scrape slightly on the floor. The quarter circle.

A light switched on automatically revealing the secret room beyond. Bosch stepped in, discovering it to be nothing more than a closet. It was a windowless space of dimensions not much larger than an interrogation room or a single-cell accommodation at Men's Central Jail downtown. The room was crowded with boxes. Some were open, revealing their contents to be books waiting to be shelved or disposed of through donation or other means. There were a couple wooden boxes with wine logos branded on them.

"Well?" Doyle said from behind.

Bosch moved in. There was a musty smell to the space.

"It looks like it's just storage."

Bosch saw a black smear on the white wall above a stack of five boxes. It looked like it might be dried blood. He lifted the top box so he could get closer to it and he heard something heavy drop down behind. He leaned in closer and quickly started moving the boxes, creating a new stack in the middle of the space. When he pulled the last box away from the wall he was looking at a fireplace poker lying against the wall trim.

"Got it," he said.

Bosch backed out of the space and told the photographer to document the poker in its position. Once that was done Bosch went back into the small space to collect the iron tool. He picked it up by its middle, careful not to touch the handle or the pointer and barb, which appeared to be covered in dried blood and hair. He walked it out of the hidden room into the library where the criminalist put plastic evidence bags over both ends and secured them with snap ties.

"So, Detective," Doyle said, "do you have what you need?"

Bosch thought a moment and then nodded.

"I think so," he said.

"Is it murder?" Doyle asked.

Bosch took a moment before answering.

"I think it's looking like she could make a case for self-defense," he said. "But she's got to lay it out for me. If her attorney is smart he'll let her talk to me. We might be able to clean this whole thing up right here and now."

"Then good luck to you," Doyle said.

Bosch thanked him and headed toward the door.

"Remember, Detective Bosch," Doyle called after him.

Bosch turned back.

"Remember what?"

"Go see your doctor about that ear."

Doyle smiled and Bosch returned it.

"Will do," he said.

When Bosch got to the library door he paused as he considered something. He decided his desire to know outweighed his desire not to give Doyle his due. He once again turned back to the deputy coroner.

"Okay, how did you know?" he asked.

Doyle feigned ignorance.

"Know what?" he asked.

"That I left a woman behind in my bed this morning."

"Oh, that was easy. When you squatted next to the body, Detective, the cuffs of your pants came up. That revealed one black sock and one blue."

Bosch resisted the urge to confirm the report by looking at his ankles.

"So?" he said.

"Elementary," Doyle said. "It confirmed your early start. You dressed before dawn. It also confirmed that you dressed without turning on the bed lamp. A man would only do that if he wished not to disturb a sleeping partner."

Bosch nodded but then thought of something and pointed at Doyle.

"You said I left a woman in bed. How do you know it wasn't a man?"

Proud of himself, Bosch smiled. He had him.

But Doyle was undaunted.

"Detective, aside from previous knowledge that you are a father and formerly married to a person of the female gender, my olfactory skills are not related to the scent of cognac exclusively. I detected on you from the earliest stage of your arrival the lingering scent of white musk. I knew you had been with a woman. The socks merely confirmed it."

A glib smile played on Doyle's face.

"Any other questions, Detective?" he asked. "We need to get Mr. Barclay packed up and off to Mission Road."

"No, I'm good," Bosch said. "No more questions."

"Then good luck with the widow."

"Thank you, Sherlock."

Bosch turned from Doyle and finally left the room.

THE CURIOUS AFFAIR OF THE ITALIAN ART DEALER

by Sara Paretsky

My wife having been called to the bedside of the governess who had been almost a mother to her, I was spending some weeks in my old lodgings on Baker Street. My wife's departure to Exeter, where her governess now resided, coincided with my own desire to spend time with my old friend and flatmate, Mr. Sherlock Holmes. On the one recent occasion when we had persuaded him to dine with us, I had seen that Holmes had fallen into that state of nervous irritability he was subject to when no case or other intellectual pursuit occupied his mind.

As was typical of him on such occasions, he screeched away on his violin at all hours. I found the sound painful enough, but the occupants of the flat above threatened an action at law if he didn't desist between the hours of two and six a.m. "We know Mr. Holmes is a great genius who has often saved our monarch from acute embarrassment, but we must beg for a few hours repose," their solicitor explained. Whereupon my old friend took up his pernicious cocaine habit once again.

I pled both as a friend and a medical attendant, to no avail: Holmes hunched himself deep in his chair and muttered that he had not inflicted his company upon mine, that I had chosen to come uninvited, when I could have been in uxorious attendance on Mary in Exeter. At times like this, my friend often displayed a petulant jealousy of my wife, or perhaps of my preference for her company: upon our marriage he was wounded by our refusal to take lodgings across the landing from his own.

In an effort to rouse him from his stupor, I tried to draw Holmes's attention to crimes reported in the sensationalist press. The stabbing of a cabman in Fleet Street "was banal beyond bearing," while the theft of the Duchess of Hoovering's emerald tiara "would prove to be the work of a criminal housemaid." When later reports confirmed he was wrong in both cases—the Hoovering cadet, bitter at the privations of a youngest son, had sold the tiara to fund a disastrous trip to Monte Carlo, while the cabman turned out to have been a Russian spy trying to overhear secrets of a Hapsburg diplomat—Holmes sank deeper into his drugged stupor.

I could not neglect my own practice, or perhaps I should say, my other patients, who were usually more willing to follow my advice than was my brilliant but capricious friend. It was at the start of the third week of my stay with him that I was summoned to the Gloucester Hotel to attend a man who had been violently assaulted in the night.

The hotel manager, a Mr. Gryce, was more anxious that my arrival should be kept a secret than he was for the welfare of his battered guest. "An Italian prince and a French countess are among our current guests," he said as he led me up to the second floor by way of the servants' staircase. "Any scandal or fear that assaults are part of every day life at the Gloucester would be most detrimental to our business."

I turned around in the middle of the stairwell. "I hope your guests believe that your solicitude for their welfare would cause you to respect the medical man you brought in to examine them. If you can't take me up by the main stairs then I will return to my surgery, where a number of patients no doubt await me already."

Mr. Gryce hurriedly begged my pardon and took me along the red-carpeted hall to the main staircase, which was filled at this hour with ladies on their way down to the street to shop or meet friends for coffee. On the second floor, the wounded guest lay in a suite near the hotel's northeast corner, a secluded part of the building which afforded but a poor view, since the flats on Cassowary Road obscured all but the tallest trees in Hyde Park. A secondary stair led from this wing to the hotel mews.

My patient was a man perhaps in his mid-twenties. Despite his Italian name—Frances Fontana, visiting from Buffalo, New York—he was a fair man, probably attractive when not swathed in bandages.

The sufferer had been badly struck around the face and had significant cuts in his fingertips. I could make no sense of the wounds, nor of the man's story. Fontana claimed he had been sound asleep when he was awakened around three by the lighting of the gas lamp in the main entrance to his suite.

"I got out of bed and instantly called out, demanding who was there. No one answered, but my attacker, his face covered by a mask, rushed through the sitting room and struck me about the head, demanding all the while where 'it' was. I hit out as hard as I could, but the man was clothed and I was in my nightshirt; he trod on my foot, demanding 'it.'

"Finally, it transpired he wanted a small painting I had brought with me from America. Family legend ascribed it to Titian and I had wanted an opinion from Carrera's on Bond Street. My assailant ransacked my luggage, looking for it, and found it in a secret compartment in my trunk. We fought for it, but he was stronger than I, and as I say, clothed and shod. As soon as he had left, I raced to the ground floor, where they thought I was perfectly demented, but when they saw my wounds, the night man bathed and dressed them. I lodged a complaint, of course, for how did the man get into my room, if not through their carelessness in giving him a key?"

Mr. Gryce looked reproachfully at Fontana. "We did not, Mr. Fontana. You know we went into this very thoroughly with the night porter and the night manager both, and no one asked for a key to your suite last night. It's possible that you yourself failed to lock the door."

Fontana protested angrily, but I cut short his outburst by unwrapping the bandages and forcing him to sit while I examined his wounds. The one on his right cheekbone was the most severe: he seemed to have been struck with some heavy object, perhaps a truncheon. I bathed the wounds with peroxide, put on a salve that contained an opiate to relieve the worst of the pain, and looked at his fingers.

"How did you come to injure your fingers? I have found a glass fragment in one of them and they all seem to have been cut with glass. At first I thought perhaps you had grasped a razor in your attacker's hands."

"What difference does it make? Are you as insensible as this man Gryce? Am I to be catechized when instead I need medical attention? I suppose the glass over the picture broke in our struggle. It's highly likely, after all."

I forbore to argue, simply checking each digit with my magnifying glass to make sure I had removed any glass fragments. I anointed his fingers with the same salve used on his face and told him that within a day he would be able to dress and eat without pain, but that for the next twenty-four hours he would do well to avoid using his hands.

He seemed to accept this with a good enough grace, and said that his man, currently lodged in the servants' wing, would take care of his most urgent needs, and would sleep in a truckle bed the hotel was bringing up so that he need not fear a second intrusion.

"And no word of this should get to my sister, mind you," he added, as I restored my implements to the bag.

"Your sister?" I inquired. "Miss Fontana is also a guest in the hotel?"

"No. She is lodging with friends in Kensington. But she is likely to call, and I would have her believe I've gone to the country for a few days. It will alarm her greatly if word of this attack should reach her."

Mr. Gryce promised to do as he asked readily as did I, in case the sister should learn that a medical man had been called in to consult with her brother. "I foresee no complications," I said as I put on my hat and coat, "but should you need me, you may send word through Mr. Sherlock Holmes, whose guest I currently am." Holmes's name acted powerfully upon Fontana, as I confess I hoped it might. He said nothing, however, and I didn't press the matter further.

As Gryce and I left, I looked around the living room of the suite and saw the signs of struggle clearly enough: drawers removed from the bureau, cushions from the divan lying at cockeyed angles, and my patient's trunk, with the secret drawer smashed into splinters. Gryce interpreted my gaze as criticism and hastily promised that a chamber maid would be sent up to put matters to rights.

I returned to Baker Street that evening greatly fatigued, for my rounds that day had included a most difficult lying-in, where I barely outwitted the Angel of Death. I had all but forgotten my American patient, and I was startled to see him fully dressed, outside our lodgings, in argument with a beggar woman.

"Ah, there you are, Doctor. This wretched woman has followed me, I swear to heaven that she has been on my trail all the way from Hyde Park Corner. Begone, you harridan, or I'll send for a constable."

"Ah, you be a sly one, b'ain't you, Mister? Thinking to do a poor beggar woman out of her widow's mite, but there be no need to call for a lawman. I ain't a going to do you no harm, no sir."

I stepped closer, to order her away from my patient, but the odor rising from her many shawls and skirts was as thick as her country accent. I took Fontana by the arm, instead, and bustled him into our entryway.

On the way up the stairs I asked how he came to be so imprudent as to rise from his couch. He said my mentioning Holmes's name had made him think his best course was to place his situation in the eminent detective's hands. "The police sent a Mr. Whicher, but I didn't care for his manner, no, not one iota. He seemed to blame me for being the victim of a crime."

The eminent detective, sprawled languidly in the armchair, still in his stained dressing gown, didn't look any more prepossessing than the beggar woman outside our door. Nor was the smell any more propitiating, although in Holmes's case it rose from the chemicals he'd been playing with all day. The dull eye he turned on me as we entered turned to anger when he realized I had brought a guest.

Fontana seemed to find nothing odd in the consulting detective's dress or manner—perhaps he had been warned that the great genius was eccentric to a degree. He plunged without invitation into a pouring out of his woes. As he spoke, my friend's eyes shut, but not, as I'd feared, in a stupor, for he pressed his fingertips together as was his habit when he was concentrating intently on a narrative.

When Fontana finished, Holmes murmured, without opening his eyes, "And who knew that you were taking the painting from America to England with you?"

"No one," Fontana said.

"Not even your sister," Holmes said.

"Oh! Beatrice. Yes, of course she knew."

"Your father was a classical scholar," Holmes said.

"My father is a banker, sir, or at least was until a stroke deprived him of his faculties a year ago. It is my mother who has a great love of the Italian classics. But why is that relevant, and how did you know?"

"You are named for one of the great Renaissance poets, and your sister for the inamorata of another," Holmes said languidly, his eyes still shut. "But your accent surprises me: I hear it on the lips of graduates from Winchester college more than from Americans."

Fontana's lips tightened, but he said with a semblance of nonchalance that his mother, whose family hailed from Guilford, had caused him to be educated at Winchester.

"Yes, I thought as much," Holmes said. "I have composed a monograph on the accents of the different public colleges of England and I am seldom mistaken. But to return to the business at hand, had you in fact called at Carrera's?"

"I stopped at the gallery yesterday morning, but Signor Carrera was not in, and I had no wish to put such an important commission in the hands of an underling. I left my card and my direction and asked that he call on me, but, though I lay in bed all day today per Dr. Watson's instructions, he never arrived." Fontana's tone was angry. "The English are famous for their manners, but few of the people I have encountered seem to have any consideration whatsoever, whether the police or the hotel manager, or even a gallery owner who might be interested in a large commission."

Holmes pointed out that Signor Carrera was not himself English, but added, "Perhaps he was your nighttime assailant. If he had wrested the painting from you, then he would know there was no need to call on you to examine it."

Fontana's eyes brightened at the idea: his shoulders relaxed and the choler in his eyes faded.

"And your sister, Miss Beatrice Fontana, she agreed with your mission to get a proper valuation of the painting?"

Fontana shifted uneasily. "She saw no point in calling public attention to it, should it prove valuable, nor of disappointing our parents, should it prove not to be the work of the great Titian."

"And she is staying with friends in Kensington, you say? Did she cross the Atlantic with you?"

"Yes; it was her voyage that decided me on my own. My mother felt that Mrs. Som—that is, an old friend of hers—could introduce my sister into society, since my mother herself is tied up wholly in care for my father." Fontana then reiterated his plea that his sister not be told; her worries for their father were sufficient. She did not need to know that her brother had been assaulted and the family's valuable painting stolen.

Holmes sat up slightly and looked at me.

"My dear fellow, you are all in—I see you have attended a difficult lying-in today—but perhaps, since he is here, you might examine your patient's wounds and change the dressing."

I wondered how he had discerned my professional duties this afternoon, but knowing him as I do, assumed there was some aspect of my dress that was habitual with me on such cases. I unwrapped Fontana's bandages and was pleased to see that healing was already underway, judging by the deepening discoloration around the wounds, as well as the incipient scabbing. Holmes actually pushed himself from his armchair and looked on gravely as I bathed and anointed the injuries. While I rewrapped them in fresh bandages, my friend withdrew, and I heard the sound of water running into the bath—a welcome signal indeed!

I escorted Fontana to the street, but it took some time to hail a hackney cab. At length, I saw my patient safely bundled inside. I rather thought that the beggar who had accosted Fontana earlier was watching from a doorway at the corner, but as the nearness of Paddington Station makes Baker Street a popular spot for women of her ilk, I could not be certain in the dark streets.

By the time I returned upstairs, Holmes had finished bathing. For the first time in days he was dressed, and in clean linen. Mrs. Hudson was just in the act of laying a plate of grilled kidneys in front of him, a sort of compromise meal of breakfast and supper, with potatoes and a dressed salad. For me she had grilled a steak.

My friend ate with all the relish of a man deprived of nourishment for some weeks.

"A very pretty problem, Watson, very pretty indeed."

"What did you make of his story?" I asked.

"It was the painting that interested me," Holmes said. "That, and the fact that his wounds were self-inflicted."

"Self-inflicted?" I repeated. "That blow on his cheek very nearly shattered the bone."

"He's left-handed, as I noted when he opened his card case," Holmes remarked. "You observed, of course, how much more severe the blow to his right cheek was than to the left, and yet the placement of the blows was symmetrical."

He picked up a sock stuffed with rags and handed it to me, instructing me to strike myself in the face. I reluctantly did so. The sock struck in both cases just beneath the eye-socket. In my case, being right-handed, I felt the blow much more on the left than on the right side, and had to concede the point.

"And the glass in his fingertips? Did he do that to himself as well?"

"Ah, that's a most interesting point. I believe we have two calls to make, one on the Carrera Gallery in Bond Street, and the other to the home of Mrs. Alicia Someringforth in Cadogan Gardens, Kensington."

At my puzzled expression, Holmes held up his directory of London boroughs and street addresses. "There are seventeen households in Kensington with owners whose last names begin with 'Som,' but only one of sufficient size to admit of enough rooms to include a young lady making her society debut. And Mr. Neil Someringforth has a position in the Foreign Office, Undersecretary of State for Oriental Affairs. He is at present in Cairo, leaving his lady with enough time to visit any number of balls and ridottos."

Now that Holmes had recovered his spirit, and had food inside him, he was ready to act on the instant, to go first to Bond Street and then to the Someringforth home in Cadogan Gardens.

I grumbled to Holmes that the gallery would be closed at this hour, that not everyone had the luxury of sleeping all day and imagining that the world was ready to conduct business at night.

"My dear chap, you've been badgering me for weeks to get up, to be active. Don't urge me to my bed now. And besides, it's Thursday, the night that new shows open in Bond Street's galleries. Carrera will be there, with wine and nuts and a desire to be accommodating. But if the fatigues of the day are such that you wish to retire, I can safely handle this business on my own."

Of course I made no further demur, but changed my own soiled linen and prepared to set forth once again. At Bond Street, it was just as Holmes had foretold: a major new exhibit of paintings from France, works by the Impressionists who are all the rage there. I wasn't much taken with the blurry mess one named Monet had made of Waterloo Station, nor of a lady painter called Morisot, but Holmes studied the painting closely, until the gallery owner came over to us.

Carrera was a tall, muscular man, who looked as though he would be more at home on a sporting field than in a gallery, but he spoke fluently about Mlle. Morisot's use of light and color.

"I find these Impressionists' work disturbing," I said. "This painting of Waterloo—the trains look as insubstantial as the smoke rising from their engines."

"I confess," Holmes said, "that my client here, Professor Sammlung, is more interested in Renaissance art. We had been told that you might have recently acquired a Titian portrait, and would be grateful for the chance to view it."

I tried to compose my features to conform to a German intellectual with a taste for Renaissance portraiture.

"Titian?" Carrera held up his hands with a laugh. "No, no, I seldom deal in old paintings. They're outside both my expertise and my finances."

"*Ach,*" I said, "*aber* Herr Fontana, he spoke to me of his Titian that he wished to sell to you. You did not visit him to inspect it, Herr Carrera?"

Carrera stared at me with narrowed eyes, and said abruptly that he knew no one named Fontana, and that he had best return to other patrons who had more interest in modern painting.

A woman of middle-age, dressed in a richly figured silk, although cut without pretense to contemporary fashion, joined us in front of the Morisot painting. "I like this," she said forthrightly, in an American accent as plain as her high-necked costume. "She gets the woman's life just right, don't you think? The sense of fatigue, although perhaps neither of you two gentlemen has ever had occasion to look at domestic work from the female point of view."

Holmes and I muttered something disjoint, and the woman nodded in good humor. "Yes, I know, meddlesome middle-aged women are the devil, aren't we? But I will confess I was surprised to hear you were a German art collector—I imagined from your waistcoat and that eminently service- able pocket watch that you were a doctor."

"Come, madam," Holmes said, "a doctor who collects art is no rarity. My dear Sammlung, there's a second gallery we should visit before we dine." He bowed slightly to the woman; I clicked my heels, and we made good our escape.

We both laughed ruefully over the encounter in the cab. "A woman of such strong observational powers," Holmes said thoughtfully. "It's rare, rare indeed. I shouldn't like her as an adversary. But the gallery owner knows rather more than he's saying. He left us abruptly when you men- tioned Carrera's name, Herr Sammlung."

"He knows I'm not German," I said with some asperity. "If you will saddle me with preposterous identities, do so before I suddenly find myself switching from fluent English to halting German!"

Holmes merely said he would set one of his street Arabs to watch Car- rera's movements. "When he left us so abruptly, it wasn't to meet with other clients as he claimed, but to go into the little office in the back of the gallery. I think we can depend upon his visiting Fontana. I had best find Charlie before we go on to Kensington."

We swung down to the river, to the docks where the boys Holmes often used could be found, scavenging among the detritus that the Thames casts along her banks. Holmes gave a peculiar whistle, and after some moments, there came an answering whistle, and one of his street urchins—his Baker Street Irregulars—appeared. While our jarvey waited, most reluctant to keep his cab standing in such a dubious spot, Holmes gave the lad a shil- ling and told him where to go and who to watch for.

To the driver's relief, Holmes directed him next to Cadogan Gardens, a much more genteel location. We alighted at the corner of the gardens, where the street connects with Pavilion Road. To my astonishment, as Holmes paid the fare, the cab was hailed by none other than our client.

"Mr. Fontana," Holmes cried, "I thought you were surely in your room at the Gloucester. You have had too much exertion for one with your recent injuries."

Fontana stared at us angrily. "What I do is none of your business, after all, and it was essential that I call on my sister."

"I thought your object was to keep your sister in ignorance of your injuries," I said.

"It was," he said, "but the attack on me was in the evening paper. That damned ineffectual manager Gryce, I suppose, although you'd think he wouldn't want his hotel to be known as a place where guests' bedchambers can be invaded in the middle of the night."

He climbed into the cab and we heard him give the driver the Gloucester as his destination.

Holmes chuckled. "It was not Gryce but I who put that story about. I telegraphed a stop-press to the evening papers and both the *Times* and the *Examiner* picked it up."

"But why?" I demanded.

"If the man injured himself, he is covering some shameful secret. Or he is protecting someone else's secret. I hoped to prod him to action."

As we approached the house at 26 Cadogan Gardens, we saw one of the housemaids in the area, talking to a shabbily dressed woman. I pointed her out to Holmes, for I thought she might be the beggar who had accosted Fontana outside the Baker Street flat earlier this evening.

Holmes looked at her with keen interest, but when we came up to the house, we both realized she was merely a charwoman looking for rough work. She bore neither the filthy rags nor the malodor of the beggar woman, and on coming up to her I saw she was altogether younger and smaller than the woman I'd seen earlier.

"They told me as how you was down a hand here," we heard her say as we climbed the shallow steps to the front entrance, "And I got good references, sure I have. Clean the area stairs, empty slop buckets, nothing ain't beneath me."

I thought of the American woman we'd encountered at Carrera's and her comment on the French woman's painting, that it captured the fatigue women experience from their domestic labors. I wondered if I had ever considered the fatigues my own dear Mary subjected herself to in order to ensure my own domestic comfort, and found my thoughts so disquieting that I was glad when a manservant answered our ring.

My friend handed him a card. "Pray tell Mrs. Someringforth that Mr. Sherlock Holmes would like a word with Miss Fontana."

The servant looked at us doubtfully. "Mrs. Someringforth is dressing and Miss Fontana is indisposed."

"Ah," Holmes said. "That is sad news indeed. We are employed by Mr. Fontana, however. Dr. Watson here is Mr. Fontana's medical advisor, and if Miss Fontana's indisposition is related to her brother's recent visit, why Dr. Watson will be delighted to assist her, I'm sure."

I produced my own card, bowing assent, much relieved that I didn't have to impersonate a Russian serf or Sufi fire-walker to suit my friend's whimsy.

The man bowed slightly and left us on the doorstep while he went to consult his mistress. The ill breeding shown by not inviting two gentlemen into the house annoyed me, but caused Holmes to knit his brow. "Something is upsetting this household. Perhaps the fact that they're 'down a hand,' as the charwoman said. Or perhaps Miss Fontana is having an hysterical fit."

We hadn't long to wait, however, before we were invited to step into a salon on the first floor. We followed the man up a flight of carpeted steps into a small room where the newly hired charwoman was hastily building a fire.

"So Fontana was ushered up to his sister's room," Holmes observed, "not treated as a common visitor."

The manservant oversaw the charwoman's fire making, ensuring she cleared the hearth of any stray ashes or kindling, then bustled her out of the theater. Shortly after, Mrs. Someringforth appeared, dressed for the theater in a low-cut gown of gold silk. The diamond drops which hung from her ears were no more lustrous than her dark eyes; she held out both hands to Holmes and, with a delightful smile, begged his pardon for keeping him waiting.

"My maid has contracted the influenza, and the housemaid filling in for her is so fearful of making a mistake that she spends twice the necessary labor on the simple job of making a middle-aged woman appear half her age."

"If she has succeeded marvelously, it can only be because she had such excellent raw materials to work with." My friend bowed over her hands. "We had come to call on your houseguest, however, and beg you not to let us keep you from your evening engagement."

"Ah, poor Beatrice!" Mrs. Someringforth cried. "I fear it's from her that my maid acquired her illness; she dressed Beatrice last night, when the poor girl was already ill. I should never have permitted her to go with me to Lady Darnley's ball, but I thought she was merely fatigued; it wasn't until our return that I realized how feverish she was."

"She saw her brother when he called?"

Mrs. Someringforth shook her head so vigorously that the diamond drops swung like pendulums. "I wouldn't permit it. He is an excitable young man, and she is so very feverish that I feared a visit from him would only make her worse, especially since he presents such a horrible vision, swathed as he is in those bandages."

"If she is indeed seriously ill, as my friend, Dr. Watson, is already here, it would be prudent to allow him to—"

"Oh, please, Mr. Holmes, just because I am going to the theater you must not think me heartless or lacking in appropriate care for my charge. My own doctor saw Beatrice this morning. He left various draughts for her, as well as for my maid, and will return this evening. Now you must not let me detain you."

She rang the bell; the manservant must have been hovering nearby, for he came at once to usher us down the stairs, handing us our hats and coats so quickly that we barely had time to assume them before he had the front door open once again.

"They're expecting another visitor," was my friend's comment. "Or concealing something they don't want us to see."

We retreated to Pavilion Road, where Holmes flagged down a passing cab, instructing the jarvey to wait. While we watched 26 Cadogan

Gardens, the charwoman left the house by the rear door. She looked up at the cab, as if puzzled by why we stood there, and we shrank back in our seats so as not to be visible from the sidewalk. The woman hurried on up Pavilion Road toward Hyde Park.

After a few minutes more, Mrs. Someringforth's carriage pulled up in front of her house; a footman helped her inside and her carriage bowled past us, heading north. Holmes told the cabman to follow her, and she led us directly to the Siddons Theatre in the Strand. Holmes proposed following her into the theater, but I pled my long day and asked the cab to return me to Baker Street.

Back at my old lodgings, I fell instantly into a deep sleep, from which I was roused a little past one in the morning by Charlie, the lad Holmes had set to watch Carrera. He had banged on the street door until the noise finally roused Mrs. Hudson, who was much incensed by his visit.

"He shoved his way past me, the little wretch." She was panting from her efforts to catch the boy before he could make it to Holmes's door.

"Never mind that, missus," Charlie said. "Is Mr. Holmes about? There's been a terrible accident, to the swell that he set me to watch, beat up, he was, on his way from his shop to wherever he was next a-heading."

I came fully awake. "How is he? Where is he?"

"I whistled up my squad and they run for help, brung a constable, *which* took some doing, I can tell you that: *None of you boys is going to be making game of I,* he says to Freddie, and Freddie has to practically swear his soul to the devil before the constable come. I stayed close by till I saw him brung into some lady's house, and then come back here to tell it all to Mr. Holmes."

Just as I was saying that Holmes had not yet returned, we heard his step on the landing. Mrs. Hudson broke into further excuses and laments about the wretched lad, but Holmes cut her short and demanded a full accounting from Charlie.

"How many assailants?"

"Just two, but they was powerful strong, they was carrying clubs or somepin' like 'em. They swung 'em at me when I tried to stop 'em but when I whistled up my lads, then they took to their heels fast enough. We sent Freddie for the constable and Oliver went for to bring a doctor, who wouldn't come at all, not for *street rabble*, and we would have been done for except this lady come along. She says to the constable, just help him into my carriage and I'll see that he gets proper care."

I looked at Holmes, startled. "Good God! Was it Mrs. Someringforth?"

"It couldn't have been," Holmes said. "I sat in the box adjacent to hers; she stayed through the entire performance and then continued to a party at Stoggett House."

"The town home of the Duke of Hoovering," I said, trying to remember where I had recently heard the name.

"Yes. Her Grace's grand ball, one of the high points of the London season. I gained admittance through the servant's entrance by passing myself off as Lady Naseby's footman, and spent the evening watching our friend. At one point she disappeared up a rear staircase, but she reappeared within a few minutes. She can't have been the person who bore off Signor Carrera. Charlie, do you have any notion where they went?"

"'Course I do, governor, like you taught me I got up behind the lady's carriage and rode with them down to the river, over Chelsea way. Ann Lane they went to."

"Excellent." Holmes gave the boy a shilling for himself and a handful of sixpenny pieces for his "squad."

When the boy had gone, shooed down the stairs at high speed by the incensed Mrs. Hudson—"Giving him money like that will just encourage him, Mr. Holmes," she'd warned, to which my friend replied, "Precisely, my dear Mrs. Hudson,"—Holmes paced up and down restlessly.

"Who could have taken him in? A good Samaritan or an accomplice? It's past two now, but she's close to the river; she could smuggle him and a valuable painting away at a moment's notice."

He rummaged through the papers for the table of tides. "Yes, the tide will turn at four-oh-nine this morning. I think, yes, I think I'd best be on my way to Chelsea."

"But she rescued him from armed assailants, Holmes," I protested, by no means willing to leave my bed after a scant four hours' sleep.

"She came along mighty promptly, whoever she is. What if the assailants are in her pay, or vice versa, and by looking like a good Samaritan, she is able to worm the Titian away from him? This must be a painting of uncommon value." He rubbed his thin hands in front of the grate. "No, I must go to Ann Lane."

I retired to my room to change once more into day clothes, half sorry my friend had been roused from his torpor: I had forgotten how exhausting it was to keep up with his fevered pace.

We reached Ann Lane easily, the streets being virtually empty at such an hour. The cab deposited us on Cheyne Walk and I was glad I had chosen to accompany my friend, for the pre-dawn denizens of the Embankment were rats and human scavengers, some hunting for easy prey among homebound revelers.

The house where Charlie had seen Signor Carrera deposited was in the middle of a row of elegant townhouses and flats. On inspection of the entryway, Holmes saw that there were three flats in the building. We assumed our quarry was on the first floor, for it alone among the buildings on the street still had a light burning.

While Holmes and I stood on the doorstep, carrying on a soft conversation about the best vantage point for watching front and rear entrances, we were surprised by the opening of the front door. Holmes had his hand in his pocket, but it was a woman at the top of the stairs, carrying a lamp.

"No need to shoot me, Mr. Holmes, and no need to fuss about keeping an eye on things, either, for I can let you come in and see the poor beat-up signor for yourself."

It was the American woman we had encountered at Carrera's gallery last evening. I was too astonished for words, but cast a glance at Holmes. His face betrayed no surprise, but a muscle was quivering in his temple as we followed the lady into the house.

She led us up the stairs to the first floor and into a drawing room that overlooked Ann Lane. One of the blinds was half drawn at a lopsided angle and our hostess excused us while she went to straighten it. She untied a single black thread from the cord.

"I worried about someone surprising me here, Mr. Holmes, so I tied a length of embroidery silk to the blind and across the railing outside. Anyone passing through it would break it at once, the thread's so fragile, and the blind would come down to alert me."

She placidly wound the thread around a spool and placed it in an outsize workbasket.

"Madam," Holmes said, "You have the advantage of us. I am certainly Sherlock Holmes and this is Dr. Watson, but—"

"My land, how rude of me, Mr. Holmes. The day has been so filled with excitement that I've forgotten my manners. I'm Amelia Butterworth of Buffalo, New York, and how I came to be involved in your adventure is quite a long story. May I make you a pot of tea, or perhaps a whisky? I believe the friend whose flat this is has one or two decanters, although I myself don't indulge."

"Tea would be welcome," I confessed, although my friend, impatient for an explanation, looked at me in annoyance.

Miss Butterworth went to the doorway and called out and a young servant, very quiet and well behaved, appeared. She reported that Signor Carrera was sleeping comfortably, and that she felt able to leave him for five minutes to bring us some tea.

"Now, you'll be wanting to know who I am, and how I came by this."

She walked over to a pianoforte and opened a massive volume whose cover proclaimed, "The Ring Cycle, scored for Pianoforte and voices." This turned out not to be a musical score, but a hollowed-out book. Recessed within it lay a painting of a woman, whose auburn hair, floating around a swan-like neck, seemed so burnished, so real, that one wished to touch it.

The servant returned with a tray, which Miss Butterworth laid on a low table. "Yes, that's the Titian, or so we're led to believe," she said as she poured out cups for me and herself.

"Now, Beatrice Fontana, she's the daughter of my good friend Alice Ellerby, who married Mr. Fontana. I don't know what the man calling himself Frances Fontana may have told you, but Mr. Fontana is a banker. He used to be in a good way of business in Buffalo, but times have been bad with the recent slump. This painting has been in the Fontana family for centuries; they say the lady was his great-grandmother's great-grand-mother and a mistress of one of those doges in Venice.

"Be that as it may, Mr. Fontana wants to prove the picture's value, for if it is by this Titian, then it will pay for a dowry for Beatrice and keep Mrs. Fontana in comfort besides. So when we learned about this Signor

Carrera being a leading authority on Renaissance painters, Mr. Fontana decided he should come over and show the painting to the signor, get an opinion and a valuation. But he couldn't leave Buffalo with his business in such a bad way, so young Beatrice said she'd undertake the commission, and, as she's my goddaughter, and I enjoy foreign travel, I fixed to come with her.

"Another old friend of ours was quite a beauty when we were all young together. She married an English gentleman and her daughter is the lady you've been following tonight, Chloë Someringforth. Chloë is a bit older than Beatrice, maybe ten years, and quite the society lady. When she learned from Mrs. Fontana that Beatrice was coming over, she offered to provide her a room and an introduction to society. That sounded good to Alice—Beatrice's ma. I have another old friend here in London who's away this winter; she offered the use of this pleasant flat."

Holmes, impatient with all the chatter about who was married, who was whose friend, and so on, demanded coldly. "How came you to have the Titian?"

"Well, Mr. Holmes, I'm coming to that, and not a pretty story it makes, either. I got my goddaughter settled at Chloë Someringforth's, but when I went to call on her a few days later, I found her in some distress. It seems that while Mr. Someringforth has been serving his country in Egypt, his lady has been entertaining a young gentleman from the Hoovering family. And it didn't take a doctor's eye to notice that Chloë will be presenting her husband with an interesting event on his return."

I was so startled that I dropped my tea cup, but when I bent to try to mop up the spill, Miss Butterworth told me not to mind it, that she would get to it after we left. "I can clean the area stairs, empty slop buckets, nothing ain't beneath me," she said.

"Yes," she laughed, seeing our amazement, "I was the charwoman looking for to help out at Someringforth's last evening, and I'd best get back there soon to light the morning fires and try to remove my poor Beatrice from their clutches, for it really is no laughing matter. And your help will be most welcome, Mr. Holmes, most welcome indeed."

"So to make a long story short, Chloë Someringforth has been entertaining this young lord who stole his mama's jewels and lost all the money at gaming. And when he learned that my young Beatrice had in her hands a valuable painting, worthy maybe twice or three times the price his mama's emeralds had fetched, first he tried to sweet-talk her, and then he tried to rob her. And Chloë apparently helped him, along with her fancy-talking personal maid, or at least that's how I interpret the stories I got from the other servants last night.

"Beatrice managed to grab the painting away from this young lord and run out into the street. She somehow made it to Bond Street and got the picture in the hands of Signor Carrera. She had left the gallery and was in Oxford Street, trying to find a cab so she could get to me when Chloë came upon her. Beatrice cried out for help, but Chloë used all her charms to explain to the crowd that the young lady was unbalanced."

"How can you possibly know this, unless you were there yourself?" I demanded.

"Some of it I had from the signor, and the rest I put together from what the other housemaids were saying when I was scrubbing the pots tonight. Chloë's maid, she put out the story that my Beatrice was delirious with fever and that Chloë picked her up in Bond Street screaming her head off. They were beside themselves with the extra work, for the first housemaid was waiting on Chloë, while the lady's maid stayed in the bedroom making sure that Beatrice didn't get out, so they told me the whole story, not holding anything back. They said they didn't think Chloë's maid was sick, they'd had to bring her up a tray themselves and she looked in the pink of health, and this made them all crosser. Then that hoity-toity man who acts as the butler came in and warned them all against spreading tales if they wanted to get paid at the quarter, so I reckon he's in on the plot, too. But anyone could guess the rest, and my word, servants do talk among themselves, as you know from your own work in disguise, Mr. Holmes."

My friend sat rigid, furious at the condescension he perceived in Miss Butterworth's compliment.

"Meanwhile, this Lord Frances Hoovering, he'd cut himself badly on the glass that was covering the painting. He checked himself into this Gloucester Hotel under an assumed name: I found his bloody gloves wadded up in the gutter before the street sweepers came by. He went into his room, beat himself about the face and then blamed it all on some intruder."

"But why would he need to disguise himself?" I asked.

"Because he knew that Beatrice was taking the painting to Carrera's—she'd let that slip before she realized what a pair of villains he and Chloë are—and he couldn't afford for the signor or anyone else to recognize him. Covered up like that in bandages, no newspaperman would have known him. I went to the gallery first thing this morning but the signor was on his guard: Beatrice had warned him that someone might try to steal the painting and he didn't know me from Adam or from Eve. The best I could do was to keep track of everyone. First I dressed up as that foul-smelling beggar following the young lord around, and then back to the gallery I went to see who might show up for the opening. And then away to Chloë's to learn what I could of my poor young Beatrice.

"I saw there was no getting near her last night, not with the manservant standing guard outside the door, so I came back to see what the art dealer was up to. He was trying to take the painting to his own home, where he could put it in a safe, when the young lord and some hired bully jumped him. The signor had buttoned the painting inside his shirt, and before they could find it on his person, those young street Arabs of Mr. Holmes up and frightened off the attackers. I was lucky enough to follow the clamor and take him up and bring him back with me here. He finally was brought to believe that I meant him no harm.

"And now, Mr. Holmes, you get out of your sulks. Even Shakespeare didn't always write perfect plays, and even you can't be right but nine hundred ninety-nine times out of a thousand. You and Dr. Watson come along with me and we'll get Miss Beatrice out of her captivity fast enough."

We did as Miss Butterworth commanded. While she changed into her charwoman's costume, I visited the unfortunate gallery owner. He had been well-treated, his wounds properly bathed, and he was in a deep, drug-induced sleep.

As soon as I had finished my inspection of the dressings, I joined Holmes and Miss Butterworth and we set out for Cadogan Gardens, dismissing our cab on Sloan Street, for what charwoman can afford a hansom cab?

As soon as the under housemaid opened the area door, Miss Butterworth, and Holmes, disguised as a coal man, followed. I came in as a doctor, claiming that I had been sent for to treat the young lady with the dangerous fever.

We freed her quickly, and not a moment too soon, for the bonds with which she was restrained were taking a toll on her circulation, as was the lack of food and water on her general health. Miss Butterworth and I escorted her back to the American woman's borrowed flat, where I tended the young lady, until I had the satisfaction of seeing her color somewhat restored. Signor Carrera was much improved as well. Indeed, he was almost exuberant for he was able to confirm that the painting was, indeed, by Titian.

Holmes, in the meantime, visited the Foreign Office, where he cabled the difficult news of his wife's treachery to the Undersecretary for Oriental Affairs in Cairo. He had returned to Baker Street and was moodily playing at his violin when I let myself into the flat. At my attempt to report on Signor Carrera's assessment of the portrait, Holmes cut me off.

"I shall retire, Watson. I am clearly no longer fit for this work. If I had taken your first suggestion to heart, and looked into the theft of the Duchess of Hoovering's tiara, none of the rest of these events need have occurred. I should not have been shown up by an untrained middle-aged American woman."

Before I could do more than mumble some incoherent phrases, Mrs. Hudson came up the stairs in great excitement to announce the Duke and Duchess of Hoovering. The noble couple did not stay long, but they wished somehow to convey the shame they felt on having a cadet who had so disgraced their lineage and their country.

"We are sending him to Kenya to work on our coffee plantation there," her grace said, "in the hopes that having to work for his livelihood will give him a greater respect for the wealth that he squanders at play. In the meantime, Mr. Holmes, we hope you will undertake a most delicate mission for us in Budapest. As you may know, my sister is one of the Empress Elizabeth's ladies in waiting. My sister believes that someone is attempting to poison Her Majesty, but it is impossible for her to mount an investigation herself."

Holmes bowed and said he was, of course, her grace's servant to command.

My wife having telegraphed her imminent return to London, I stayed at Baker Street only long enough to help my friend pack his bag. I escorted him to Waterloo for the night train to Paris and returned to my own home. You may imagine how eager I was to put the sorry business of Lord Frances Hoovering and Chloë Someringforth out of my mind, although I was of course delighted that my friend's weakness for royalty had caused him to put down his violin and return to the chase. My one cause of unease was the sight of a beggar woman wrapped in numerous shawls boarding the third-class carriage of the Paris train. But surely, I thought as I sped through the streets, Miss Butterworth would not leave her young charge alone in London.

⊰◈⊱

NOTE: Amelia Butterworth was the amateur detective created by American crime novelist Anna Katherine Green (1846-1935). Miss Butterworth assisted and, indeed, outshone Green's investigative detective Ebenezer Gryce, whose methods of observation and deduction were similar to Holmes. The first Gryce novel, *The Leavenworth Case*, was published almost a decade before Sherlock Holmes first appeared. At the height of her popularity, Green's novels sold in the millions of copies; she was Woodrow Wilson's favorite popular writer.

THE MEMOIRS OF SILVER BLAZE

by Michael Sims

I shall not soon forget that awful night on the moors.

I was happy in King's Pyland. At the time of my story, I was in my fifth year. I had already been an eminent racer for years, but at heart I am still a romantic colt, and northern Dartmoor is wild and free. Not that Colonel Ross permitted me to race across the moors. No, I was too valuable for that. But I breathed the bold spirit of the moors from dawn to dusk. I loved the rugged hillsides, the towering granite tors, and the mists that often veiled it all for hours before the sun could make headway.

My mother taught me that a gentleman never boasts, and thus I face a quandary. I hope that mentioning a fact won't brand me a braggart; possibly you have been on the continent and failed to recognize the name Silver Blaze. (I have a white forehead but no other white markings except a mottled off foreleg.) Thistle was my dam and Isonomy my sire. Yes, *the*

Isonomy, who in 1878 won the Cambridgeshire at Newmarket, and the next year both the Ascot Gold Cup and the Manchester Plate, and the next the Ascot again. It was a legacy to trip even the most cocksure colt, yet I fancy I showed myself worthy. Foaled in 1885, I barely perspired in winning the Two Thousand Guinea Stake in my third year. At Ascot I won the St. James Place Stakes in a canter. At the time I speak of, I was the favorite in the Wessex Cup, with odds of three to one.

The Devonshire moor country round the stables is bleak and windy. About half a mile to the north there is a small cluster of villas which seem to be reserved as barns for lame and winded people. I have seen them seated in chairs on the lawn, their expressions reminding me of Black Simon after he broke his off foreleg in the St. Leger—wondering when they would come for him. Two miles distant across the moor lay Capleton, which a sly trainer named Silas Brown ran for Lord Backwater. Two miles to the west was the only sign of civilization: the village of Tavistock rising above the bracken and furze. Wild moors sprawled in every other direction, populated only by the occasional gypsies, who smell delightfully of pungent smoke but whose livestock is not of the highest class.

Mr. Straker, our groom, was a small man, light on his feet, who moved too quickly. He had been the colonel's jockey for five years. But one cannot remain a colt forever; he had put on weight and could no longer ride as before, so he became a trainer for the colonel, and had served in this job for seven years. He had a bitterness about him that he tried to hide from Colonel Ross. Apparently he succeeded. Sure in his views of the world, the colonel accepted much without examination and, like dogs who have been unchallenged in their yard for too long, he never doubted his own bark. Indeed, with his trim whiskers and dapper alertness, the old colonel seemed like a terrier in gaiters and frock coat.

Mr. Straker's modest house, where he lived with his wife and a single wan servant girl, was a couple of hundred yards from my stable. Three boys worked under Mr. Straker, tending my three friends and myself. At night two slept up in the chaff-cutting loft above the harness room and the third down with us horses. I liked the boys more than I liked Mr. Straker, who was gentle with us only when Colonel Ross was near. He was a hard man and solemn. Something was terribly amiss with Mr. Straker. Late one night I had glimpsed him in the paddock, laming a couple of sheep with a fierce little curved knife. The cries of the animals would have broken his heart if he had had one.

◆

I remember it was late September, with the brambles and ferns bronzing the low hillsides. At nine on that fateful evening, they locked the stables. The other two boys went up to the house for supper, leaving Ned Hunter to wait for his as he combed and brushed us. A gentle lad, Ned, and steadfast. I felt safe in the stable with him. There also were Bayard, another winning colt, smug but plucky; the other two horses, Plym and Meavy, cousins bought together from Major Ignatius at Widecombe-in-the-Moor; and growly old Sharp, a hound with the bark of a sergeant-major but the heart of a butler.

Shortly afterward the maid, Edith Baxter, strolled down the lonely path from the house, with her lantern casting swinging shadows as she brought Ned his supper. I could smell that tonight it was curried mutton, as occasionally it had been before. She carried no beer, because the boys were permitted to drink only water, which they drew from a tap in the stable.

Ned had just led me in from my evening constitutional. He offered me a bucket of water, but I drank little because it was too cool for my taste and tickled my nostrils with the stench of tin. I was near the small open window, through which I could see Edith's approach about to intersect that of a man who was stumbling awkwardly across the moor toward the stable. At that moment, Sharp rose suddenly from a nap and began to bark.

Apparently Edith had neither seen nor heard the stranger. She was less than a hundred feet from the stable—far enough that I could not yet smell her particular aroma of soap and sweat and a hint of lavender—when the man drew near and called for her to wait. Voices carry far around here.

Moor-born but not without qualities is our Edith. Wary but unafraid, she held up the lantern. Within its circle of light I could see a pale, nervy fellow in a gentlemanly cloth cap and gray tweeds. Gaiters guarded his trouser legs from mud and from the yellow furze blossoms that crouched in every nook among the lichen-mottled boulders of the moor. At his neck he wore an attention-getting cravat of black-and-red silk. He was somewhere over thirty years old and carried a heavy stick with a weighted knob—the kind that I have heard described as a Penang lawyer. A man of that stripe bears watching, and so does his stick.

"Can you tell me where I am?" he asked the maid.

Edith regarded him skeptically, as well she might.

"I had almost made up my mind to sleep on the moor," he continued with an unconvincing friendliness, "when I saw the light of your lantern."

"You are close to the King's Pyland training stables," said Edith at last.

"Oh, indeed!" exclaimed he. "What a stroke of luck!" He was not much of an actor. He looked at the dish in her hand and said, "I understand that a stable-boy sleeps there alone every night. Perhaps that is his supper which you are carrying to him. Now I am sure that you would not be too proud to earn the price of a new dress, would you?"

Despite Edith's unwelcoming expression, he reached between the lapels of his tweed coat to a waistcoat pocket and withdrew a folded paper. "See that the boy has this tonight, and you shall have the prettiest frock that money can buy."

Edith is no fool. Without another word she dodged around the man. Because the stable was locked, she ran to the little open window through which she usually passed the supper dish to the boy on duty. Her sudden appearance started Sharp barking again. Ned was at the window and Edith thrust the laden plate into his hands as she began describing her encounter. They did not seem aware that the tweedy man was walking up to the window in the dark, crunching across the ground and smelling of wool and pipe smoke. They were caught off guard when he appeared at the window. He held cupped in his hand a single folded bank note. Sharp was growling deep in his throat and the man watched him carefully.

In a hail-fellow-well-met tone, he said immediately to Ned, "Good evening. I want to have a word with you." I heard him rest his heavy stick against the outside wall.

Brave Ned is not one to cower. "What business have you here?" he demanded.

"It's business that may put something into your pocket," the man replied in an oily tone. "You've two horses in for the Wessex Cup—Silver Blaze and Bayard. Let me have the straight tip, and you won't be a loser. Is it a fact that at the weights Bayard could give the other a hundred yards in five furlongs, and that the stable have put their money on him?"

I don't mean to slight young Bayard, who from fetlock to mane is fully two-thirds the foal he imagines himself to be, but that is a base prevarication over which I will not linger.

"So you're one of those damned touts!" cried Ned. I fear that working in a stable does not refine one's language. Yet, as Mater always said, a horse must remain a gentleman or lady no matter how one's servants behave.

"I'll show you how we serve them in King's Pyland!" cried impetuous Ned. He leaped up and dashed across the stable to free Sharp, who rose to the occasion with a fearful bellow. Edith was already running back to the house.

As the boy unlocked the front door, Sharp raced out, bellowing, "I was half asleep! How dare you interrupt me? I eat strangers for supper!" Sharp tends to exaggerate, but his gruff bark was convincing.

Ned locked the door behind them and raced into the darkness. Soon, panting, he returned without the stranger. Later I heard him tell the other boys that he had lost him in the darkness.

⋘◈⋙

That night it rained hard. Without a wind, it fell straight down from the sagging clouds and drenched moor and farmyard alike. In the middle of the night, I heard someone sloshing through the mud from the direction of Straker's house, just before I smelled Straker himself. He was always surrounded by the scent of Cavendish tobacco, which he smoked in a briar-root pipe clamped between his yellow teeth.

Soon Straker quietly unlocked the door and came in almost without a sound, his wet mackintosh waterproof dripping onto the straw. Sharp looked up and wagged his tail but did not bark.

Ned sprawled in his chair, snoring. He had fallen into a deep sleep shortly after eating his mutton; he had actually dropped his water cup, which lay sideways on the straw floor. For some time I had entertained myself with trying to guess when Ned would slide to the ground in his stupor, which I thought would result in an amusing surprise. But he must have been more deeply asleep than ever before, because not even the trainer's arrival in the barn woke him. Straker watched the boy closely for a minute, then finally turned toward me. He paused again when one of the boys in the loft stirred, but apparently neither had awakened. I had known both to sleep through thunderstorms.

To my surprise—and, I admit, my alarm—Straker came over to me and, without the hypocritical murmurs and gentle pats he gave me in Colonel Ross's presence, he roughly pulled a bridle over my head and inserted the bit. I tossed my head and instantly he slapped my cheek, making me bite my tongue. I yelped. He twisted the reins in his left hand and gathered them close under my chin. I ought to have fought back then, but training and manners slowed my reaction. From his bed in the straw, Sharp watched us with concern, his tail still but his eyes following our every move.

Slowly Straker opened the barn door and led me out into the mud and rain, toward the moor. As Sharp rose to follow, Straker latched the door behind us. We headed into the night. The rain was cold. My tongue hurt from biting it and my cheek burned where the man had slapped me. I am ashamed to admit that I watched for an opportunity for revenge.

Along one path Straker found the black and red silk cravat that had been worn the night before by the stranger who came to the barn. It was now drenched and muddy but he scooped it up and carried it along with us. He led me about a quarter of a mile from the house, into a bowl-shaped depression below the knoll from which, during daylight, all the neighboring moor could be seen. There he took off his mackintosh, which the wind was flapping around his legs, and draped it across a furze bush. Cupping his hands over it, he struck three wax vestas, trying again and again to light a stub of tallow candle and angrily flinging each spent vesta off into the wet night. He began to curse in a worried, angry voice.

It was then that I saw another figure at a distance, standing alone in the rain, watching. Straker had been leading me toward this other man, and as he stopped he looked up and waved rudely to him. The other fellow briefly raised a hand in reply but did not come closer.

Like every other horse, even your vulgar hansom slavey—perhaps especially those unfortunates—I am well versed in watching the hands of men. Even in the rain that night, I saw Straker pull from his pocket an ivory-handled surgical knife with a stiff but delicate blade, its evil point sheathed only in a chunk of cork. The instant I saw it I began to snort and toss. I knew Straker and I knew that knife. I had seen him use it on the sheep.

I knew then what Straker had in mind for me. I have not spent my life around race tracks and paddocks without paying attention. Feigning a comforting murmur, which was patently false and also lost in the rain, he walked beside me, patting my flank, until he stood beside my tail. He held the black-and-red cravat twisted like a rope.

Like a blacksmith, he bent to grasp my left hind leg and raise the hoof. Instead I twisted aside and kicked as hard as I could. To my astonishment I felt his skull cave in, and as I danced around I saw that his hand brought the evil little knife not to my leg but to his own. I smelled blood and knew real fear. Without even a moan, Straker slid into the mud as I fled across the moor.

I saw the other man slosh after me but soon I lost him in the rain and mist.

⊸◇⊷

We are taught always to accept the sufferings foisted upon us by our often ignorant servants. Perhaps Mater would have argued that I ought not to have kicked my treacherous trainer. But times change; mine is not the world in which she foaled. I fought back and I shan't claim that I regret it. Even as I galloped away, I suspected that Mr. Straker would never torment another sheep or horse, but my heart was pounding with the realization of how close I myself came to never seeing another autumn day in Dartmoor. Finally I stood still in the rain until my breathing slowed and my sides stopped aching.

Then I saw the other man—he who had witnessed my kicking of Mr. Straker—approaching from a distance. I watched him cautiously. I thought the movement and silhouette seemed familiar. Finally I realized that it was Silas Brown, the black-eyed, terrier-browed old man who ran the Capleton stables for Lord Backwater. Brown was in charge of Desborough, whom reckless gossip ranked as comparable to myself in speed and form. Two or three times when Straker exercised me out on the moor, he secretly met with Brown. As Desborough and I exchanged superficial pleasantries, Straker had complained about his debts and Brown had told him ways to vanquish them—which included betrayal of Colonel Ross. It appeared that they had planned tonight's shenanigans for some time.

I was tired and wet, and I confess that I was somewhat relieved when I saw that it was only Silas Brown who approached. I considered running away, but where was I to go? I am not a fallow deer. I am a horse, a race horse. At night I sleep in a stable.

"Here, my lad," called Brown in a voice that was, for him, soft and comforting. "Not to worry, me lad."

I turned to look at him.

"A bit of a change in plan, that's what we have here," he continued, appraising me but pausing in his tracks as I turned. "Ye're a fierce one, an't you, Mr. Silver Blaze? Well, ole Silas is no meater himself. Not half. Well, we be calm and straight, lad. I won't hurt ye. But also," and he actually chuckled to himself, "also I won't be standin' behind ye." He pretended to casually glance around. "Tonight I would trade every fancy racer for a hansom nag, or even for a rain napper." Again he laughed. He did not seem disturbed by the death of his co-conspirator.

I sigh to recall how easily I let this coarse oaf take my reins and lead me toward the Capleton stable. I relished the shelter. I welcomed the grain and water. I was delighted to be dried and combed. But I was hobbled and reined before I realized what was happening next. Scurrying in the dawn light, Brown opened jars and bottles and pumped water into a bucket and was soon dyeing my beautiful black coat—forgive my vanity—a drab brown.

⬥

A few days later, I was standing at the stable's front window at sunset beside Desborough, my rival and new house mate, peering out at the road that led through the Capleton gates when I saw two men walking up from across the moor.

The taller man was obviously the leader. He strode purposefully ahead, his gaze darting from grass to road, from stable to gate. He had a presence about him, a kind of confidence and poise, from his strong hands to his high forehead. The other man looked like a former soldier, himself strong and broad-shouldered, his gait equal to that of his companion but his posture a bit subservient.

Dawson, Brown's battered and spiritless lackey, ran out of the stable to confront them. "We don't want any loiterers about here!"

The taller of the two stood with his finger insolently hooked in his waistcoat pocket. "I only wish to ask a question," he said lazily. "Should I be too early to see your master, Mr. Silas Brown, if I were to call at five o'clock tomorrow morning?" Belying his tone was his piercing gaze, which I soon realized had observed me at the window of the stable. Our eyes met.

"Bless you, sir," Dawson said, falling into a peasant tone in response to the man's confidence, "if anyone is about he will be, for he is always the first stirring."

He glanced back over his shoulder with what I already knew was his perpetual worried expression. "But here he is, sir, to answer your questions for himself."

The tall man held out a coin, but Dawson quickly murmured, "No, sir, no; it is as much as my place is worth to let him see me touch your money. Afterwards, if you like."

The man replaced the coin and waited calmly as Brown stamped across the asphalt, swinging his hunting crop threateningly.

"What's this, Dawson? No gossiping! Go about your business!" He turned to the strangers. "And you—what the devil do you want here?"

"Ten minutes' talk with you, my good sir," the slender man said calmly. He did not deign to glance at the swinging crop.

"I've no time to talk to every gadabout," snapped Brown. "We want no strangers here. Be off, or you may find a dog at your heels."

Calmly the man leaned forward and whispered into Brown's ear.

His cheeks flushed and he snarled angrily, "It's a lie! An infernal lie!"

"Very good. Shall we argue about it here in public or talk it over in your stable?"

Brown's bluster passed like a shower on the moor. "Oh, come in if you wish to."

The man smiled. "I shall not keep you more than a few minutes, Watson," said he to his companion. "Now, Mr. Brown, I am quite at your disposal."

Brown took a deep breath, failed to restore his swagger, and quietly, almost meekly, turned to lead the way into the stable. As the one called Watson wandered about outdoors, I turned from the window to watch Brown and the tall stranger in the stable, so near my stall. My heart was pounding with anxiety. Desborough seemed bored.

"I am Sherlock Holmes," the man said calmly. "Perhaps you have heard my name."

Brown shook his head.

Mr. Holmes raised his eyebrows and said, "I'm sorry I left Watson outside. He would enjoy this. I come, Mr. Brown, to tell you a little story."

"I'm not interested in stories."

"I fancy you shall find this one fascinating. Shall we sit? No? Fine. As you told the constable and Inspector Gregory, you were out on the moor very early one morning recently. You were wearing those same square-toed boots you have on now."

Brown glanced down at his muddy boots.

"What you did not tell anyone is that while there you spied a lone horse wandering about. You crept closer and discovered, to your disbelief, a large white blaze on his forehead. It was your own Desborough's chief rival—Silver Blaze."

"I have no idea what ye mean."

"Let us not waste time. You saw Silver Blaze but he was alone. There was no John Straker, no Ned Hunter, no Colonel Ross. What you could not have known was that Straker was already dead on the moor."

Brown's expression did not change. It was one of the rare moments when I yearned for the ability to speak to people.

"You stood in disbelief. You started back toward Capleton. You walked in a circle and thought."

Brown was no longer able to keep his face without expression. "Where the devil were you hiding, sir?"

"You took the dragging reins of Silver Blaze and walked him around a few minutes. Then you headed toward King's Pyland."

Brown stared.

"You then realized that fate had delivered into your hands the opportunity you had dreamed of throughout your conniving, petty life. Under cover of the dawn mists, you decided to lead Silver Blaze back here to Capleton."

Brown laughed as if he had been storing up energy for a final protest. "Then where is he now, sir?"

Mr. Holmes sighed and, without turning toward me, waved a hand in my direction.

"I don't see a blaze on that bay," said Brown, but almost choked on his attempt at bravado.

"Mr. Brown, we are not children. This is not a game. I have it in my power to destroy you and I will not hesitate to do so unless you follow my instructions to the letter."

Brown tried to meet Mr. Holmes's gaze but failed. He looked down at the straw and sighed. Sweat stood out on his forehead and upper lip.

"You will keep Silver Blaze here."

Brown's eyebrows shot up.

"You will keep him dyed."

"What?"

"This is not a discussion. These are your instructions. You will prepare him for the Wessex Cup race at Winchester four days hence. You will not inform Lord Backwater. Nor will you cease to exercise both horses and to treat them well." Mr. Holmes's tone darkened. "If Silver Blaze is harmed in any way—in the slightest way—I will personally see you in court for horse-stealing and tampering with a race, and I might enjoy throwing in suspicion of murder."

"Murder! I have no—"

"It doesn't matter what you have none of." Mr. Holmes strode toward the door. "I shall send you a telegram with further instructions." He stepped outside.

Fascinated by the spectacle of this man calmly overpowering the bullying Brown without a blow, I turned to watch them through the window again.

His spirit broken, Brown scurried along behind the other man as he returned to his companion. "Your instructions will be done. It shall all be done."

"There must be no mistake," said Mr. Holmes, looking round at him. The one called Dr. Watson watched them closely.

Brown read the threat in Mr. Holmes's gaze and swallowed. "Oh no, there shall be no mistake. It shall be there. Should I change it first or not?"

Mr. Holmes thought a moment and chuckled. "No, don't. I shall write to you about it. No tricks, now, or—"

"Oh, you can trust me, you can trust me!"

To my astonishment, Brown held out a quivering hand to shake.

And to my delight, Mr. Holmes ignored it, saying over his shoulder as he turned away, "Yes, I think I can. Well, you shall hear from me tomorrow."

Brown marched as steadily as he could into the stable, then almost collapsed against the wall, leaning against it for support as he looked out the window to watch the two men stride across the moor toward King's Pyland. He breathed deeply and I smelled his stale cigars and whiskey.

Then suddenly he turned and kicked the door of my stall. I squealed and turned so I could fight back if he opened the door, but he dashed from the stable like a frightened rat.

⬥

I ran a good race at Winchester. I was uncomfortably itchy with my coat still dyed, and embarrassed to not be recognized at a distance. Only when close enough to smell me did my fellow horses know me as Silver Blaze.

I loved the roaring crowd. I was raised to this world, as was my father before me. The shouts, the waved hats and scarves, the glint of spyglasses raised to follow our progress—I loved it all. As always, however, I ignored the men's calls such as, "Five to four against Silver Blaze! Fifteen to five against Desborough! Five to four on the field!" To win you have to think only of the race.

They were a worthy lot, the other horses. I had just spent several days in the company of Desborough. He acted as if somehow we were co-conspirators—until just before the bell he whickered, "No need to push yourself, my dear Blaze. You can't keep up."

"Sir," I protested, shocked, "may the best horse win."

"Indeed."

The other horses were not so rude as Desborough. I had not seen Iris, who runs for the Duke of Balmoral, in almost a year, and I discovered that my admiration for her lean flanks had not diminished. Pugilist, Colonel Wardlaw's famous roan, I had run against before and we had a respectful, collegial relationship. I had never before crossed paths with Rasper, Lord Singleford's proud bay with the haughty gaze and restless tail. The Negro, Heath Newton's big black, was also new to me—and, I must admit, a handsome fellow, with his jockey riding lightly in cinnamon jacket and red cap.

None too soon for me, because I had never felt so restless, there came the gun. The six of us ran neck and neck for a couple of long minutes, with my heart and hooves both pounding. Soon, though, Rasper, The Negro, and Pugilist fell behind. For a minute Iris and Desborough ran on each side of me. But beautiful Iris was spent and fell back to a respectable third place. Then Desborough, cursing me in language I shall not repeat and choking on the dust from my hooves, fell half a length behind, then a length, then more. I was six lengths ahead when I passed the finish line.

After all that had happened to me over the last weeks, I had never felt more triumphant.

<hr />

"Here he is," I heard the hawk-nosed Mr. Holmes say as he led the way into the owners-only weighing enclosure. Ned Hunter was combing me and wiping me down as I drank water from a bucket. He took off his cap and Mr. Holmes and Dr. Watson nodded to him. Glowering Colonel Ross did not.

Mr. Holmes still smelled of strong tobacco. He indicated me. "You have only to wash his face and his leg in spirits of wine, and you will find that he is the same old Silver Blaze as ever."

"You take my breath away!" exclaimed the colonel.

"I found him in the hands of a faker, and took the liberty of running him just as he was sent over."

"My dear sir, you have done wonders." The colonel walked round me, looking me up and down, fetlock to mane. He patted my flank. "The horse looks very fit and well. It never went better in its life. I owe you a thousand apologies for having doubted your ability. You have done me a great service by recovering my horse. You would do me a greater still if you could lay your hands on the murderer of John Straker."

"I have done so," said Mr. Holmes quietly.

"You have got him! Where is he, then?"

"He is here."

"Here! Where?"

"In my company at the present moment."

Colonel Ross bristled like a teased dog. "I quite recognize that I am under obligations to you, Mr. Holmes," he said coldly, and the hand gripping his riding crop twitched, "but I must regard what you have just said as either a very bad joke or an insult."

"I assure you that I have not associated you with the crime, colonel," the man said with a mocking sort of laugh that matched his fierce eyes and aristocratic nose. "The real murderer is standing immediately behind you." He stepped past the colonel and, with surprising gentleness in a man so clearly strong, rested his hand upon my neck. It was the first time I had touched the man who rescued me. I learned then that respect and gratitude can suddenly feel like affection.

"The horse!" the two men exclaimed simultaneously.

"Yes, the horse."

Mr. Holmes looked at me sympathetically and I held my head high. I dislike pity.

"And it may lessen his guilt if I say that it was done in self-defense, and that John Straker was a man who was entirely unworthy of your confidence. But there goes the bell, and as I stand to win a little on this next race, I shall defer a lengthy explanation until a more fitting time."

I realized then that, knowing where I was and that I would be brought over to race—as he had commanded that simpering coward, Silas

Brown—Mr. Holmes had placed a bet on my race. I was flattered, but I knew that this kind of betting knowledge was illegal at the track.

No one seemed to care.

⚬◈⚬

The next day, Ned Hunter drove me home along the familiar lanes, with the rented cart horses jostling my wagon but my stance steady and proud as befits a returning conqueror. I saw Silas Brown, dirty and meek, standing by the roadside. He appraised me coolly as the wagon passed. I met his gaze with an expression I imagine he could not read.

When Colonel Ross glanced at him, the sly old cowardly groom doffed his cap respectfully. Ned clucked to the other horses and we drove on up the lane.

Dr. Watson's Casebook

by Andrew Grant

John H. Watson, MD

Dr. James Mortimer was at 221B Baker Street, London.

   ◊ **Sherlock Holmes** likes this.

Sherlock Holmes Now is the dramatic moment of fate! I hear a step upon the stair, but know not whether for good or ill . . .

Dr. James Mortimer

Finding myself confronted with a most serious and extraordinary problem, I realise I require the services of the second highest expert in Europe . . .

   ✎ **Sherlock Holmes** does not like this.

Dr. James Mortimer

This **Sherlock Holmes** fellow is a little touchy! He does possess the most exquisite skull, however. How I long to touch his parietal fissure! I wonder if he would allow me to take a cast, until the original becomes available? Anyway, in the meantime I must say I'm very happy to have back the stick

I inadvertently left at his door last night when I unsuccessfully attempted to call on him.

  👍 **Dr. Mortimer's Spaniel** likes this.

  👎 **Dr. Watson** does not like this.

Dr. Watson How was I to know he was so young? Deducing that Mortimer was elderly seemed perfectly reasonable to me. After all, I only had his stick to work with . . .

Sherlock Holmes On the contrary, it was elementary to deduce that Mortimer was under thirty, amiable, unambitious, and absent minded. The clues were clear to see.

Mrs. Hudson How clearly would he see without me to polish the coffee pot he uses to observe Watson's reflection—that's what I'd like to know!

Dr. James Mortimer shared a link to the manuscript **The Legend of the Baskerville** Family.

  👎 **Sherlock Holmes** does not like this.

Sherlock Holmes Only a fool would entertain such a fairy tale! A supernatural hound? Complete nonsense.

Dr. James Mortimer We have numerous reports of people sighting a hound which could not possibly be any animal known to science. Huge, luminous, ghastly, spectral—exactly corresponding to the legend.

Sherlock Holmes The superstitious ramblings of imbeciles, no doubt. And perfectly healthy people dying of fright? No, sir. A sound, scientific explanation must exist.

Dr. James Mortimer Perhaps. But Sir Charles Baskerville believed the legend, and look what happened to him!

Dr. James Mortimer shared a link to **The Devon County Chronicle**.

  🔥 **Sherlock Holmes** likes this.

Sherlock Holmes Much better! A concise account of the recent death of Sir Charles Baskerville, the head of the family. The circumstances of his death may not have been completely cleared up—I was not there to investigate, after all—but there's certainly no reason to suspect the unworldly. Sir Charles had, I note, a history of heart problems . . .

Dr. James Mortimer True. And the coroner's prosaic findings should finally dispel the romantic whisperings which may otherwise have discouraged Sir Charles' heir from settling at Baskerville Hall and continuing his most excellent renovations.

  🔥 **The Association of Devon Building Contractors** likes this.

Sherlock Holmes
The more I hear of the facts of this case, the more intrigued I become. I vaguely remember reading about it at the time, but I was too busy with an engagement in Italy to pay full attention.

  🔥 **The Pope** likes this.

Dr. James Mortimer
I fear I may have inadvertently misled poor **Holmes**! I do not wish to engage his investigative services in this matter. Indeed, I only wish

to seek his advice as to whether it is safe for Sir Charles' heir—**Sir Henry Baskerville**, who is due to arrive in London from America in seventy-five minutes' time—to take up his ancestral home.

Sherlock Holmes Matters are a little more complicated than our new medical friend seems to grasp. I will need a little time to consider them . . .

Sherlock Holmes has invited **Dr. James Mortimer, Sir Henry Baskerville**, and **Dr. John Watson** to the event **Breakfast at my Rooms,** tomorrow at 10:00.

Attending: **Dr. James Mortimer, Dr. John Watson.**

Possibly Attending: **Sir Henry Baskerville.**

Dr. John Watson was at **The Diogenes Club.**

It's always best to leave **Holmes** alone when he needs time to think . . .

  👍 **Baker Street Tobacco Supplies** likes this.

  👍 **Marylebone Coffee Importers** likes this.

Dr. John Watson was at **221B Baker Street, London.**

9:00 p.m. If I open the window immediately, there's still a chance **Holmes** may not suffocate!

  👎 **Sherlock Holmes** does not like this.

Sherlock Holmes Enough of thinking for the day. Time for the violin!

  👍 **Dr. John Watson** likes this.

Sir Henry Baskerville, Dr. James Mortimer, and **Dr. John Watson** were at 221B Baker Street, London.

Sir Henry Baskerville 10:00 a.m., and this **Holmes** fellow is still in his dressing gown? Mighty strange behaviour.

☙ **Jermyn Street Gentlemen's Accessories** does not like this.

Sir Henry Baskerville I'd probably have come to sound the chap out anyway, even without the good offices of **Dr. James Mortimer**, because of a queer letter I received at my hotel this morning. It's just one line of letters cut from a newspaper, but it warns me to keep away from the moor!

🖒 **Sherlock Holmes** likes this.

Sherlock Holmes If I'm not much mistaken, gentlemen, I think you'll find the letters are taken from the Leader in yesterday's Times . . .

🖒 **Sir Henry Baskerville** and **Dr. James Mortimer** like this.

Sir Henry Baskerville
With all this talk of hounds and violent deaths, I'm not sure if I need the assistance of a clergyman or a policeman! And I certainly seem to have come into an inheritance with a vengeance! A little time to absorb all this information is needed, I think . . .

Sir Henry Baskerville has invited **Sherlock Holmes, Dr. John Watson,** and **Dr. James Mortimer** to the event **Lunch at my Hotel** at 2:00 p.m.
Attending: **Sherlock Holmes, Dr. John Watson, Dr. James Mortimer.**

Sir Henry Baskerville I wish I knew somewhere better to take them! The hotel's a terrible place. A den of thieves. Already one of my boots has been stolen—and I'd only just bought it! The pair was brand new. Not even worn yet.

Dr. John Watson

One of my favourite things about working with **Sherlock Holmes?** How quickly he can change his mind. Not to mention his clothes! One moment—we were taking coffee in his dining room with guests. The next—we were vigorously but discretely pursuing them down Regent Street, despite the attentions of a mysterious bearded gentleman in a hansom cab . . .

🖐 **Sherlock Holmes** does not like this.

Sherlock Holmes Why are there never any cabs available when you need them? The canny devil spying on **Sir Henry Baskerville** became aware of our observation, and fled. Allowing him to slip away in such a manner is bad luck and bad management, but must surely also be counted as a failure on my account.

Sherlock Holmes and **Dr. John Watson** were at the **District Messenger Office.**

Dr. John Watson You never know when a good turn will be repaid! **Sherlock Holmes** had previously assisted the manager of the place, and now he was only too happy to lend us the services of one of the brighter boys in his employ: **Cartwright.**

👍 **Cartwright** likes this.

Cartwright Working for **Sherlock Holmes** is much more exciting than delivering messages! I just hope I can find the cut-up newspaper he instructed me to look for at the local hotels. As long as I don't lose the bribe money he provided me with . . .

Sir Henry Baskerville, Sherlock Holmes, Dr. James Mortimer, and **Dr. John Watson** were at the **Northumberland Hotel** for Lunch.

Dr. John Watson I'd venture that lunch with a baronet is more enjoyable when he hasn't just suffered the theft of a second boot in less than a day . . .

🖋 **Sir Henry Baskerville** does not like this.

Dr. John Watson

Sir Henry Baskerville took the news of the spy on his tail very calmly, in the circumstances. The revelation that the butler from Baskerville Hall, Barrymore, has a beard was very interesting. And **Sherlock Holmes'** ruse—using a bogus telegram to find out if he's currently at the Hall—was brilliant!

🖋 **Sherlock Holmes** likes this.

Dr. John Watson

Modern technology certainly speeds up the process of detection, even if the satisfaction of the answers it brings does not match its rapidity. We have learned that **Barrymore** was indeed at **Baskerville Hall** at the time the spy was marauding the streets of London, and that young **Cartwright** was unable to unearth any trace of a dismembered *Times*.

🖋 **Sherlock Holmes** likes this.

Sherlock Holmes There's nothing more stimulating than a case where everything goes against you!

Dr. John Watson
Sherlock Holmes is sending me to Devon with **Sir Henry Baskerville** as he is occupied with a blackmail case. He must hold me in higher esteem than I'd realised!

  ✿ **Dr. John Watson** likes this.

  ❧ **Sherlock Holmes** does not like this.

Sherlock Holmes I will be very glad to have my friend **Watson** back safe and sound in **Baker Street** once more. New revelations regarding the adroit handling of the cabbie by the bearded spy only serve to underline the extreme threat he poses. In truth, I feel a foil as quick and supple as my own . . .

Dr. John Watson
There's nothing like traveling first class! Especially with good conversation, good scenery, and a good dog, to boot.

  ✿ **Sir Henry Baskerville** likes this.

Sir Henry Baskerville I love Devon! It's in my blood. But, you know, despite all the thousands of miles I've travelled and the dozens of countries I've visited, I've never once set eyes on Baskerville Hall . . .

Dr. John Watson
Soldiers add even more drama to the Devon landscape! Apparently a convict has escaped from a nearby jail.

  ✿ **Mrs. Barrymore** likes this.

Sir Henry Baskerville

Baskerville Hall's beautiful, but the old girl could sure use some electric light . . . .

🔥 **Devon Electric Co.** likes this.

Dr. John Watson

Portraits don't make good dinner companions! Elizabethan, Regency, or any era in between, their silent company is plain daunting.

🔥 **Sir Henry Baskerville** likes this.

Sir Henry Baskerville No wonder my uncle was so jumpy!

Dr. John Watson has left the group Physicians Who Like Atmospheric Country Houses.

Dr. John Watson has re-joined the group Physicians Who Like Atmospheric Country Houses.

Dr. John Watson It's true! Things always seem better in daylight . . .

Dr. John Watson has joined the group Physicians Who Are Confused By Current Events.

Dr. John Watson A woman's sobs in the night, that may or may not have been a dream? **Barrymore** denying all knowledge, but **Mrs. Barrymore**'s face red and tearful in the morning?

A postmaster who can no longer confirm whether **Sherlock Holmes'** test telegram was put directly into **Barrymore's** hand, or not? Somebody—Help!

Dr. John Watson

I wish **Sherlock Holmes** were here! I cannot avoid the sense of a deep and subtle scheme weaving an invisible net around the young baronet, and I fear I lack the skills to unpick it alone.

🖋 **Dr. John Watson** does not like this.

Dr. John Watson

Sir Henry Baskerville may not have many neighbours, but at least the ones he does have are interesting! I met **Stapleton**, today. He collects insects, and claims to know the moors better than anyone around here. I'll certainly heed his warning to steer clear of **Grimpen Mire**! Even as he pointed it out to me, we heard the appalling, haunting sound of a pony drowning in its treacherous clutches. A sound I won't soon forget, I assure you.

🖋 **Miss Beryl Stapleton** does not like this.

Miss Beryl Stapleton Sir Henry Baskerville should go back to London instantly! He is not safe here.

🖋 **Stapleton** does not like this.

Dr. John Watson

I must confess I do not devote as much attention to physical fitness as perhaps I might, but I must be doing something right—**Miss Beryl Stapleton** mistook me for the baronet!

🖋 **Stapleton** and **Miss Beryl Stapleton** do not like this.

Dr. John Watson

Sherlock Holmes may possess the ultimate deductive faculties, but I'd like to think there's still a place for good, old fashioned questioning—judiciously applied—in the investigative process. Take today as an example. I was able to ascertain that as educated a man as **Stapleton**, and as beautiful a woman as his sister, washed up in this particular backwater as the result of a tragic epidemic which ravaged the school they had previously operated in Yorkshire. Three boys were killed, and the majority of their capital was absorbed by the aftermath.

⚘ **Miss Beryl Stapleton** does not like this.

Stapleton Don't shed any tears for us. Teaching is far too uninteresting and mechanical an occupation for a man of my temperament.

Stapleton has invited **Sir Henry Baskerville**, **Dr. John Watson**, and **Miss Beryl Stapleton** to the event **Walk to the Scene of the Origin of the Baskerville Legend**.

Attending: Stapleton, Sir Henry Baskerville, Dr. John Watson, Miss Beryl Stapleton.

Dr. John Watson The spot was utterly dismal—completely in keeping with the diabolical theme of the legend—but there was one pleasant aspect to our outing. The burgeoning friendship—and possibly more—between **Sir Henry Baskerville** and **Miss Beryl Stapleton**.

👍 **Sir Henry Baskerville** likes this.

⚘ **Stapleton** does not like this.

Dr. John Watson

Could it be possible that my prolonged exposure to **Sherlock Holmes'** company is, in one way at least, detrimental to my expectations of the ordinary people I encounter? **Sherlock Holmes** expends all of his prodigious powers in the service of others, so when I meet—as I did today in the person of **Frankland**, another of **Sir Henry Baskerville**'s neighbours and a repugnant, litigious busybody—individuals who devote themselves to denigrating their fellows, it leaves me excessively disappointed.

❦ **Frankland** does not like this.

⚖ **Battles**, **Browne**, **and Rhoades**, **Attorneys at Law** likes this.

Dr. John Watson

Look—it's hard enough to sleep in a creaky old mansion at the best of times, without ghostly hounds and weeping women and drowning ponies on your mind, so do you really have to stomp along the corridor outside my room in the dead of night? And yes, **Barrymore**—I mean you!

And you disturbed **Sir Henry Baskerville**, too.

The only good that came of it is that one of little mysteries is solved! I saw you sneak into the empty bedroom and signal with your candle, and then I heard the kitchen door being unlocked. Add that to **Mrs. Barrymore**'s tears, and there's only one explanation. A love intrigue! You rat.

❦ **Barrymore** and **Mrs. Barrymore** do not like this.

Sir Henry Baskerville We should lie in wait for the cad one night and follow him . . .

Dr. John Watson

On the subject of love intrigue, and in deference to **Sherlock Holmes'** instructions never to allow the baronet to stray into danger rather than out of any bizarre voyeuristic impulse, I followed **Sir Henry Baskerville** to a clandestine meeting he had arranged with **Miss Beryl Stapleton** . . .

 ⚐ **Sir Henry Baskerville** does not like this.

Sir Henry Baskerville Watson's actions aren't really what upset me. I understand his motives were upright. It's more that the rendezvous was a complete fiasco! First, **Miss Stapleton** warned me to leave the moor. Then, when I was on the verge of proposing marriage, her brother came charging out of nowhere, eyes blazing like a madman, and dragged her away. What's wrong with me? Would I really make such an objectionable husband?

Dr. John Watson I'm sorry, my friend. This is one area in which I am ill equipped to help . . .

Sherlock Holmes With your experience of women extending over many nations and three separate continents? The fair sex is your department!

Dr. John Watson
While I applaud the strength of character required to admit one's mistakes and offer an apology where necessary, it would make my task of keeping **Sherlock Holmes** informed of developments much easier if people would kindly refrain from doing this in private!

Sir Henry Baskerville Don't fret, old chap! There are no secrets between us. **Stapleton** simply blamed his intemperate behaviour on a deep attachment to his sister, and asked me to defer my courtship for three months in order for him to prepare for living alone. Not unreasonable in the circumstances!

Stapleton has invited **Sir Henry Baskerville**, **Dr. John Watson**, and **Miss Beryl Stapleton** to the event Apology Dinner.

Attending: Stapleton, Sir Henry Baskerville, Dr. John Watson, Miss Beryl Stapleton.

Dr. John Watson

I take my hat off to **Sir Henry Baskerville**. When he says he'll do something, he does it! Although, in this case—lying in wait to apprehend **Barrymore** on one of his suspicious and noisy nocturnal expeditions—the potential sadly outweighed the outcome. We ended up with little more to show for our resolve than the imprint of **Sir Henry**'s armchairs in our backs.

> **Sir Henry Baskerville** Have no fear! We'll keep trying until we catch the wretch red handed . . .
>
> ❧ **Barrymore** does not like this.

Dr. John Watson

Once again, **Sir Henry** was as good as his word. We set ourselves up in his room, but this time instead of an uncomfortable night's sleep we were rewarded with the sound of footsteps in the corridor. As **Barrymore**'s employer **Sir Henry** was able to take a very firm approach with the miscreant butler but the servant's resolve was such that he was prepared to accept the threat of the sack until his wife appeared and intervened on his behalf. **Mrs. Barrymore** admitted that the escaped convict—**Selden**—was her brother and with **Barrymore**'s assistance she'd been smuggling him food.

Sir Henry and I raced outside in the hope of apprehending the fugitive and returning him to custody before he could harm anyone else, but alas he eluded us in the dark. I did, however, spot the outline of a tall figure silhouetted against the sky when the moon unexpectedly broke through the clouds to provide an instant's illumination.

Sir Henry Baskerville I'm sure it was a prison warden or policeman, chasing their quarry.

We were right not to give any further chase . . .

🕯 **Sherlock Holmes** does not like this.

Sir Henry Baskerville

Adjusting to the ways of the staff in this country is taking longer than I'd expected! Take **Barrymore**, for example. Fortunate not to be jailed, I'd say, let alone sacked. But I took a lenient stance, only to find the man complaining that **Watson** and I had broken his confidence by attempting to capture his brother in law, **Selden**. In the end I had to give him a parcel of clothes I no longer required, just to silence his grievances.

👍 **Barrymore** and **Selden** like this.

Dr. John Watson Outrageous! But I hope we did the right thing, agreeing not to call the police. Still, if Selden does leave the country by ship as **Barrymore** promised he would, it will be much cheaper for the British taxpayer than continuing to house him in jail . . .

Barrymore

It was very decent of **Sir Henry** to give me that parcel of clothes. I could never afford that kind of quality myself, and if they're not quite this year's style I don't think **Selden** will mind as long as they keep him warm on the moor. One good turn deserves another, my old mum used to say, so I reckoned it was only right I told **Sir Henry** about the letter—well, the burned fragment of the letter—his uncle **Sir Charles** had received from someone who signed themselves "LL." It was a very strange thing really, arranging to meet him the day he died . . .

👍 **Sir Henry Baskerville** and **Dr. John Watson** like this.

🕯 **Mrs. Laura Lyons** does not like this.

Dr. John Watson

I'm very sorry to report yet another tragedy has occurred in our midst. **Dr. Mortimer**'s Spaniel is missing on the moor and the poor chap is convinced the animal will never be seen again.

👍 **The Hound** likes this.

Dr. John Watson As a mark of the man's mettle, despite his grief **Dr. Mortimer** was able to call on his encyclopedic knowledge of the local population and suggest that "LL" could be a **Mrs. Laura Lyons** from Coombe Tracey. **Mrs. Lyons** is actually the objectionable **Frankland**'s daughter—abandoned by her blackguard artist husband, neglected by her misanthropic father, but set up in business through the charity of concerned local citizens.

Mrs. Laura Lyons has shared a link to **Lyons' Typing Services** (Local Business)

👍 **Dr. James Mortimer, Stapleton**, and **Sir Charles Baskerville's ghost** like this.

Dr. John Watson

Although I feel a little guilty at profiting from the demise of so lovely an animal as **Dr. Mortimer**'s Spaniel, another valuable opportunity presented itself to me as a consequence of his grief. While **Sir Henry** was occupied playing him at cards in an attempt to raise his spirits I had occasion to speak with **Barrymore** at greater length than normal. During our conversation he let slip that **Selden**, his fugitive brother in law, had reported seeing a second man somehow scraping a living on the moors. A possible witness! And a piece of information that, along with the details of the letter from "LL" brought the total of useful leads recently provided by Barrymore to two . . .

Dr. John Watson was at Lyons' Typing Services, Coombe Tracey. Life has a way of finding occasions to remind me how fortunate I am to have avoided matrimonial difficulties, and my visit with **Mrs. Laura Lyons** was undoubtedly one of these times. I felt deep pity—mixed with a touch of cynical distrust—as she recounted details of her miserable married life, culminating with the unorthodox appointment, which she swore not to have kept, with the late **Sir Charles**. She claimed that its purpose was to petition **Sir Charles** for funds with which to procure a divorce, and that after news of his death reached her she attempted to prevent anyone finding out about the arrangement for fear of misunderstanding leading to scandal.

🖢 **Dr. John Watson** does not like this.

Frankland shared links to **Frankland v Middleton** and **Frankland v Fernworth**, at **Court of Queen's Bench**.

👍 **Frankland** likes this.

🖢 **1,000 others** do not like this.

Frankland Two cases, two results in my favour! I WON!!! My case against the constabulary is next. I'll win that, too! But if the police treated me with the respect I deserve, I'd be helping them, not fighting them. I could tell them where to find the missing convict. I could tell them how to watch the boy who delivers his food every day. But they don't, so I won't. Ha!

👍 **The West Country Telescope Emporium** likes this.

Dr. John Watson was at A Neolithic Stone Hut.

👍 **Sherlock Holmes** likes this.

Dr. John Watson I followed the path the mystery boy uses to deliver food, and found my way to this hut. There's no one here, but it shows signs of occupation—clothes, bedding, remnants of meals—plus a report on MY movements! Someone's been watching me! But who? A malignant enemy? Or a guardian angel? There's only one way to find out. I'll wait.

Sherlock Holmes was at **A Neolithic Stone Hut.**
☞ **Dr. John Watson** does not like this.

Dr. John Watson Holmes was on the moor all this time? There was no blackmail case to keep him in London? He lied to me. He didn't trust me, after all. And all the time I spent sending him reports was wasted.

Sherlock Holmes No! Your reports were vital. I had them all forwarded to Coombe Tracey. I have them in my pocket! Look—thumbed through and well read. I only operated incognito to avoid forewarning our enemies . . .

    👍 **Dr. John Watson** likes this.

Dr. John Watson
Working with **Sherlock Holmes** is a little like climbing one of the country's highest mountains: every time you think you're about to reach the summit, you realise another taller, more impressive peak is behind it, hidden from your sight until the last minute.

    👍 **Sherlock Holmes** likes this.

Sherlock Holmes When you met **Mrs. Lyons**, I take it you discovered she's close to **Stapleton?**

Dr. John Watson That depends what you mean by close . . .

Sherlock Holmes They write. They meet, and so on. And of course you know that **Beryl** isn't really **Stapleton**'s sister?

Dr. John Watson Not his sister?

Sherlock Holmes No! His wife. He must have felt a "sister" would afford him a significant advantage. For example, I'd wager that posing as a single, available man he entreated **Mrs. Lyons** to approach **Sir Charles** regarding the funds for her divorce, holding out the prospect of marrying her himself, and in so doing ensuring that the cautious old man was lured out into a vulnerable position at a predetermined time.

Dr. John Watson But why? What motive could **Stapleton** have for doing away with **Sir Charles**? And how did he do it?

Sherlock Holmes I will soon be in a position to answer both questions.

Dr. John Watson It was **Stapleton** in the cab in London?

Sherlock Holmes I think it's safe to assume so, though I have no definite proof.

Dr. John Watson What will **Mrs. Lyons** do when she discovers Stapleton is married? And that he used her as an unwitting accomplice in the murder of **Sir Charles**—if your hypothesis is correct?

Sherlock Holmes That, my dear **Watson**, is an excellent question!

Dr. John Watson I was so misguided, **Holmes**! Only now do I begin to see **Stapleton** as a creature of infinite patience and craft, with a smiling face and a murderous heart . . .

Sherlock Holmes has invited **Dr. John Watson** to the event Invoking the Fury of the Scorned Woman at Lyons' Typing Services.

Attending: Sherlock Holmes and Dr. John Watson.

Possibly Attending: Mrs. Laura Lyons.

Sherlock Holmes has invited **Dr. John Watson** to the event Keeping Sir Henry Baskerville out of Danger at Baskerville Hall.

Attending: Dr. John Watson.

Possibly Attending: Sir Henry Baskerville.

Sherlock Holmes has cancelled the event Keeping Sir Henry Baskerville out of Danger at Baskerville Hall.

👎 **Sherlock Holmes** and **Dr. John Watson** do not like this.

Sherlock Holmes has invited **Dr. John Watson** to the event Removing Sir Henry Baskerville's Dead Body at A Sheer Cliff, The Moor.

Attending: Sherlock Holmes and Dr. John Watson.

Possibly Attending: Sir Henry Baskerville.

👎 **Sherlock Holmes**, **Dr. John Watson** and **Sir Henry Baskerville** do not like this.

Sherlock Holmes This is terrible! It's my fault. The greatest failure of my career. I swear to bring the culprit to justice!

Dr. John Watson Why was Sir Henry out on the moors alone? He knew the danger.

Sherlock Holmes has edited his event, which is now **Removing Selden (the escaped convict's) Dead Body** at **A Sheer Cliff, The Moor.**

Attending: **Sherlock Holmes** and **Dr. John Watson.**

Possibly Attending: **Selden.**

🖋 **Selden** and **Mrs. Barrymore** do not like this.

Dr. John Watson He was wearing Sir Henry's clothes! That's why we didn't recognise him at first!

Sherlock Holmes It's also why he's dead. Sir Henry's clothes carried his scent. And that explains why his boots were stolen in London.

Stapleton was at **The Scene of Selden's Death, A Sheer Cliff, The Moor.**

🖋 **Sherlock Holmes** and **Dr. John Watson** do not like this.

Stapleton Oh my goodness! Is **Sir Henry** dead?

Dr. John Watson No. This is some other chap who was wearing his cast-off clothes for some reason. Poor devil probably fell from the cliff, suffering from exposure.

👍 **Stapleton** likes this.

Sherlock Holmes I don't know about you fellows, but I'm fed up with this case. In fact, I'm heading back to London first thing in the morning.

👍 👍 👍 **Stapleton** LOVES this.

Sherlock Holmes and **Dr. John Watson** were at Baskerville Hall for **Supper**.

🕯 **Sir Henry Baskerville** likes this.

Sherlock Holmes Has anyone noticed that, allowing for the hair, **Stapleton** looks exactly like the portrait of the evil **Hugo Baskerville**, the progenitor of the curse?

Sir Henry Baskerville By goodness **Holmes**, you're right!

👎 **Dr. John Watson** does not like this.

Dr. John Watson It was pitch dark, most times I was in here. I was tired! How could I tell . . . ?

Sherlock Holmes This could account for another piece of the puzzle, gentlemen! I wager that some conscientious research will reveal that **Sir Charles'** disgraced brother, **Rodger**, did not perish without issue in South America, after all . . .

Stapleton has joined the group **Inconvenient Heirs No One Knew Existed—Until Now!**

Sherlock Holmes and **Dr. John Watson** were at **Coombe Tracey** railway station.

👎 **Sir Henry Baskerville** does not like this.

Dr. John Watson has changed his status for **Stapleton**'s event **Apology Dinner** to Not Attending.

   👍 **Stapleton** likes this.

   👎 **Sir Henry Baskerville** does not like this.

Inspector Lestrade was at Coombe Tracey railway station.

   👍 **Sherlock Holmes** and **Dr. John Watson** like this.

Inspector Lestrade Time to feel some collars . . . ?

Sir Henry Baskerville was at Stapleton's event Apology Dinner.

   👍 **Stapleton** and **The Hound** like this.

Sir Henry Baskerville The food wasn't too unpalatable, fortunately, but I was sad not to see **Miss Stapleton**. I wonder where she is? And why does **Stapleton** keep retreating to his outhouse? And what's making that strange scratching sound from inside it?

Sherlock Holmes, **Dr. John Watson**, and **Inspector Lestrade** were at Rocky Ambush Position, The Moor.

   👎 **Inspector Lestrade** does not like this.

Inspector Lestrade Not a very cheerful place . . .

Dr. John Watson has shared a link to the **London Meteorological Service**—Likelihood of Severe Fog: 90%

    👍 **The Hound** likes this.

    👎 **Sherlock Holmes** does not like this.

Sir Henry Baskerville
Not a very nice night to walk home from **Stapleton**'s. I hope I don't get lost on the way . . .

    👍 **Stapleton** and **The Hound** like this.

The Hound was at His Teeth at Sir Henry Baskerville's Throat.

    👍 **Stapleton** and **The Hound** like this.

    👎 **Sir Henry Baskerville, Sherlock Holmes, Dr. John Watson,** and **Inspector Lestrade** do not like this.

Dr. John Watson
I'm reckoned fleet of foot, but on this occasion **Sherlock Holmes** outpaced me as much as I outpaced little **Inspector Lestrade**. I burst through the blanket of fog just in time to see **Holmes** empty five barrels of his revolver into **The Hound**'s flank, and with a last howl of agony and a vicious snap in the air, it rolled upon its back and fell limp, finally releasing **Sir Henry** from its monstrous jaws.

    👍 **Sir Henry Baskerville, Sherlock Holmes, Dr. John Watson,** and **Inspector Lestrade** like this.

    👎 **Stapleton, The British Phosphorus Company,** and **The Devon and Cornwall Animal Feed Cooperative** do not like this.

Stapleton has joined the group **Entomologists Who Don't Know Deadly Mires As Well As They Thought They Did.**

 🔥 **Beryl Stapleton** likes this.

Sir Henry Baskerville has joined the group **Hound Attack Survivors in need of a Stiff Brandy.**

 🔥 **Everyone** likes this.

THE ADVENTURE OF THE LAUGHING FISHERMAN

by Jeffery Deaver

❖

Sometimes it's overwhelming: the burden of knowing that the man you most admire isn't real.

Then the depression that you've fought all your life creeps in, the anxiety. The borders of your life contract, stifling, suffocating.

And so slim Paul Winslow, twenty-eight, was presently walking into the neat, unadorned office of his on-again, off-again therapist, Dr. Levine, on the Upper West Side of Manhattan.

"Hello, Paul, come on in. Sit down."

Dr. Levine was one of those shrinks who offered basic armchairs, not couches, for his patients. He spoke frequently during the sessions, wasn't afraid to offer advice and asked, "How do you feel about that?" only when it was important to know how his patients felt. Which was pretty rare.

He never used the verb "explore."

Paul had read Freud's *Psychopathology of Everyday Life* (not bad, though a bit repetitive) and the works of Jung and Horney and some of the other biggies. He knew that a lot of what brain docs told you was a crock. But Dr. Levine was a good man.

"I did the best I could," Paul now explained to him. "Everything was going along okay, pretty much okay, but over the past couple of months it got worse and I couldn't shake it, you know, the sadness. I guess I need a tune-up," Paul added, smiling ruefully. Even at the worst of times, his humor never wholly deserted him.

A laugh came from the mouth of the clean-shaven, trim physician, who wore slacks and a shirt during the appointments. His glasses were unstylish wire rims, but that seemed to fit his casual style and friendly demeanor.

Paul had not been here for nearly eight months and the doctor now glanced through his patient's file to refresh his memory. The folder was thick. Paul had seen Dr. Levine off and on for the past five years and had been to other shrinks before that. Diagnosed from a young age with bipolar and anxiety disorders, Paul had worked hard to control his malady. He didn't self-medicate with illegal drugs or liquor. He'd seen therapists, attended workshops, taken medicine—though not regularly and only those run-of-the-mill antidepressants ingested by the ton in the New York metro area. He'd never been institutionalized, never had any breaks with reality.

Still, the condition—which his mother also suffered from—had side-lined him. Never one to get along well with others, Paul was impatient, had little respect for authority, could be acerbic and never hesitated to verbally eviscerate the prejudiced and the stupid.

Oh, he was brilliant, with an IQ way up in the stratosphere. He'd zipped through university in three years, grad school in one. But then came the brick wall: the real world. Teaching at community colleges hadn't worked out (you don't necessarily have to get along with fellow professors, but a modicum of tolerance for your students' foibles is a requirement). Editing for scientific publishers was equally disastrous (the same problem with his bosses and authors). Recently he'd taken up freelance copyediting for one of his former employers and this solitary job more or less suited, at least for the time being.

Not that money was important; his parents, both bankers, were well off and, sympathetic to their son's condition, established a trust fund for him, which supported him nicely. Given these resources, he was free to live a simple, stress-free life, working part time, playing chess at a club in the Village, dating occasionally (though without much enthusiasm) and doing plenty of what he loved most: reading.

Paul Winslow didn't care much for real people but he loved the characters in fiction. He always had.

Lou Ford and Anna Wulf and Sam Spade and Clyde Griffiths and Frank Chambers and Mike Hammer and Pierre Bezukhov and Huck Finn . . . a hundred others made up Paul's circle of intimates. Harry Potter was a good friend; Frodo Baggins, a better one.

As for vampires and zombies . . . well, better not to get Paul started.

Yet no fiction, high-brow or -low, captivated him like the short stories and novels of one author in particular: Arthur Conan Doyle, the creator of Sherlock Holmes.

Upon his first reading, some years ago, he knew instantly that he'd found his hero—a man who reflected his personality, his outlook, his soul.

His passion extended beyond the printed page. He collected Victorian memorabilia and artwork. Sitting prominently on the wall in his living room was a very fine reproduction of Sidney Paget's pen and ink drawing of arch enemies Holmes and Professor Moriarty grappling on a narrow ledge above Reichenbach Falls, a scene from the short story "The Final Problem," in which Moriarty dies and Holmes appears to. Paul owned all of the various filmed versions of the Holmes adventures, though he believed the old Granada version with Jeremy Brett was the only one that got it right.

Yet in recent months Paul had found that spending time in the world of the printed page was growing less and less comforting. And as the allure of the books wore off, the depression and anxiety seeped in to fill its place.

Now, sitting back in Dr. Levine's bright office—shrink contempo, Paul had once described it—he ran a hand through his unruly black curly hair, which he often forgot to comb. He explained that the high he got from reading the books and stories had faded dramatically.

"It hit me today that, well, it's lame, totally lame, having a hero who's fictional. I was so, I don't know, *confined* within the covers of the books,

I'm missing out on . . . everything." He exhaled slowly through puffed cheeks. "And I thought maybe it's too late. The best part of my life is over."

Paul didn't mind the doctor's smile. "Paul, you're a young man. You've made huge strides. You have your whole life ahead of you."

Paul's eyes, in his gaunt, narrow face, closed momentarily. Then sprung open. "But how stupid is that, having this hero who's made up? I mean, they're only books."

"Don't dismiss the legitimate emotional attraction between readers and literature, Paul. Did you know tens of thousands of Victorians were inconsolable when one character in a Dickens book died?"

"Which one?"

"Little Nell."

"Oh, *The Old Curiosity Shop.* I didn't know about the reaction."

"All over the world. People were sobbing, milling around in the streets, talking about it."

Paul nodded. "And when it looked like Sherlock Holmes died in 'The Final Problem,' Doyle was so hounded, one might say, that he had to write a sequel that brought him back."

"Exactly. People love their characters. But apart from the valid role that fiction plays in our lives, in your case I think your diminished response to Sherlock Holmes stories is a huge step forward." The doctor seemed unusually enthusiastic.

"It is?"

"It's a sign that you're willing—and *prepared*—to step from a fictional existence to a real one."

This was intriguing. Paul found his heart beating a bit faster.

"Your goal in coming to see me and the other therapists in the past has always been to lead a less solitary, more social existence. Find a job, a partner, possibly have a family. And this is a perfect opportunity."

"How?"

"The Sherlock Holmes stories resonated with you for several reasons. I think primarily because of your talents: your intelligence, your natural skills at analysis, your powers of deduction—just like his."

"My mind does kind of work that way."

Dr. Levine said, "I remember the first time you came to see me. You asked about my wife and son—how was he doing in kindergarten? But I didn't wear a wedding ring and had no pictures of family here. I never mentioned my family and I don't put any personal information on the internet. I assumed at the time you were just guessing—you were right, by the way—but now I suspect you deduced those facts about me, right?"

Paul cocked his head. "That's right."

"How?"

"Well, as for the fact you had a child and their age, there was a tiny jelly or jam fingerprint on the side of your slacks—about the height of a four or five year old hugging daddy at breakfast. And you never have appointments before eleven a.m., which told me that you probably were the spouse who took your child to school; if he'd been in first grade or older you would have gotten him to school much earlier and could see patients at nine or ten. You did the school run, I was assuming, because you have more flexible hours than your wife, working for yourself. I was sure she had a full-time job. This *is* Manhattan, of course—two incomes are the rule.

"Now, why a son? I thought the odds were that a girl of that age would be more careful about wiping her fingers before hugging you. Why an only child? Your office and this building are pretty modest, you know. I guessed you weren't a millionaire. That and your age told me it was more likely than not you had only one child. As to the wife, I suspected that even if you had had marital problems, as a therapist you'd work hard to keep the marriage together, so divorce was very unlikely. There was the widower factor, but the odds seemed against that."

Dr. Levine shook his head, laughing. "Sherlock Holmes would be proud of you, Paul. Tell me, that comes naturally to you?"

"Totally natural. It's kind of a game I play. A hobby. When I'm out, I deduce things about people."

"I think you should consider using these skills of yours in the real world."

"How do you mean?"

"I've always thought you were misplaced in academia and publishing. I think you should find a job where you can put those skills to work."

"Like what?"

"Maybe the law. Or . . . Well, how's this: You studied math and science."

"That's right."

"Maybe forensics would be a good choice."

"I've thought about that," Paul said uncertainly. "But do you think I'm ready? I mean, ready to get out in the real world?"

The doctor didn't hesitate. "I absolutely do."

❈

Several days later Paul was doing what he often did at 10 a.m. on a weekday: having a coffee at Starbucks near his apartment on the Upper West Side and reading. Today, however, it was not fiction he was engrossed in, but the local newspapers.

He was considering what Dr. Levine had told him and was trying to find some way to use his skills in a practical way. He wasn't having much luck.

Occasionally he would look around and make deductions about people sitting near him—a woman had broken up with a boyfriend, one man was an artistic painter, another was very likely a petty criminal.

Yes, this was a talent.

Just how to put it to use.

It was as he was pondering this that he happened to overhear one patron, looking down at her Mac screen, turn to her friend say, "Oh, my God. They found another one!"

"What?" the companion asked.

"Another, you know, stabbing victim. In the park. It happened last night. They just found the body." She waved at the screen. "It's in the *Times*."

"Jesus. Who was it?"

"Doesn't say, doesn't give her name, I mean." The blonde, hair pulled back in a ponytail, read. "Twenty nine, financial advisor. They shouldn't say what she does without giving her name. Now everybody who knows a woman like that's going to worry."

Paul realized this would be the man—*surely* a man, according to typical criminal profile—who was dubbed the "East Side Slasher." Over the course of several months he'd killed two, now three, women. The killer took trophies. From the first two victims, at least, he cut off the left index finger. Post mortem, after he'd slashed their jugulars. There'd been no obvious sexual overtones to the crimes. Police could find no motives.

"Where?" Paul asked the Starbucks blonde.

"What?" She turned, frowning.

"Where did they find the body?" he repeated impatiently.

She looked put out, nearly offended.

Paul lifted his eyebrows. "It's not eavesdropping when you make a statement loud enough for the whole place to hear. Now. *Where* is the body?"

"Near Turtle Pond."

"How near?" Paul persisted.

"It doesn't say." She turned away in a huff.

Paul rose quickly, feeling his pulse start to pound.

He tossed out his half-finished coffee and headed for the door. He gave a faint laugh, thinking to himself: the game's afoot.

⬥

"Sir, what're you doing?"

Crouching on the ground, Paul glanced up at a heavyset man, white, pale white, with slicked back, thinning hair. Paul rose slowly. "I'm sorry?"

"Could I see some identification?"

"I guess, sure. Could I?" Paul held the man's eyes evenly.

The man coolly displayed his NYPD detective's shield. The detective said his name was Carrera.

Paul handed over his driver's license.

"You live in the area?"

"It's on my license."

"Doesn't mean it's current," the detective responded, handing it back.

He'd renewed two months ago. He said, "It is. West Eighty-Second. Near Broadway."

They were just north of the traverse road in Central Park, near the pond where the Starbucks woman had told him the body had been found. The area was filled with trees and bushes and rock formations. Grass fields, trisected by paths bordered with mini shoulders of dirt—which is what Paul had been examining. Yellow police tape fluttered but the body and crime scene people were gone.

A few spectators milled nearby, taking mobile phone pictures or just staring, waiting to glimpse some fancy *CSI* gadgets perhaps. Though not everyone was playing voyeur. Two nannies pushed perambulators and chatted. One worker in dungarees was taking a break, sipping coffee and reading the sports section. Two college-age girls roller-bladed past. All were oblivious to the carnage that had occurred only fifty feet away.

The detective asked, "How long have you been here, Mr. Winslow?"

"I heard it about the murder about a half hour ago and I came over. I've never seen a crime scene before. I was curious."

"Did you happen to be in the park at around midnight?"

"Was that the time of death?"

The detective persisted. "Sir? Midnight?"

"No."

"Have you seen anyone in the park recently, wearing a Yankees jacket and red shoes?"

"Is that what the killer was wearing last night? . . . Sorry, no I haven't. But is that what the killer was wearing?"

The detective seemed to debate. He said, "A witness from a street-sweeping crew reported seeing somebody walk out of bushes there about twelve-thirty this morning in a Yankees jacket and red shoes."

Paul squinted. "There?"

The detective sighed. "Yeah, there."

"And he was in his street-sweeping truck?"

"That's right."

"Then he's wrong," Paul said dismissively.

"I'm sorry?"

"Look." Paul nodded, walking to the traverse. "His truck was over there, right?"

The detective joined him. "Yeah. So?"

"That streetlight would've been right in his face and I'd be very surprised if he'd been able to see writing on the jacket. As for the shoes, I'd guess they were blue, not red."

"What?"

"He would only have seen them for a second or two as he drove past. An instant later his mind would have registered them as red—because of the after image. That means they were really blue. And, by the way, they weren't shoes at all. He was wearing coverings of some kind. Booties, like surgeons wear. Those are usually blue or green."

"Covering? What're you talking about?" Carrera was rocking between interested and irritated.

"Look at this." Paul returned to dirt he'd been crouching over. "See these footprints? Somebody walked from the body through the grass, then onto the dirt here. He stopped—you can see that here—and stood in a pattern that suggests he pulled something off his shoes. The same size prints start up again here, but they're much more distinct. So your suspect wore booties to keep you from finding out the brand of shoe he was wearing. But he made a mistake. He figured it was safe to take them off once he was away from the body."

Carrera was staring down. Then he jotted notes.

Paul added, "And as for the brand? I guess your crime scene people have data bases."

"Yessir. Thanks for that. We'll check it out." He was gruff but seemed genuinely appreciative. He pulled out his mobile and made a call.

"Oh, Detective," Paul interrupted, "remember that just because the shoe's big—it looks like a twelve—doesn't mean his *foot* is that size. It's a lot less painful to wear two sizes large than two sizes smaller, if you want to fool somebody about your stature."

Paul's impression was that the cop had just been about to say that the suspect had to be huge.

After Carrera had ordered the crime scene team back and disconnected, Paul said, "Oh, one other thing, Detective?"

"Yessir?"

"See that bud there?"

"That flower?"

"Right. It's from a knapweed. The only place it grows that grows in the park is in the Shakespeare Garden."

"How do you know that?"

"I observe things," Paul said dismissively. "Now. There's a small rock formation there. It'd be a good place to hide and I'll bet that's where he waited for the victim."

"Why?"

"It's not unreasonable to speculate that his cuff scooped up the bud while he was crouched down, waiting for his victim. When he lifted his foot to pull off the booties here, the bud fell out."

"But that's two hundred yards away, the garden."

"Which means you haven't searched it."

Carrera stiffened, but then admitted, "No."

"Just like he thought. I'd have your people search the garden for trace evidence—or whatever your forensic people look for nowadays. You see so much on TV. You never know what's real or not."

After he'd finished jotting notes, Carrera asked, "Are you in law enforcement?"

"No, I just read a lot of murder mysteries."

"Uh-huh. You have a card?"

"No. But I'll give you my number." Paul wrote it down on the back of one of the detective's cards and handed it back. He looked up into the man's eyes; the cop was about six inches taller. "You think this is suspicious, I'm sure. I also wrote down the name of the chess club where I play, down in Greenwich Village. I was there last night until midnight. And I'd guess the CCTV cameras in the subway—I took the Number One train to Seventy-second—would show me getting off around one thirty. And then went to Alonzo's deli. I know the counterman. He can identify me."

"Yessir." Carrera tried to sound like he hadn't suspected Paul, but in fact even Lestrade in the Sherlock Holmes books would have had him checked out.

Still, at the moment, the detective actually offered what seemed to be a warm handshake. "Thanks for your help, Mr. Winslow. We don't always find such cooperative citizens. And helpful ones too."

"My pleasure."

Carrera pulled on gloves and put the bud in a plastic bag. He then walked toward the garden.

As Paul turned back to examine the scene a voice behind him asked, "Excuse me?"

He turned to see a balding man, stocky and tall, in tan slacks and a Polo jacket. Topsiders. He looked like a Connecticut businessman on the weekend. He was holding a digital recorder.

"I'm Franklyn Moss. I'm a reporter for the *Daily Feed*."

"Is that an agricultural newspaper?" Paul asked.

Moss blinked. "Blog. Feed. Like RSS. Oh, that was a joke."

Paul gave no response.

Moss asked, "Can I ask your name?"

"I don't know. What do you want?" He looked at the recorder. Something about the man's eager eyes, too eager, made him uneasy.

"I saw you talking to the cop, Carrera. He's not real cooperative. Kind of a prick. Between you and I."

You and me, Paul silently corrected the journalist. "Well, he was just asking me if I saw anything—about the murder, you know. They call that canvassing, I think."

"So, did you?"

"No. I just live near here. I came by forty-five minutes ago."

Moss looked around in frustration. "Not much good stuff, this one. Everything was gone before we heard about it."

"Good stuff? You mean the body?"

"Yeah. I wanted to get some pics. But no luck this time." Moss stared at the shadowy ring of bushes where the woman had died. "He rape this one? Cut off anything other than the finger?"

"I don't know. The detective—"

"Didn't say."

"Right."

"They always play it so close to the damn chest. Prick, I was saying. You mind if I interview you?"

"I don't really have anything to say."

"Most people don't. Who cares? Gotta fill the stories with something. If you want your fifteen minutes of fame, gimme a call. Here's my card." He handed one over. Paul glanced at and then pocketed it. "I'm writing a sidebar on what people think about somebody getting killed like this."

Paul cocked his head. "I'll bet the general consensus is they're against it."

◆

All the next day, Paul had been in and out of the apartment constantly, visiting the crime scenes of the Upper East Side Slasher, getting as close as he could, observing, taking notes. Then returning and, as he was now, sitting at his computer, continuing his research and thinking hard about how to put into practical use everything he'd learned from his immersion in the Sherlock Holmes books.

His doorbell rang.

"Yes?" he asked into the intercom.

"Yeah, hi. Paul Winslow?"

"Yes."

"It's Detective Carrera. We met the other day. In Central Park?"

Hm.

"Sure. Come on up." He hit the button to unlock the door.

A moment later there came a knock on the door. Paul admitted the detective. Breathing heavily from the two-story walkup—he apparently hadn't waited for the elevator—the man looked around the apartment. Maybe his cop training precluded him from saying, "Nice digs,'" or whatever he would say, but Paul could tell he was impressed at the small but elegant place.

His trust fund was really quite substantial.

"So," Paul said. "Did you check me out? I'm guessing you did, 'cause you don't have your handcuffs out."

Carrera, who was carrying a thick, dark-brown folder, started to deny it but then laughed. "Yeah. You weren't much of a suspect."

"Perps *do* come back to the scene of the crime, though."

"Yeah, but only the stupid ones give the cops advice. . . . and good advice, in your case. The shoe was a Ferragamo, size twelve—you got a good eye. So our perp's pretty well off."

"And you checked the indentation?"

"It was pretty deep. He's a big man, so the shoe's probably the right fit."

"How old was the shoe?"

"They couldn't tell wear patterns."

"Too bad."

"And you were right about the jacket. The street cleaner didn't really see the logo. He was speculating—because it was black and had the cut of a Yankees jacket his kid owns. Trying to be helpful. Happens with witnesses a lot."

"Remember the back lighting. It might not have been black at all. It could have been any dark color. Can I get you anything?"

"Water, yeah. Thanks."

"I'm having milk. I love milk. I drink a glass a day, sometimes two. You want some milk?"

"Water's fine."

Paul got a glass of milk for himself and a bottle of Dannon for the detective.

He returned to find the man studying the shelves. "Man, you got a lot of books. And that whole wall there: True crime, forensics."

"I'm thinking maybe someday I'll study it. Go to school, I mean. I've got degrees in math and science."

"That's a good start. All the good crime scene cops I know have science backgrounds. Hey, let me know if you need advice on where to go, what courses to take."

"Yeah? Thanks."

Carrera turned away and said, "Mr. Winslow?"

"Paul."

"Okay, and I'm Al. Paul, have you heard that sometimes police departments use civilians when there's a tough investigation going. Like psychics."

"I've heard that. I don't believe in psychics. I'm a rationalist."

"Is that somebody who doesn't believe in the supernatural?"

"That's right."

"Well, that's me too. But one thing I *have* done in the past is use consultants. Specialists. Like in computer work. Or if there's been an art theft, we'll bring in somebody from a museum to help us."

"And you want me to be a consultant?" Paul asked, feeling his heart pounding hard.

"I was impressed, what you told me in the park. I've brought some files from the UNSUB two-eight-seven homicides—that's what we call the perp."

"Police don't really use the word 'slasher' much, I'd guess."

"Not too, you know, professional. So, Paul. I was wondering if you could take a look at them and tell us what you thought."

"You bet I would."

❖

George Lassiter was upset.

The forty year old Manhattanite, whose nickname in the press was the sensationalist but admittedly accurate "Upper East Side Slasher," had a problem.

No one was more meticulous than he was when it came to planning out and committing his crimes. In fact, part of the relaxation he experienced from murder derived from the planning. (The actual killing—the *execution*, he sometimes joked—could be a letdown, compared with the meticulous planning, if, say, the victim didn't scream or fight as much as he'd hoped.

Taking scrupulous care to select the right kill zone, to leave minimal or confusing evidence, to learn all he could about the victim so there'd be no surprises when he attacked . . . this was the way he approached all his crimes.

But apparently he'd screwed up in the latest Central Park murder near Shakespeare Garden and Turtle Pond a few nights ago.

The solidly built man, dressed in slacks and a black sweater, was now outside an apartment on Eighty-Second Street, on the Upper West Side of Manhattan. Lassiter had returned to the crime scene the next morning, to see how far the police were getting in the investigation, when he'd noted a skinny young man talking to Albert Carrera, whom Lassiter had identified as the lead detective on the case. The man seemed to be giving advice, which Carrera was obviously impressed with.

That wasn't good.

After the young man had left the crime scene, Lassiter had followed him to his apartment. He'd waited a half hour for someone to exit the building and, when an elderly woman walked down the stairs, Lassiter had approached her with a big smile. He'd described the man and had asked his name, saying he looked like somebody Lassiter had been in the army with. The neighbor had said he was Paul Winslow. Lassiter had shaken his head and said that, no, it wasn't him. He thanked her and headed off.

Once home, he'd researched Paul Winslow at the address he tracked him to. Very little came up. No Facebook page, Instagram, Twitter, Flickr, LinkedIn . . . no social media. A criminal background check came back negative too. At the least, it was pretty clear the young man wasn't a professional law enforcer, just a private meddler.

Which didn't mean he wasn't dangerous.

He might even have seen Lassiter step out of the hiding place in the Shakespeare Garden and grab Ms. Rachel Garner around the neck, throttling her to unconsciousness and then carry her into the park. For the knife work.

Or seen him slip away from the scene around midnight after he was through. That was more likely; after all, Lassiter had seen Paul staring at the very spot where he'd slipped away from the bloody murder site.

Why hadn't Paul called the police then? Well, possibly he'd spent the night debating the pros and cons of getting involved.

It was Paul's apartment that he was surreptitiously checking out at the moment. His intention had been to follow the young man again and find out where he worked, perhaps learning more about him.

But then, lo and behold, who came knocking at the front door, carrying a big fat file folder?

Detective Carrera, in need of a tan and a workout regimen.

What to do, what to do?

Several thoughts came to mind. But, as always, Lassiter didn't leap to any conclusions right away.

Think, plan. And think some more.

Only then could you act safely and your crimes be successful.

◈

"We did find something," Al Carrera was telling Paul, as he spread the contents of the case file out before them on the coffee table. "In the rocks, where you said the UNSUB waited—Shakespeare Garden."

"What was it?"

"Indentations that match the bootie prints. And a tiny bit of wrapper, food wrapper. Forensics found it was from one of those energy bars that campers and hikers eat. From the paper and ink analysis we found it was a Sports Plus bar—their four ounce, peanut butter and raisin one. Probably the perp's because of the dew content analysis. That told us it'd been dropped on the ground about midnight."

"Your people are good," Paul said. He was impressed. He recalled that Sherlock Holmes had his own laboratory. Conan Doyle, a man of science himself, had been quite prescient when it came to forensics.

The detective lifted an envelope, eight and a half by eleven. "These're the pictures of the crimes scenes—and the victims. But I have to warn you. They're a little disturbing."

"I don't know that I've even seen a picture of real body. I mean, on the news I have, but not up close." He stared at the envelope, hesitated. Finally he nodded. "Okay, go ahead."

Carrera spread them out.

Paul was surprised to find they were in color—vivid color. He supposed he shouldn't have been. Why would police photographers use black and white, when nobody else did nowadays?

As he stared at the unfiltered, bloody images Paul felt squeamish. But he thought back to the Sherlock Holmes stories and reminded himself to be as detached and professional as his hero.

He bent forward and concentrated.

Finally he offered, "Some observations. He's really strong. You can see the bruises on their necks. He didn't have to reposition his hands. He just gripped and squeezed and they went unconscious—not dead, mind you. The amount of blood loss tells us they were stabbed while still alive. Let's see, let's see . . . All right, he's right handed. A lefty pretending to be right wouldn't have gotten the cuts so even in the soft tissue."

"Good."

"Also he's cautious, very aware and observant. Look at his footprints in the dirt at all three scenes. He's constantly standing up and walking to the perimeter and looking for threats. Smart."

Carrera wrote.

Paul tapped the picture that showed the perp's bloody hand print on the ground, perhaps as he pushed himself up to a standing position. "Look at the thumb. Interesting."

"What?

"It's not spread out very far—which you'd think it would be if he was using the hand for leverage to rise."

"I see it."

"That might mean that he spends a lot of time on a computer."

"Why?"

"People who regularly type tend to keep their thumbs close in, to hit the spacebar."

Carrera's eyebrow rose and he jotted this down too.

Paul gave a faint smile. "He's a fisherman."

"What?"

"I'm fairly certain. See those marks on the victims' wrists?"

"Ligature marks."

Paul squinted as he shuffled through the pictures. "They're about the thickness of fishing line. And see how he made those incisions *before* he removed the victims' fingers. That's how you skin fish. And, yes, the energy bar—just the sort of food a fisherman would take with him for lunch or a midmorning snack."

Paul sat back and glanced at Carrera, who was writing feverishly. The young man said, "If he *is* a fisherman, which I'm pretty sure he is, he probably has a lake house somewhere in the Tri-State area. We know he's got money. He's not fishing with the locals in the East River. He'll go out to the country in his BMW. Wait," Paul said quickly with a smile, noting Carrera had started to write. "The Beemer's just a guess. But I'm sure his car's a nice one. We know he's upper income. And the arrogance of the crimes suggests that he'd have an ostentatious car. Mercedes, BMW, Porsche."

After he finished writing, Carrera asked, "Is there any reason he'd take the index finger?"

Paul said, "Oh, I think it's an insult."

"Insult. To who?"

"Well, to you. The police. He's contemptuous of authority. He's saying someone could point directly to the killer and you'd still miss it. He's laughing at you."

Carrera shook his head at this. "Son of a bitch."

Paul looked over the pictures once more. "The laughing fisherman," he mused, thinking that make a good title for a Sherlock Holmes story: "The Adventure of the Laughing Fisherman."

Carrera snapped, "Laughing at us, the prick."

Then Paul cocked his head. "Fish . . ."

"What?" Carrera was looking at Paul's focused eyes, as the young man strode to his computer and began typing. After a moment of browsing he said, "There's fishing in Central Park—the Lake, the Pond and Harlem Meer. Yes! I'll bet that's where your perp goes fishing . . . for his victims." He glanced at Carrera eagerly. "Let's go take a look, maybe see if we can find another wrapper or some other evidence. We could set up surveillance."

"It's not authorized for a civilian to go on field operations."

"I'll just tag along. To observe. Offer suggestions."

Carrera debated. "Okay. But if you see anyone or anything that looks suspicious, I take over."

"Fine with me."

Paul collected his jacket and from the den and returned to the living room. Pulling it on, he frowned. "There's something else that just occurred to me. I'll bet he knows about you."

"Me? Personally?"

"You and the other investigators."

"How?"

"I'm thinking he's been to the crime scenes, checking out the investigation. That means you could be in danger. All of you. You should let everyone on your team know." He added gravely, "Sooner rather than later."

Carrera sent a text. "My partner. He'll tell everybody to keep an eye out. You should be careful too, Paul."

"Me? I'm just a civilian. I'm sure I don't have anything to worry about."

◀◆▶

Paul Winslow's apartment was pitifully easy to break into

After James Lassiter had seen Paul and Detective Carrera leave the place—it was about two hours ago—he'd had slipped around back and jimmied the basement door. Then up a few flights of stairs to the apartment itself. The lock-pick gun had done the job in five seconds, and he'd slipped inside, pleased to note that the place didn't have an alarm.

Piece of cake.

He now stood in the bay window of the dim living room, scanning the street. He was wearing latex gloves and stocking cap. Lassiter had been impressed with the fancy apartment; the opulence worked to his advantage. Having so many nice things in an un-alarmed house? Just the place for a robbery. He'd decided that Paul couldn't be a victim of the Upper East Slasher, because then Carrera and the other investigators would know immediately that Paul's advice—which might lead to Lassiter—was accurate. No, the crime would be your basic break-in, the burglar surprised when Paul stepped into his apartment.

His plan was that if Carrera returned with Paul he'd slip out the back and wait another day. But if the young man returned alone, Lassiter would throw him to the floor and pistol whip him. Blind him, shatter his jaw. Put him in the hospital for months and render him useless as a witness. Murder ups the ante exponentially in a crime. Police frankly don't care so much about a beating, however serious.

Jesus, look at all the books . . . Lassiter almost felt bad thinking that blinding him would pretty much finish his days as a reader.

But it's your own fault, Mr. Meddling Winslow.

A half hour later, Lassiter tensed. Yes, there was Paul returning from the direction of Central Park. Alone. The cop wasn't with him. When the young man stepped into a quick mart, Lassiter drew his gun and hid behind the front door, which opened onto the hallway of Paul's building.

Three minutes passed, then four. He was awaiting the key in the latch, but instead heard the sound of the buzzer.

Lassiter cautiously peered through the eyehole. He was looking at a fisheye image of a pizza-delivery man, holding a box.

He nearly laughed. But then wondered, *Wait, how had the guy gotten through the front security door without hitting the intercom from outside?*

Oh, shit. Because Paul had given him the key and told him to ring the buzzer, to draw Lassiter's attention to the front door. Which meant—

The gun muzzle touched the back of Lassiter's neck, the metal cold. Painfully cold.

"Settle down there, Lassiter," Paul said in a calm voice. "Drop the gun, put your hands behind your back."

Lassiter sighed. The pistol bounced nosily on the wood floor.

In an instant, expertly, Paul had cuffed his hands and picked up the gun. Lassiter turned and grimaced. The young man did not, it turned out, have a weapon of his own. He'd bluffed, using a piece of pipe. Paul nodded to the door and said, "I gave him the key outside and told him to let himself in the front door. If you were wondering. But you probably figured."

The buzzer rang again and Paul eased Lassiter onto the floor.

"Don't move. All right?" The young man checked the gun to see that it was loaded and ready to fire, which it was. He aimed at Lassiter's head.

"Yes. Right. I won't."

Paul pocketed the gun and turned the apartment lights on. He stepped to the door, opened it.

He took the pizza box and paid. He must've left a real nice tip; the young man said an effusive, "Well, thank you, sir! You have a good night! Wow, thanks!"

❖

Paul didn't care much for pizza. Or for any food really. He'd only placed the order to distract Lassiter and give him the chance to sneak in the back door. He did, however, have a thirst. "I could use a glass of milk. You?"

"Milk?"

"Or water? That's about all I can offer you. I don't have any liquor or soda."

Lassiter didn't respond. Paul walked into the kitchen and poured a glass of milk. He returned and helped Lassiter onto a chair. He sipped from the tall glass, reflecting on how different he felt, how confident. The depression was gone completely, the anxiety too.

Thank you, Dr. Levine.

Paul regarded the glass. "Did you know milk has a terroir too, just like wine? You can tell, by analysis of the milk, what the cows were eating during the lactation period: the substances in the soil, chemical residues, even insect activity. Why do you wrap your trophies in silk? The fingers you cut off your victims? That's one thing I couldn't deduce."

Lassiter gasped and his eyes, wide, cut into Paul's like a torch.

"I know it wasn't on the news. The police don't even know that." He explained, "There was a single bloody thread at one of the scenes. It couldn't have come from a silk garment you were wearing. That would be too ostentatious and obvious for a man on a killing mission. Silk is used for cold-weather undergarments, yes, but you wouldn't have worn anything like that in these temperatures; very bad idea to sweat at a crime scene. Weren't the days better for people like you when there was no DNA analysis?"

Did a moan issue from Lassiter's throat? Paul couldn't be sure. He smiled. "Well, I'm not too concerned about the silk. Merely curious. Not relevant to our purposes here. The more vital question you have surely is how I found *you*. Understandable. The short answer is that I learned from the newspaper accounts of the murders that you're an organized offender. I deduced you plan everything out ahead of time. And you plan the sites of the killings and the escape routes meticulously.

"Someone like that would also want to know about the people tracking him down. I decided you'd be at the scene the morning after the killing. I observed everyone who was there. I was suspicious of the man sipping coffee and reading the sports section of the *Post*. I was pretty sure it was you. I'd known that the clue about the Ferragamo shoe was fake—why take off the booties in the dirt, when you could have walked three feet farther onto the asphalt and pulled them off there, not leaving any impressions for the police. That meant you weren't rich at all but middle class—the shoes were to misdirect the cops. I knew you were strong and solidly built. All of those described the *Post*-reader pretty well.

"When I left the scene I was aware that you followed me back here. As soon as I got inside I grabbed a hat and new jacket and sunglasses and went out the back door. I started following *you*—right back to your apartment in Queens. A few internet searches and I got your identity."

Paul enjoyed a long sip of milk. "An average cow in the U.S. produces nearly twenty thousand pounds of milk a year. I find that amazing." He regarded the unfortunate man for a moment. "I'm a great fan of the Sherlock Holmes stories." He nodded around the room at his shelves. "As you can probably see."

"So that's why the police aren't here," his prisoner muttered. "You're going play the big hero, like Holmes, showing up the police with your brilliance. Who're you going to turn me over to? The mayor? The police commissioner?"

"Not at all." Paul added, "What I want is to *employ* you. As my assistant."

"*Assistant?*"

"I want you to work for me. Be my sidekick. Though that's a word I've never cared for, I must say."

Lassiter gave a sour laugh. "This's all pretty messed up. You think you're some kind of Sherlock Holmes and you want me to be your Watson?"

Paul grimaced. "No, no, no. My hero in the books—" He waved at his shelves. "—isn't *Holmes*. It's *Moriarty*. Professor James Moriarty."

"But wasn't he, what do they say? Holmes's nemesis."

Paul quoted Holmes's word from memory, "'In calling Moriarty a criminal you are uttering libel in the eyes of the law—and there lie the glory and the wonder of it! The greatest schemer of all time, the organizer of every deviltry, the controlling brain of the underworld, a brain which might have made or marred the destiny of nations—that's the man!'"

He continued, "Holmes was brilliant, yes, but he had no grand design, no drive. He was passive. Moriarty, on the other hand, was ambition personified. Always making plans for plots and conspiracies. He's been my hero ever since I first read about him." Paul's eyes gazed affectionately at the books on his shelves that contained the stories involving Moriarty. "I studied math and science because of him. I became a professor, just like my hero."

Paul thought back to his session with Dr. Levine not long ago

The Sherlock Holmes stories resonated with you for several reasons. I think primarily because of your talents: your intelligence, your natural skills at analysis, your powers of deduction—just like his. . . .

Dr. Levine had assumed Paul worshipped Holmes, and the patient didn't think it wise to correct him; therapists presumably take role modeling of perpetrators like Moriarty, even if fictional, rather seriously.

"Moriarty only appeared in two stories as a character, was mentioned in just five others. But the shadow of his evil runs throughout the entire series and you get the impression that Holmes was always aware that a villain even smarter and more resourceful than he was always hovering nearby. *He* was my idol." Paul smiled, his expression filled with reverent admiration. "So. I've decided to become a modern-day Moriarty. And that means having an assistant just like my hero did."

"Like Watson?"

"No. Moriarty's sidekick was Colonel Sebastian Moran, a retired military man, who specialized in murder. Exactly what I need. I wondered whom to pick. I don't exactly hang out in criminal circles. So I began studying recent crimes in the city and read about the Upper East Side Slasher. You had the most promise. Oh, you made some mistakes, but I thought I could help you overcome your flaws—like returning to visit the scene of the crime, not planting enough fake evidence to shift the blame, attacking victims who were very similar, which establishes patterns and makes profiling easier. And for heaven's sake, eating a power bar while you waited for your victim? Please. You *are* capable of better, Lassiter."

The man was silent. His expression said he acknowledged that Paul was correct.

"But first I needed to save you from the police. I helped Detective Carrera come up with a profile of the perp that was very specific, very credible . . . and described someone completely different from you."

"Maybe, but they're out there looking for me."

"Oh, they are?" Paul asked wryly.

"What do you mean?"

He found the cable box remote. He fiddled for a moment. "You know, in the past we'd have to wait until the top of the hour to see the news.

Now, they've got that twenty-four/seven cycle. Tedious usually but helpful occasionally."

The TV came to life.

Actually it was a Geico commercial.

"Can't do much about those," Paul said with a grimacing nod at the screen. "Though they can be funny. The squirrels're the best."

A moment later an anchorwoman appeared. "If you're just joining us—"

"Which we are," Paul chimed in.

"'NYPD officials have reported that the so-called Upper East Side Slasher, allegedly responsible for the murders of three women in Manhattan and, earlier tonight, of Detective Albert Carrera of the NYPD, has been arrested. He's been identified as Franklyn Moss, a journalist and blogger."

"Jesus! What?"

Paul shushed Lassiter.

"Detective Carrera was found stabbed to death about 5 p.m. near the Harlem Meer fishing area in Central Park. An anonymous tip—"

"*Moi*," Paul said.

"—led authorities to Moss's apartment in Brooklyn, where police found evidence implicating him in the murder of Detective Carrera and the other victims. He is being held without bond in the Manhattan Detention Center."

Paul shut the set off.

He turned and was amused to see Lassiter's expression was one of pure bewilderment. "I think we don't need these anymore." He rose and unhooked the handcuffs. "Just to let you know, though, my lawyer has plenty of evidence implicating you in the crimes, so don't do anything foolish."

"No, I'm cool."

"Good. Now when I decided I wanted you as an assistant I had to make sure somebody else took the fall for the killings. Whom to pick? I've never liked reporters very much, and I found Franklyn Moss particularly irritating. So I datamined him. I learned he was quite the fisherman, so I fed Carrera this mumbo jumbo that that was the killer's hobby.

"Earlier today I convinced Carrera we should go to Central Park, one of the fishing preserves there, to look for clues. When we were alone at the Meer I slit his throat and sawed off his index finger. That's a lot of work, by the way. Couldn't you have picked the pinkie? Never mind. Then I went to Moss's apartment and hid the knife and finger in his garage and car, along with some physical evidence from the other scenes, a pair of Ferragamos I bought yesterday and a packet of those energy bars you like. I left some of Carrera's blood on the doorstep so the police would have probable cause to get a warrant."

Paul enjoyed another long sip of milk.

"The evidence's circumstantial, but compelling: He drives a BMW, which I told Carrera was his vehicle—because I'd seen it earlier. Public records show he has a lake house in Westchester—which I also told Carrera. And I suggested that the ligature marks were from fishing line, which Moss had plenty of in his garage and basement . . . You used bell wire, right?"

"Um, yes."

Paul continued, "I also fed the detective this nonsense that the killer probably spent a lot of time keyboarding at a computer—like a blogger would do. So our friend Moss is going away forever. You're clean."

Lassiter frowned. "But wouldn't Carrera have told other officers *you* gave him the profile? That'd make you a suspect."

"Good point, Lassiter. But I knew he wouldn't. Why bring the file to me here in my house to review, rather than invite me downtown to examine it? And why did he come alone, not with his partners? No, he asked my advice *privately*—so he could steal my ideas and take credit for them himself." Paul ran his hand through his hair and regarded the killer with a coy smile. "Now, tell me about the assignment—about the person who hired you. I'm really curious about that."

"Assignment?"

But the feigned surprise didn't work.

"Please, Lassiter. You're not a serial killer. I wouldn't want you if you were—they're far too capricious. Too driven by emotion." Paul said the last word as if it were tainted food. "No, you came up with the plan for the multiple murders to cover up your real crime. You'd been hired to murder a particular individual—one of the three victims."

Lassiter's mouth was actually gaping open. He slowly pressed his lips back together.

Paul continued, "It was so obvious. There was no sexual component to the killings, which there always is in serial murders. And there's no psychopathological archetype for taking an index finger trophy—you improvised because you thought it would look suitably spooky. Now, which of the three was the woman you'd been hired to kill?"

The man gave a why-bother shrug. "Rachel Garner. The last one. She was going to blow the whistle on her boss. He runs a hedge fund that's waist deep in money laundering."

"Or—alternative spelling—'waste deep,' if it needs *laundering*." Paul couldn't help the play on words. "I thought it was something like that."

Lassiter said, "I'd met the guy in the army. He knew I did a few dirty tricks, and he called me up."

"So, it was a one-time job?"

"Right."

"Good. So you can come to work for me."

Lassiter debated.

Paul leaned forward. "Ah, there's a lot of carnage out there to perpetrate. Lots of foolish men and women on Wall Street who need to be relieved of some of their gains, ill- or well-gotten. There're illegal arms sales waiting to be made, and cheating politicians to extort and humans to traffic and terrorists who may hold intellectually indefensible views but have very large bank accounts and are willing to write checks to people like us, who can provide what they need."

Paul's eyes narrowed. "And, you know, Lassiter, sometimes you just need to slice a throat or two for the fun of it."

Lassiter's eyes fixed on the carpet. After a long moment he whispered, "The silk?"

"Yes?"

"My mother would stuff a silk handkerchief in my mouth when she beat me. To mute the screams, you know."

"Ah, I see," Paul replied softly. "I'm sorry. But I can guarantee you plenty of opportunities to get even for that tragedy, Lassiter. So. Do you want the job?"

The killer debated for merely a few seconds. He smiled broadly. "I do, Professor. I sure do." The men shook hands.

ART IN THE BLOOD

by Laura Caldwell

When the reporter from the *Post*, a young woman with a garishly severe haircut, tried to tell him that the Gargeau he'd sold last month was a fake, Dekalb swallowed his disgust, took his bone china cup out of her hand and asked her, as politely as possible, to leave his office. Drew Dekalb Van-Werden was his full name, but he preferred Dekalb. And Dekalb did not take well to contradiction or confrontation, certainly not from the *Post*.

The reporter had gotten an appointment by telling his assistant, a boy named Tad who would now have to be fired, that the *Post* wanted to do a profile on him. Movers and shakers of the art world, she'd apparently said. "A follow-up to *Art in the Blood*."

She had clinched his interest with that comment. The decades-old article in the *New Yorker*, naming him as the Sherlock Holmes of the art world, was still the favored link on his website. The moniker was one he'd gladly accepted.

But now she wouldn't get up from his chair, the Victorian wing chair he'd just had refinished.

"Look, Mr. Van Weird," she said.

"Van*Werden*." He said this too quickly, too harshly. "Van Weird" was what they used to call him in Manautaukee, Pennsylvania, the zit of a town where he'd been raised.

"Yes, Van*Werden*," she said.

He reminded himself that she was mimicking him on purpose, that she wanted a reaction. The realization calmed him. He would find out what she wanted and get her the hell out. He took a seat at his desk and nodded at her to continue.

"We believe our information is correct," she said. "What we believe is that *Wheels of a Rogue*, a painting that you sold for . . ." She stopped talking and leaned forward, her ear cocked in his direction as if he might supply this information.

When he was silent, she sat back and said, "Well, anyway, we believe it's a forgery."

He almost laughed. He stood and moved around his desk, forcing her to twist in order to follow him. He stopped at one of the arched windows that overlooked Madison Avenue, one hand on his hip, the other on the walnut window frame.

"Have you talked to the owner of the piece?" He was careful not to say the name of Barbara Baden-Shore—BB as she was called—although they could find out easily enough.

"Not yet. We've received tips."

"I see. And have you viewed the painting?"

He glanced back and saw her squirm in the chair.

"I see," he said again.

Then he fell silent. They stared at each other. And stared.

"I'm from San Francisco," she said.

"And . . . ?"

"I'm just saying, we don't let stories drop."

He nodded at her, graciously he thought, then he let his own silence stand.

Finally, she muttered something and collected her battered purse from the floor.

He walked across the room and held open the door for her.

"Tad," he said. "Come here."

✦

A week later, the vellum envelope was waiting on his chair when he returned from a meeting at Sotheby's. He was between assistants, so the office had been locked and empty during his absence, yet there was the envelope, sitting shamelessly on his chair where he couldn't miss it.

Then he saw Binny Moriarty's handwriting. And he became irritated. No, more than irritated. Binny's impudence was staggering. He'd loved that about him at one point. It was Binny's audacity that made him stand out from the other assistants, made Dekalb break his ironclad rule about never dating the help (and the rule about always getting his keys back). Stupid, but then love can be incredibly stupid.

He sliced the flap open with a silver letter opener by Robert Garrard, circa 1867, a gift to himself after he'd sold his first painting more than twenty years ago.

Inside was a piece of filmy vellum paper in a hideous sea-green color. Binny's sharp, scratchy scribble covered the page.

> *Dear Dekalb,*
> I have the Gargeau.
> It's a little piece of you, I guess you could say, which was all
> I ever wanted.
> *Au revoir,*
> *Binny*

Dekalb dropped the letter with a quick flick of his hand as if it were a used tissue. It fluttered instead of sinking out of sight the way he'd hoped. Finally, it came to rest on his tulipwood marquetry desk, right on top of a pile of invitations to lunches and cocktail parties and gallery openings. He'd been trying to ignore those invitations. Without an assistant, he'd have to respond to all of them himself, a task he relished with as much enthusiasm as picking up cigarettes in the Vietnamese grocery. It struck him now that if Binny was telling the truth, he'd never get another one of those pathetic invitations again.

He snatched the letter off his desk, appalled at the way his hand trembled. With the other hand, he plucked a cigarette from the black lacquer box on his desk and lit it. After a few deep, lung-filling drags, he read the letter again, then again. Binny *had* the Gargeau? The real one? Binny must be lying—a sophomoric grab for attention, that was all. But then what about that reporter from the *Post*? Coincidence?

That *damned* Binny.

"It's short for Benjamin," he'd said the first day when he walked into Dekalb's office.

He was in his late twenties, not a smooth-faced, backpack-carrying kid like the other boys and girls who usually applied for the position. He wore black scuffed loafers—Armani rip-offs, Dekalb could tell—and a black wool blazer. His hair was black, too, blue-black and curly. His eyes, though, were a deep, jeweled green. One of his front teeth was just barely crooked, like a canvas hanging an eighth of an inch too low on one side.

They'd shaken hands, and Binny sank into the Victorian wing chair, crossing a leg so that one cheap shoe rested on his knee.

"You say that Binny is short for Benjamin," Dekalb said, "but it's your last name, Moriarty, I'm curious about."

After the *New Yorker* anointed him the Holmes of art forgery, discussing his ability to suss out fakes (at least three confirmed at that point), he'd gone back and reread many of the Holmes stories. And he'd always enjoyed the stories with Professor Moriarty, the great nemesis to Holmes. There was something about the way Holmes was thought to have been dead, outwitted by Professor Moriarty, only to later be resurrected.

"Yes, Moriarty," Binny said with a smile. "It's Irish."

"Or English by way of Ireland."

"Well, they do say we're descendants of William the Conqueror." Binny paused. "But, you know how it is . . ."

"Everyone says they're from William the Conqueror."

They said the sentence at the same time, and although true, it was a very odd thing to say simultaneously. Dekalb laughed, then raised his hand to his mouth to stop the momentum. Generally, he didn't laugh. It didn't suit him. But he was charmed by this lad. Binny laughed too, and Dekalb felt the rolling of the wheel of laughter again, hard to halt.

But halt it he did. Charming or no, Dekalb had to establish control. And so he held up his hand, and then he launched into his usual spiel about the unique pieces he dealt with, how he liked to work alone, how he wasn't like any other dealer in the New York art world.

Binny nodded, eyes bright. "I can't tell you what a pleasure it is to meet you," he'd said when Dekalb gave him a pause. "I've been following your career ever since you sold the Vernet. It set you on the map. You're one of the best."

Dekalb felt something bulky catch in his throat, and he swallowed hard. The Vernet was his gleaming moment of dealerdom, one that was a step onto other greats, but one that he hadn't exactly been able to replicate since. It wasn't that he hadn't sold other such painters or Old Masters. He had. But nothing topped the Vernet in terms of sheer, unadulterated excitement—the find, the initial secrecy, then the perfectly-placed rumors at the perfectly-placed time to send the price soaring. He wasn't sure why the others had been a slowly sloping hill downward. Not even the forgeries he'd detected could flag the same enthusiasm, that same joy he'd had with the Vernet.

Sherlock Holmes was said to be a descendant of Vernet, the *New Yorker* journalist had mentioned, and now here was this man-boy, with a Sherlock Holmes kind of a name. It seemed the universe was circling back around, bringing Dekalb back to that state of mind he'd enjoyed early in his career.

Later, it struck Dekalb that Binny couldn't have followed his career since the Vernet sold. The boy had probably been thirteen years old— thirteen and living in a shabby walk-up in the Bronx with his mother and his scruffy pack of sisters, where the sale of a rare Vernet certainly could not have been news.

But he didn't pick up on that at the time, too flattered by Binny's words, Binny's apparent art knowledge, his mischievous good looks, and the fact that he didn't travel in any of Dekalb's circles (past or present). All that had converged like planets aligning to get Dekalb to hire him, and in truth, those things had probably made him fall for Binny, too, which was why Dekalb hadn't seen the almost malevolent power that Binny possessed. Because like Professor Moriarty in the tales of his adopted namesake, Binny had hereditary tendencies of the most diabolical kind.

◈

"Dekalb! How lovely," BB said, as she pulled him into a loose, false hug. The aroma of her signature perfume—some spicy, Asian fragrance made just for her in Thailand—overpowered him. He *hated* women's perfume, especially BB's, but inhaling it was one of the sacrifices he made for his business.

"Thank you for having me, BB." Dekalb stepped into her foyer with its gold and white marble floor. High above them, ornate moldings carved with cherubs framed the room.

"Well, it's about time," she said, as if she'd been inviting him without response for years, when he'd practically had to beg his way into this lunch.

Dekalb attempted to discreetly shake the damp from his right leg. Before he'd come, he'd visited the Vietnamese grocery, a filthy place that smelled of old fish. Dekalb had spent an eternity trying to point the seemingly mute and illiterate clerk toward his French cigarettes. There was only one pack left, he could see, and he was terrified that another patron would somehow claim them first. Once they were in his hands, he was so grateful he decided to light one as he left the store. The clerk had given him matches, which he rarely used, and he fussed with them instead of digging for his lighter. He'd stepped off the curb, ready to hail a cab, but his right foot sunk into a pothole filled with swampy sewage water. Now, he felt the still-wet pant leg clinging to his calf. He prayed BB wouldn't look down.

Luckily, she swung an arm up and around his shoulder, an arm that managed to be both bony and taut with muscles. It was the look that all BB's crowd went for these days—anorexically thin but with a light layer of brawn. BB had to be at least sixty, probably eight years older than he was, but the combination of the hard body, perfect clothes, and a symbiotic relationship with a plastic surgeon made her look in her forties.

Strangely, BB reminded him of his mother. It was partly due to the blond hair and the heavy-lidded eyes. Of course, his mother's eyes were swollen really, regularly pummeled into shape by her boyfriends, while BB's were surgically crafted to give her a sexy, Veronica Lake look. But BB, like his mother, could be sweet and playful toward him one minute, icy-cold the next.

She led him down a hallway where millions of dollars of paintings hung on the walls, one right next to another, as if they were posters, not rare originals. Dekalb's eyes flashed on each one, searching for the Gargeau, which was, of course, his whole reason for coming to this lunch. He had to see for himself if what Binny and the *Post* reporter claimed was true—that a painting worth over two million dollars had been replaced with a fake.

Dekalb did use faux masterpieces occasionally, just never for the Gargeau. All dealers used them for those times when a painting needed to be shown but the insurance would be too high. The forgers who did these copies—*maîtres copistes*—truly were artists, *masters*, because the results were flawless. Unless you were actually looking for the forger's signature mark, such as a minuscule white dot or an excruciatingly small black check mark, you might never know the difference. But no matter how good the piece, they were always destroyed immediately after use so there'd be no mix-up. Accidentally shipping a forged painting to a client was unforgivable in Dekalb's world. It branded you an amateur, and people in this town had no patience for amateurs.

He was fairly certain he could identify if the Gargeau was a fake. He simply needed to turn on his investigative Sherlockian skills once more. The gut-turning reality was obvious to him though—this time, discovering a forgery could mean his own demise rather than someone else's.

But there was no sign of *Wheels of a Rogue* in BB's front hallway, just the European landscapes that BB seemed to favor so much—an Edouard Cortes showing a rainy Paris street, a James Kay with its myriad fuzzy browns and blues depicting turn-of-the-century London, even a Cézanne landscape of the French countryside. Although BB considered herself superior to everyone in this city, everyone in the country for that matter, Dekalb had found that most of her type felt decidedly inferior to Europeans. BB's way of compensating for that, apparently, was to acquire these paintings and practically line her drawers with them. Normally, they gave Dekalb a thrill, these paintings, making him want to stand close to the walls and breathe in the faint oily, dusty scent of old canvases, but today he noticed only the absence of the Gargeau.

"You know Char and Tommy," BB said as they walked into her sitting room, a vast space where the walls were plastered with salmon-colored damask silk and then more landscapes. BB pointed to Charlotte Raford-Jennings and Tomasina Winters, both of whom jumped from their gold leaf chairs and took turns squeezing him around his middle with more of those tiny, rock-hard arms.

"Hello, ladies. You look *fabulous*," he said, dialing up the effeminate act. Women like BB, Char, and Tommy still loved to have a gay male friend around, a man who could talk clothes and spas and haircuts, unlike their husbands.

And so talk he did, all through the tea service (a European tradition that BB liked to call her own, although she mistakenly served it before the meal instead of mid-afternoon) and all through the lunch of sea bass and some kind of exotic greens. The women stayed away from the food, but BB had a wine cellar bigger than most studio apartments, and they soon got rather drunk on the Fumé Blanc. They usually did at these lunches—something Dekalb had counted on, since he needed to search the apartment at some point for the Gargeau. He needed to see it by himself, to study it.

The anticipation of seeing *Wheels of a Rogue* was killing him, and so he drank too much as well. It was impossible to tell exactly how much he imbibed since BB's waitstaff kept filling up his glass whenever he took so much as a sip.

Finally, when he could take it no longer, he pushed his chair back. "*Mesdames.*" He stood and made a slight bow, knowing BB would love that. "I must use the little boy's room."

BB waved a bejeweled hand. "You know where it is, Dekalb. Help yourself."

He tried not to run down the hallway as the ladies' laughter trilled behind him. He didn't need to examine the paintings in this area, since BB probably wouldn't hang the Gargeau in a short hall that led to a guest bath. No, it had to be somewhere more prominent. The formal dining room, perhaps, or maybe over the fireplace in the living room? He couldn't ask BB. That was out of the question, for BB didn't like to talk about where or how she acquired something; she liked to pretend it was always hers.

He ducked in the powder room, planning on relieving himself in a lightning fast way, then giving himself a few minutes to prowl the rest of the apartment before BB noticed him gone and sent one of the servants looking.

As he flicked on the lights, he saw a figure lurking in the corner, and he felt a clench and then a pounding in his heart. "Good Lord!" he said, a hand flying to cover his chest.

He tittered when he saw what it was—a white marble statue of an angel, standing at least six feet tall. He shut the door, berating himself for being so jumpy. While he urinated, he stared at the statue. A Benzoni, if he wasn't mistaken, probably 1852 or so. God knew BB had taste—a Benzoni this size was hard to come by—but she had absolutely no sense of placement, and this reminder made him even more nervous. The Gargeau could be anywhere.

When he was done, he left the bathroom light on and closed the door so that someone might think he was in there. He tiptoed down the hall, trying to minimize the squishing sound his shoe made every time his still slightly-wet sock rubbed against it. He turned right, moving away from the sitting room where BB and the ladies were still giggling. He poked his head in a large yellow living room cluttered with amber inlaid commodes and French clock garniture, thinking he definitely might find *Wheels of a Rogue* on the walls, but there were only more European cityscapes and such. As he continued on, he saw two bedrooms, both of them guest rooms with canopied beds and the antiques BB had relegated to second tier. No Gargeau.

At the end of the hallway, there were two doors, one of them open. He popped his head in the room, seeing a study painted a rich, dark gray and filled with leather furniture that had a red sheen. The husband's room, Dekalb thought. Probably the only place he could relax in this mausoleum, the poor bastard. He quickly scanned the walls before moving back into the hallway and staring at the last remaining door. Closed.

He knew he shouldn't. He'd already overstepped his bounds. You didn't go traipsing around one of these apartments unless you were invited to do so. Space and privacy traded at a premium in Manhattan, and lurking about was the social equivalent of putting your hands in your host's underwear drawer.

He stayed still a moment and strained his ears. Were the women still carrying on—swirling wine glasses and making promises of double workouts to banish the calories? He couldn't hear anything, but he was sure he was too far away now. Just a quick peek was all he needed to see if the Gargeau was real.

The door to the master opened silently as he turned the gold doorknob. Inside was an enormous bed with footstools on either side. And, above it, *Wheels of a Rogue*.

Rogue depicted a pair of men's shoes at the foot of a bed. One lay on its side, the other at an angle. Between the two were a glittery blue handbag and a white lace bra.

Rogue was a sexy piece, despite the fact that it portrayed just a floor with shoes and such, because you couldn't help but wonder about the man, the rogue, who'd enticed a woman to throw her jeweled handbag and lingerie on the floor. You couldn't help but imagine what they were doing on that bed.

Dekalb moved further into the room until he reached the end of the bed. It was so bloody big he still couldn't get a close look at the painting. He tilted his body forward, leaning over the fluffy yellow linens that looked like lemon chiffon, but still he couldn't get near enough to inspect it for marks. He walked to the side and strained his neck forward. Everything looked fine from that angle, yet he couldn't be absolutely sure. And he had to be sure, or he'd never sleep again.

He glanced over his shoulder, heard nothing, and after a quick intake of breath, moved to the side of the bed and crept up one of the foot stools until he towered over the bed, his face nearly even with the painting now. His eyes flicked over the canvas. Top left quadrant, fine. Top right, no problem. Mid portion, fine. Bottom left, okay. Bottom right . . .

There it was. Right under the corner of the golden-brown bed was an equally golden dash. It was only a fraction of an inch at most and so close to the bottom of the bed that no one would notice. But there it was.

Fuck, fuck, *fuck*. He bent farther over the bed for a better look, just to make sure. He leaned one hand on the lemon yellow pillows, making a deep indentation in the linens, his ass high in the air, his nose close to the painting.

His breath was coming faster now, his chest rising and falling under his cashmere sweater.

The fingers of his free hand squeezed and unclenched and then squeezed again repeatedly. He felt a familiar ping somewhere in his chest, somewhere high near the top of his lungs, and it caused him to freeze, his hand sinking like a stone into the bedding. He wasn't eating the way he'd promised the doctors, and he hadn't quit smoking, but he thought he had his heart problems under control. Binny's letter must have brought it back. It was *all* about Binny. That first ping, a year ago, the one accompanied by the flames shooting down his arm, had happened at the beginning of the end of their relationship, when Binny asked to become his partner.

"Not just like this," Binny had said, stroking Dekalb's forearm, "but in the business, too."

By that time, they had worked together for years. Binny no longer bought designer rip-offs, but instead saved his pennies, or waited for Dekalb to get in a generous mood, and took home the real thing—the Prada shoes with leather as soft as silk, the sport coats from Gucci. With the smart clothes and the job that gave him a ticket inside the art world had come a new sort of confidence. Oh, Binny had always been confident. He'd probably been confident when he was a pimply prepubescent in the boroughs, but after a few years with Dekalb he carried himself with a different kind of self-possession, no longer hanging back at the parties but rather jumping right into conversations, letting his newly acquired knowledge and his newly acquired garments, carry his inherent good looks until a little circle fell around him, both men and women beaming at him, the women whispering about the way his jet-black locks fell over his eyes, the men wondering if they could take him home for just one night.

As Binny spoke that day, talking about how much he'd learned from Dekalb, how much he loved him, how all this made him believe that they could be partners in every facet of their lives including the business, Dekalb had an explosion of an awareness—the dawn of a recognition. That was when he'd seen the malevolence that Binny Moriarty possessed. And like Holmes with Professor Moriarty, he was both appalled and impressed. But mostly betrayed. And so he sat, staring with dead eyes at the one person in his whole life who he'd thought had truly loved him, the whole of him. He'd been wrong, he saw that. Binny hadn't loved him, he'd just played him, wheedled his way into Dekalb's life and home, and hoped for Dekalb's business and checkbook as well.

That was when the pain started.

And now it tinged his chest again. Then the flames flared and pain soaked his chest, his being.

Fucking Binny. How *could* he?

He heard a brittle cough behind him, and the shock of it dispelled the chest pain.

"Dekalb," BB said. "What in the hell are you doing?"

❖

Binny came in his apartment using his old set of keys, the keys that had allowed him to snatch the Gargeau and maim Dekalb's business, making it a limping horse that would soon have to be shot.

He'd called an hour ago, saying simply that he would like to stop by.

Dekalb said only one word. "Okay."

He'd been caught in BB's bedroom only two days ago, yammering excuses about wanting to visit a favorite painting, and yet already the rumors had started. Customers he called on sounded odd, the Christie's appraiser he spoke to made a crack about having too much to drink at the Shore house, and Char Raford-Jennings admitted that BB was talking, whispering hopes that the pressure of the art scene wasn't leading to an emotional breakdown. The irony, of course, was that now he did feel on the verge of a breakdown, on the very edge of a tremendous abyss with the bottom nowhere in sight.

After the phone call, Dekalb sat on his balcony, his back to the door, not caring that the sun snuck around the building and soon shone on his face, probably making him look old and haggard.

He'd been reviewing, again, his meager options and once again decided that none of them would do any good. Even if he could get the original Gargeau from Binny, he couldn't envision how he could sneak in BB's apartment and switch it. Not after getting caught with his ass in the air, staring at the painting. And he couldn't simply tell BB what had happened, because that would amount to professional suicide. No one would ever buy from him again, too afraid that they were being peddled a fake. He considered getting the original back and hiding it somewhere in the hopes that BB would never find out. But she would. When she divorced the current husband or when she simply tired of the painting, it would be appraised and the truth would come out. Dekalb couldn't stand the thought of waiting for the ax to fall like that. So now he just sat, his hands lifeless on his lap.

After the key turned, he heard the soft *tap, tap, tap* of Binny's loafers across the wood floor, coming closer.

"Deck?" he heard from behind him.

Still he didn't move.

When he felt the weight of Binny's hands on his shoulders, he stood and shook them off, spinning around, one fist raised.

The sight of Binny—his green eyes no longer glinting but dull, no smile playing over the off-center teeth—startled him for a moment, but then it fueled his anger, and he raised the other fist too, a boxer's pose.

A coarse chuckle escaped Binny's mouth. "Jesus, Deck, you look like a fool." He batted down Dekalb's hands. "Come inside before your nose gets pink."

Binny turned and walked inside, leaving Dekalb standing there, his arms limp now, flattened by Binny's words and the familiar coddling tone.

He followed Binny through the French doors and into the kitchen. Binny opened the Sub-Zero refrigerator with the knotty pine exterior, bending down to peer inside like he still lived here, reaching in for the peach juice, pouring them both a glass.

Dekalb ignored the offering. "How did you do it?"

Binny made a face as if that were a silly question. "Took it from the racks late one Friday night, before you delivered to the Shores."

Dekalb dialed his mind back. BB Shore and her husband had taken delivery of the Gargeau after his recovery, after he thought Binny was gone from his life. "And then?

"And then I gave it to Sharton, replaced it two nights later." William Sharton was one of the best, and undisputedly the fastest, forger in the city.

Dekalb felt a pulse of anger in his temples that Binny could be so nonchalant. "So tell me your price, Binny. Let's get on with it."

Binny sipped his juice, his long fingers wrapped around the small, bubbled-glass tumbler. They were as physically close to each other now as they'd been in over a year, and Dekalb could see the little U shape in the middle of Binny's upper lip, the cinnamon-brown freckles in a curved trail below his eyes, the long black lashes. Binny pursed his mouth, and at the same time lifted his shoulders in a shrug.

It was that shrug that got him.

"Don't!" Dekalb said to Binny.

"Don't what?" A desperate, angry tone.

"Don't play any more games with me!" Dekalb's volume rose, and without moving his feet he strained himself toward Binny, feeling his face growing purplish. He couldn't take this—Binny back in his kitchen, acting like he hadn't orchestrated Dekalb's personal destruction. "You're hustling me for a reason. Tell me what in the hell you want."

Another rough chuckle from Binny. "Hustling you? Is that what you think?"

"Blackmail then. Call it what you like."

Binny leaned back against the counter. "This is what I want," he said, waving the tumbler in an arc in front of his body.

Dekalb clenched his hands, his nails digging into the soft flesh of his palms, liking the thought that he might dig enough to draw his own blood. "My apartment? My furniture?"

"You, Deck, you idiot." Binny set the glass down.

Dekalb swallowed, felt himself stall. "What?"

Binny's eyes roamed his face. "Do you remember, after the hospital, how many times I called you, how many vases of lilies I sent, how many visits I tried to make to your office?"

Of course he remembered. He'd been trying to expunge Binny from his world, cleanse him from his pores, wanting to forget that the man he adored was just a con artist trying to get at his business.

"You used me," Dekalb said.

"I loved you." The flat, green eyes seemed to sink into Binny's face, his mouth hung open a little, making him look out of breath. "I know you think you're infallible, Deck, but you messed up there. I only wanted us to be closer, to share everything. I didn't want half of your business, just to share a fraction, but you wouldn't fucking listen. You jumped to conclusions, Deck, and you destroyed everything."

Dekalb felt a prickle along his scalp, an inkling of fear that maybe he could have read it all wrong. He scoffed to show Binny he didn't buy it, but the doubt crept in like smoke, making him flush with rage again. "Don't do this to me."

"Don't do this to *you*?" Binny stood away from the counter, his face coloring, too. "*You* fucked it all up, Deck. Do you know where I'm working now? Do you know what you've reduced me to by spreading your lies about me?"

Dekalb didn't move. He didn't breathe. The pulsing in his temples grew stronger, almost thunderous.

"I'm working at the fucking Met." Binny's words got louder. "I'm selling scarves in the gift shop!" Binny waved his arm, and his hand connected with the tumbler on the counter, sending the glass skidding, peach juice lapping over the side. "You destroyed me, Deck, because you were too insecure to see what I was really asking you. I only took the Gargeau to make you hurt a little, to make you see that you couldn't forget me."

Dekalb wanted to pummel the sneer that twisted Binny's mouth, the mouth that had once seemed so luscious. He wanted to smash the gleam that had crept back into Binny's eyes.

"Name your price!" Dekalb screamed, enunciating each word, the shrill of his voice surprising him because he never screamed. Never. And yet now his reputation was flitting away on the easy words of BB Shore and her pack, and it was all disintegrating, all because of Binny.

"A thousand, twenty thousand, maybe a hundred thousand? Will that make you feel better?" Binny said, coming closer, and Dekalb saw a tear bead at the corner of one eye. Binny blinked fast, and it rolled down his pale cheek.

Dekalb coughed, nearly choked on air that seemed stuck in his throat. Was Binny telling the truth? Had he been proposing a marriage of sorts, a marriage of their lives, both professional *and* personal? No, he couldn't let his mind roam there.

"Will that do it?" Binny was shouting now too, leaning nearer. "Will writing me a check and getting the Gargeau back make you feel safe? Will that do it, Deck? Is that all you need?"

Dekalb turned away, opening the drawer where Binny had left his carving knives, a drawer he rarely opened anymore because it reminded him of Binny, of those bleak days after the hospital when the knives sang to him, asking to be drawn, length-wise, from his wrists and up his arms. The silver steel of the largest blade was shining, glinting at him like Binny's eyes used to. The handle was smooth polished wood with little brass posts screwed into it. Dekalb lifted it, the cool of the wood tucking perfectly in his grasp.

❖

He'd get out in six years, four months and fourteen days, although parole was a possibility, too. Dekalb was a prisoner who no one worried about, who kept to himself. He liked tending to his cell, liked the ritual.

He spent his free time reading, keeping quiet until his weekly art lecture, where he often discussed Vernet, and the monthly book club, where he often asked the other inmates to read Sherlock Holmes. These groups were held in the rear of the cafeteria, and they were poorly attended. But the men who did come? They were good men, mostly because once a week or once a month, they'd chosen to be so. Dekalb was learning from them all the time.

He no longer cared that his stabbing of Binny and his own subsequent confession, had been sensationalized, exposing the art fraud. He wasn't bothered that his assets had been liquidated to pay for criminal defense lawyers, his apartment sold, his paintings, furniture, and collectibles purchased by an auction house in London. He didn't care that he'd never have lunch with BB Shore again.

The only thing he did care about, other than the other men he learned from, was Binny. Binny, who'd refused to testify against him even though he'd never breathe properly again. Binny, who was his only visitor, the only person who wrote or sent packages.

Binny.

DUNKIRK

by John Lescroart

(This story is dedicated to my father-in-law,
Robert F. Sawyer, who at 78 years of age
can still out run, out hike, out ski, out work
and out think just about everybody else out there.)

May, 1940

In full dark and shrouded in fog, the *Dover Doll* rose and fell in the still waters of the English Channel.

The *Doll*, an 18-meter former fishing boat converted to pleasure yacht, had disembarked from her berth in Dover at a few minutes before 7 p.m. that night, the 26th, one of the 161 British vessels that proved to be available on the first day of Operation Dynamo. The *Doll* carried a crew of four. Two of them—Harry and George– were boys under sixteen years of age, nephews of Duffy Black, a clerk from Churchill's War Office who, because he'd spent much of his youth on the water, had volunteered to act as the captain of his brother-in-law's boat during this crisis.

The last crew member, lately arrived from the Sussex Downs, was a elderly man who had, with great formality, identified himself to Duffy only as Mr. Sigerson. Taciturn and close to emaciated, Sigerson struck Duffy as a potential if not likely liability, but Churchill had called for volunteers post haste without regard to rank or age, and Duffy wasn't in a position to turn away an able hand.

If, Duffy thought, he was in fact, able.

As they'd readied the *Doll* for its new mission, the last couple of days had laid that qualm to rest. The four of them had spent all day Saturday and Sunday stripping the boat of its deck chairs, footlockers, beach umbrellas and personal items, adding a supplementary gasoline tank, tuning the engine, preparing the boat for action. As far as Duffy could tell, Sigerson never even slowed down, much less took an actual break. He could carry more equipment than Duffy himself, or either of the boys; he knew his way around a radio; he radiated a calm and seemingly endless confidence and energy that seemed to motivate the boys and keep them on track. Beyond that, Sigerson had come with an extra duffel bag filled with a good quantity of canned food along with gauze, medicines, and other first aid supplies, prompting Duffy to inquire if he'd been a doctor during his working life.

"No," Sigerson had replied, "although I did live with one for a number of years." And then he struck a note that, obsessed with refitting the boat for its mission, Duffy hadn't yet really considered. "This evacuation is not going to be accomplished without casualties. It's best to be prepared."

The mission was no less than to save what was left of the British Expeditionary Force under General Lord Gort before it was annihilated by the advancing German army. The BEF was now stranded in a ten-kilometer perimeter on either side of Dunkirk. Three days earlier, the Germans had turned north and west to the coast out of Abbeville on the Somme Estuary and taken first the city of Boulogne and, earlier today, the port at Calais. Now the panzers were moving north to the tip of the wedge at Dunkirk, although inexplicably they had paused at the Aa Canal, sixteen kilometers south of that city.

❖

Mr. Sigerson, tall and thin, stood alone on the bow of the *Doll*, his smoked-out pipe clamped firmly in his teeth, the eyes above his angular nose searching for the shoreline in the black night. Off to his left, the oil tanks of Dunkirk, bombed earlier in the day by German Junkers Ju 87s—the famous Stukas—burned brightly even through the night-time fog.

They had already passed a dozen or more boats returning to England laden with troops, and all had suggested using the fires as beacons to direct them to their destination. In the flickering dim light, Sigerson could make out five or six other boats, none larger than the *Doll*, within about a two hundred meter circle.

A whiff of Duffy Black's cigarette—a Balkan Sobranie tobacco mixture about which Sigerson had once written a scholarly monograph—preceded the captain's sudden appearance at his elbow. "Awfully decent of Jerry to light our way like this," he said. "And just when you've about come to believe there's nothing good to be said for 'em." He laughed shrilly and blew a long plume of smoke into the air.

Sigerson said, "I wouldn't worry about it. It's perfectly natural to be nervous."

"It's just that I don't want to spread my worries to the lads when . . ." He stopped, let out a brittle chuckle. "It shows, does it?"

"There are signs, yes."

"Well, I'd be obliged if you could let me know what they are. Between you and me, I don't mind telling you that I'm terrified, but I want to keep that hidden from the boys if I can."

Sigerson nodded. "The laughter when you speak. The long exhale of your smoke. The cigarette all but crumbling between your fingers."

Duffy looked down at his hand, brought the cigarette to his mouth, took a drag, exhaled out normally. "Thank you," he said, without any accompanying chuckle. "All easily corrected."

Sigerson threw a glance out to the water, then looked back over his shoulder. "I take it the boys are skilled at steering? It's getting crowded out here."

"They've both been on the water since before they wore long pants. I'd worry more about me when we get close in. So how about you? If you're nervous, I must say you've got it well under control."

Sigerson pulled his pipe from his mouth, put it in his pocket. "I'd be a fool if I wasn't concerned. But I'm more surprised than anything. I wasn't expecting the Boche would let us drive right up like this."

"It may be they don't know we're here yet."

But Sigerson, who had spent some of his time aboard at the two-way radio in the hold below, shook his head. "No. They're monitoring our chatter and have reported it back to Guderian." The German commander. "They even got Churchill's speech. So they know what we're trying to do, anyway."

"You speak German?"

"I can get by." He scanned the sky left to right. "But there's no sign of them."

Duffy trained his eyes in front of him. "I'm betting there will be plenty of sign come daylight, which is why I hope to be loaded up and long gone by then." Suddenly, Sigerson grabbed him by the arm, pointed with his other hand. "There! Do you see that? We're getting close."

Squinting into the night, Duffy could now make out what looked at first to be a darker patch in the fog. To their right, a disembodied voice carried over the water. "Comin' up on it." The flaming oil fire to their left was no longer at eleven o'clock. It had moved down closer to nine. They were nearly to the shore.

Duffy turned and spoke up to the bridge. "Back it down half slow, Harry. I'm coming up. Georgie, give Mr. Sigerson another pair of eyes and hands down here, would you? I expect we're gettin' close."

Another boat, low in the water, appeared out of the mist at under fifty meters, on a collision course straight for them. On the bridge, Harry gave a whistle and both boats jerked to the right.

As they drew alongside, Sigerson was close enough to see the faces of troops—fifty or sixty men stood on the deck, and who knew how many more below? They were a silent bunch for the most part, and when the captain called across, his words were clear. "Keep your hull up and slow, mate. Sand bars all the way in. Tide's dead low."

"How much more ahead of us?"

"Two hundred meters. More or less. They're off the beach. Look for the queue. You're coming up on them."

By now Duffy was back at the wheel and he slowed the boat. Within seconds, Sigerson felt the tug of bottom drag that meant they'd touched, but only just touched, a sand bar. They kept moving forward, over it.

Sigerson looked overboard into the black water. The *Doll* drew a little over a meter—if it was loaded with men, it would draw more. Sigerson, hyper-aware, knew that they were about as close in to shore as they dared go.

His voice shrill with excitement, 13-year-old George called out. "There they are, uncle! One o'clock."

Sigerson looked over to his right and sure enough, here was the classic British queue heading out from the shoreline. The men were up to their waists and deeper in the very cold water, their weapons at their shoulders, to all appearances patiently waiting for a boat to come about and invite them aboard. Perpendicular to the shoreline, all the way up as far as the eye could see in the flickering light from the oil fires, similar lines of men waited in the water at roughly thirty meter intervals.

Sigerson felt the now familiar tug from another sand bar. At the same time, he felt a subtle shift in the swell and knew that if they continued forward they would run aground. With no time for any hesitation, he yelled this information up to the bridge.

In an instant, Duffy had the *Doll* turned around and was backing it toward the line of men. Sigerson and Georgie rushed back to the stern and the boy threw the rope ladder overboard just as the motor cut to neutral.

The crew fell to their assigned tasks. Since Sigerson was far taller than Duffy or either of the boys, he had insisted that he was the logical choice to drop into the freezing water where he could stand and guide the troops in the darkness to the ladder. Georgie made sure that those aboard moved away for the others behind them. Harry kept the count of them, getting them arranged first below decks and then up on top; each of them keeping up a steady consoling patter. "Easy now, men. Watch the steps. Plenty more boats on the way. We'll get you on the outside of some hot tea in a couple of hours." Talking them forward. Moving them along. There was no time to be lost.

Duffy had calculated that they could recross the Channel with fairly decent control of the craft as long as they didn't bring more than forty men on board. But the queue stretched unbroken from the boat to the shoreline, a distance of at least a hundred and fifty meters, and Sigerson, glancing toward the beach, realized that there was an endless supply of men. He kept handing troops up to the ladder, urging them to climb aboard. Without actually counting, he knew that he'd helped sixty-seven men by now.

In the tension and activity, Duffy their captain seemed to have lost control of the larger picture. Sigerson realized that if they brought on many more men, all of them might perish. He had to take command from back here in the water. "Five more, lads," he called out. "Sorry. Five more. We're full up."

"Five more."

"Five more."

The call went down the ranks of men, and the sixth man stopped in his tracks, turned and bellowed to the men behind him. "It stops with me, mates. Hold the queue, please. Another boat will be along shortly." Then, to Sigerson's astonishment, he broke into a popular ditty, "Oh, I *do* like to be by the seaside."

And the men behind them in the queue first laughed, then picked up the lyrics and sang along.

Meanwhile, an all-business Sigerson counted the last men down. "Three, two, one, up and over. There you go now."

The old man himself stood up to his chest in the water. He knew how cold he was, and realized that these men had been standing out in the water for hours. How many of them would still be alive in seven more hours, when morning finally came? The first man among those left stood five meters from him, still leading with his singing, his face barely visible in the dark. He lifted a hand to his helmet in salute.

Duffy gunned the engine—the signal—and Sigerson stepped to the ladder himself, up and over the side. Men were packed like cordwood over every inch of the deck. When Sigerson reached over to pull up the ladder, he looked down over the boat's railing. They were riding deeper in the water than when they'd come in—and they'd dragged a sand bar then. But that had been nearly a half hour before, and the tide was rising.

Duffy didn't hesitate. Slamming the boat into forward, he started out to the open water. They hadn't gone more than two hundred meters when they came upon another boat—this one a fairly-decent sized trawler—moving north parallel to the shoreline.

Duffy yelled across the water, describing the line of men waiting directly in from where they now were.

"We pull too much draft," came the reply. "We're touching bottom out here as it is. We've got to pick up at the mole,"—the rock jetty that formed Dunkirk's harbor—"but we'll pass the word back."

Sigerson looked behind him, hoping that they'd put enough distance between themselves and the men they'd had to abandon that the latter wouldn't have heard the trawler's response. He needn't have worried. The men they'd left were already out of sight—one of hundreds of identical lines of men, each waiting for a small boat to appear out of the black and trackless sea, to pick them up and take them home.

━◆━

They got back to Dover by about 4:00 a.m. It would have been sooner, but they were so overloaded that Duffy ran at half speed or less as the chop came up with the rising tide. They'd boarded seventy-two men, almost twice Duffy's maximum allowance. For future trips—and they'd be going around the clock until Operation Dynamo ended—Sigerson and Duffy pegged the number they'd allow aboard firmly at sixty. They were hearing rumors at the docks that the numbers of troops who'd made it back to England during these first hours was already in the thousands.

This was galvanizing news.

After they'd filled the petrol tanks and again cleared the harbor at Dover, the eastern sky lightened to a gunmetal gray. Duffy had the wheel while Sigerson put the boys to sleep below, then mounted to the bridge.

The huge high plumes of smoke from the oil fires, which had been so helpful during the night, continued to mark their destination by day. Duffy corrected his steering, then stood off the seat and stretched. "How are you holding up?"

The old man nodded. "The dry clothes help."

"Not too tired to take us halfway over?"

"All the way if needed."

Duffy shook his head. "And here I thought—meaning no disrespect—that you'd be a burden. What about your own sleep?"

"There'll be time later, I'm sure."

"All right. You're a tough old bird, I'll grant you that. Give me one hour, then wake me up and I'll take us in. I want to let the boys get as much rest as they can. It might be a long few days."

Sigerson moved into the seat behind the wheel, pushed the speed up a couple of knots. All around them now, in the dull gray morning, other boats of all sizes, designs, and draughts were making their way east.

In spite of his admitted fatigue, Duffy made no move to go below. Instead, he walked across the cabin and stood looking out over the water. He rubbed the back of his neck, glanced below to where the boys slept, shook a cigarette from his pack, and lit it.

"They'll be all right," Sigerson said. "The boys."

Duffy wheeled on him. "How did you . . .? Did I say something about the boys?"

"Not aloud, no. But clearly."

"You're a very observant fellow, Mr. Sigerson. Has anyone ever mentioned that to you?"

A small smile lifted Sigerson's lips. "I've heard it remarked on," he said. "And you are worried about the boys."

The captain sighed. "My sister will kill me if anything happens to either of them. But I didn't see any way I could leave 'em—they wouldn't hear of it. And they do know this old crate better than anyone."

"They do good work."

"Oh, sure and that. I'm not worried about that. They're fine boys and good seamen. But it might get ugly as sin over there any time now. This trip."

"You could assign them both below."

"That's what I'm thinking. If there's shooting. Any of the regular troops can handle the ladder once they're aboard." Duffy, now obviously relieved by the adjustment in their plans, drew heavily on his cigarette.

Until Friday, he'd been working as a clerk in Churchill's War Office under Whitehall, taking dictation for orders, dispatches, and reports, and then typing them up. He still looked the quintessential bureaucrat. Sallow in complexion and thin-chested, he was swimming in a black slicker sea coat.

The responsibility of what they were doing was clearly starting to weigh on him. Operation Dynamo wasn't intended to be one quick trip to save seventy-five men, but a concerted operation to bring hundreds of thousands of troops back over the water to England. They might be doing this for a week or more if the Germans could be held up in their relentless advance on Dunkirk. And at some point—perhaps already—as Duffy had said, it seemed destined to become more a battle than a mere rescue operation.

"Go below and get some sleep," Sigerson said. "You're going to need it. I can get us to those plumes."

—◇—

The first wave of Stukas appeared out of the smoke to Sigerson's left, banking steeply as they cleared the covering oil smoke and diving in formation down nearly to the waterline. The *Doll* had convoyed with a couple of dozen other small craft on the way over, all of them running more or less in the wake of the larger British naval vessel, *The Canterbury*, whose guns now opened fire at the approaching fighter planes.

"Scatter, man, scatter," Duffy yelled as he appeared on the bridge. "Get out of their line!"

"Already done, sir."

Duffy clapped Sigerson on the shoulder. "I might have known. Of course you'd know what to do. Do you mind letting me get back at the wheel?"

"You're the captain, sir." Sigerson stepped to one side, letting Duffy once again take control of the boat.

The German planes were coming in from the north, strafing *The Canterbury*, and continuing straight on into the line of the smaller companion boats to the *Doll*. The entire convoy was still several kilometers from shore and had plenty of sea room, but the individual boats were close enough to one another that the maneuvering was tricky.

Beyond that, the chop came up in a hurry as the vessels began to scatter. Foam flew over the *Doll*'s bow and into the windshield in front of Sigerson—the bridge on the *Doll* was not fully enclosed—as Duffy turned the boat south. And then suddenly, directly crossing into their path, another boat from behind them careened at full speed. Duffy swore as he pulled back on the throttle, stalling the *Doll* as she lay. He reached for the key and gave it a turn, but the engine didn't catch. He tried it again.

"You damned fool, you've flooded her!" Duffy swore to himself, looking out behind them. "But get us movin', man, get us movin'."

More than twenty Stukas made up the strike formation, and most were concentrating on *The Canterbury*—sweeping low to strafe, then banking up for another run. But one fighting group of three coordinated wing to wing and continued straight on low over the water, firing on the smaller boats as they came to bear. Even as Sigerson and Duffy both watched, one of their companion boats exploded into a ball of flame two hundred meters off their stern.

"C'mon, c'mon!" Duffy was pleading with the ignition, which rolled over and over, unresponsive.

"Captain," Sigerson stepped in next to him, "excuse me." He reached down and closed the choke all the way. His voice tense but controlled, he said. "Let it sit a minute."

Looking back over his shoulder as the trio of fighters rose and turned for another run, Duffy shook his head. "We don't have a minute. If we're not moving, we're sitting ducks." He tried the key again, with the same results.

Wrrr . . . wrrr. . . wrrr . . .

"Let me."

Sigerson's tone was commanding and made Duffy shrug reluctantly out of the seat. Behind them, adjusting their line, the birds were now heading straight for the *Doll*. Behind Sigerson, Duffy called below for the boys to open the hatch, get some air in over the engine, let some of the gas evaporate.

Sigerson did not even try the ignition.

"They're leveling right at us, man! We've got to move."

"We will." Then, out the window over the side, he yelled with a real urgency. "You boys stay down! Don't even look out! Hit the deck!"

In the distance, the sound of the first strafings reached Sigerson's ears, deep staccato poppings blending into an uneven roar over the deeper scream of the fighters' engines. They had almost closed the gap now. In seconds, the *Doll* would be in range—he could already see the water stitching up with their rounds approaching.

Another second. Two seconds. At last he reached out tried the ignition. The engine caught!

"Yaahh!" Duffy yelled.

Sigerson threw the boat into gear. The strafing line boiled the water behind them as the Stukas streaked by overhead with a deafening roar.

Duffy turned and yelled to Sigerson. "We hit?"

"Missed. Just."

Sigerson wasn't about to slow *Doll* down and admire their position. They'd escaped one pass, but were still sitting unarmed in the open ocean, and now with their prolonged stall, they were all alone in an ever-widening circle of fleeing watercraft.

But Sigerson realized what perhaps Duffy did not—that this was to their advantage. The Stukas would be more efficient attacking groups of boats in almost any type of formation. One lone craft would be a tougher target, and more difficult to hit. The fighters would be wiser to leave the solo boats alone, and instead attack where the vessels had concentrated.

Duffy was back at his side. "Where are you going?" he yelled over the sound of the engine.

"The smoke cover's thicker in toward shore. They won't be so much strafing there." He moved to one side. "The wheel is yours, captain."

Duffy nodded and stepped in to take over. He cast his eyes to his left— "Well, you haven't been wrong yet"—and swung the wheel around. A little way north, the Stukas were still concentrating on both *The Canterbury* and another regular British navy ship that they could now see in the water about two kilometers beyond, up close to the Dunkirk mole. The noise of cannon and strafing fire was continuous, though now more distant, as the *Doll* broke at near full-speed for the shoreline.

Almost immediately the queues waiting in the water came into sight. Another very small navy vessel—only slightly larger than a battleship's lifeboat—was suddenly on their port side running alongside them. Both boats pulled up to adjacent queues and both swung around to face away from the shore just as a lone Stuka broke under the cover of cloud and smoke and dove toward the troops packing every inch of the beach.

Sigerson had spent all of this time and attention so far on the aerial attack and only incidentally on the queues in the water. Now he looked up and saw the enormous concentration of the troop convergence at the shoreline. He'd never seen so many people assembled in one place.

The lone Stuka, now at treetop height although there were no trees, cut across his line of sight from left to right, its machine guns raining death down on the men who stood waiting for one of the boats to approach their queue.

And then Sigerson was overboard again, at his place in the water behind the boat, grabbing the hand of the nearest man, directing him to the boat's ladder. He was surprised to discover that this man—in fact, this entire queue—was French.

At the southern horizon, the Stuka banked high with a whining scream, then turned back and cut low for another run at the massed men on the beach. *"Bâtard,"* the lead man said, and got answering nods from the men behind him in the queue.

Still, in spite of the extreme danger, there was no panic. Sigerson announced the number of men that the *Doll* could accommodate— *soixante hommes*—and the men seemed to understand. They were counting themselves off aloud as they got up the boat's ladder and aboard onto the deck.

". . . dix neuf, vingt, vingt-et-un . . ."

As Sigerson had suggested, one of the soldiers had replaced George at the ladder.

But by now Sigerson and everyone else was preoccupied with the Stuka's next strafing run. There were a few machine guns on the beach, and now they heard the sound of steady return fire, which was welcome but did little to hamper the fighter's effectiveness. The plane ducked and rolled and its gun continued to fire in regular and devastating bursts.

Then the sixty troops were aboard the *Doll,* and Sigerson was over the ladder on board with them. At the next queue, only fifteen or twenty meters away, the boarding had obviously been going less smoothly than their own, possibly because the boat was so small, with a steep hull and a different kind of makeshift ladder. Whatever the cause, though, friction obviously was high.

At the back of the boat where the men were loading, someone in a British navy uniform now was yelling, panic in his voice. "I don't care about your rank, sir. The boat can't accommodate everybody back to where you stood. There's just not room. You've got to get back in your place in the queue. You're holding us all up."

"I'm not going back. I've been standing here all night . . ."

"So've we all, mate!" From the queue.

The queue-breaker turned and fumed back. "I'm not your mate. I'm a major in the British Expeditionary Force."

"You're a horse's ass!" someone yelled. "Mate!"

At that moment, the Stuka dove out of the sky again and opened fire at the waterline perhaps thirty meters directly behind them. Men at the water's edge fell like sheaved wheat. The cries of those who'd been wounded carried over the water.

On the boat next to them, the major had a foot on the ladder and was pulling himself up, now halfway aboard. The man in charge of the lifeboat screamed over the declining roar of the airplane. "I'm warning you, sir, I can't allow you to board. There are men in the queue before you."

Those men were pressing forward now, shouting obscenities, terrified by the Stuka's attack and, perhaps more so, by the breakdown in discipline. The mood in the queues all along the shore that were hearing all this was beginning to turn now and in the closer lines was becoming decidedly ugly.

Sigerson had pulled the *Doll*'s ladder up. But meanwhile, they had drifted close enough to the boat next to them to make out faces and hear the individual strained voices.

"I'm telling you, sir. This is my last warning."

"God damn your eyes, son. I'm coming aboard." The major got a leg over the side of the boat, and this added weight forced the stern low enough to break the pitching surface of the water. Seawater spilled over onto the deck.

The young commander's voice rose a notch as it took on an even more terrified tone. "By God, you're swamping us, major! Get down! I order you to get down."

"I won't, blast you! I'm coming aboard."

"Sir, we're taking water. You'll get us all killed."

"Shoot the bugger!" someone in line yelled.

And then—it was very fast—Sigerson saw the young man raise his arm. He heard the sharp crack of a pistol shot. And the major's body pitched back into the water.

The men in their queue broke into a cheer.

With a despairing gesture, holding up his pistol, the commander of the dinghy glanced over at the *Doll* and yelled over. "He was going to sink us! We'd all have gone down!" Then, over the stern to the rest of the waiting men. "All right, now, next six men is all we have room for. Step lively, please, and keep your places."

Duffy put the boat into gear as the Stuka turned again through the smoke cover. Dead low in the water, the *Doll* started throwing a low wake as she picked up what speed she would be able to handle on the westward crossing.

❖

They had run out of the food tins by the fourth crossing. All of the blankets were either gone or soaked. There was no more medicine left, and no gauze.

For all of Sigerson's planning and forethought, for all of his observations and cleverness, he realized that he hadn't made much difference after all. A bit of solace or comfort for a very few men, perhaps.

He was at the wheel, approaching Dover with a full boat for the seventh time. They would be going out again. It felt endless.

He did not think in terms of being glad, or of being disappointed, that he had come. He was, and had habitually throughout his life been, all but completely unaware of his emotions. He had spent much of his life in the intellectual pursuit of solving crimes, coming upon murder victims long after the fact. He had joined this quixotic mission so late in his life because he believed that evil was on the march in the world, and that perhaps he could play some role in thwarting it.

As he had done in the first World War.

But now, in the aftermath of what he'd witnessed in the past few days—the firsthand carnage, the Stuka strafings, the heroism of both the soldiers and other volunteer civilians who, like his old partner Dr. Watson, had actually fought in battles—he found himself ill-equipped to deal with death on this scale, or with this immediacy.

This was a new world, a new reality, and for once he felt truly unprepared. His vaunted intellect and his prodigious powers of observation suddenly felt if not useless, then at least seriously marginalized.

And this made him realize that he was, quite literally, in the same boat as his fellow human beings. He felt this connection, for the first time in his very long life, in the very core of his being.

The emotive force of belonging.

◈

Four days later, on May 30, Sigerson sat at the two-way radio in the lower cabin of the *Doll*, which was fighting high seas and a vicious tail wind.

Sigerson had no real memory of the last time he'd eaten or slept, of how many times they'd crossed the same expanse of water, of how many men they'd taken on board and offloaded, either at Dover or on one of the navy's destroyers closer in. Over the radio, he'd established communications with many other boats and had heard many, many numbers bandied about. He didn't know if he believed them—some twenty-seven thousand men saved the first day; eighteen thousand on the third.

It seemed impossible.

The Germans had sunk two large British battleships in Dunkirk harbor itself, but Dynamo operations were still going on off the mole to the south of it. A tremendous number of small craft were plying the Channel taking part in the rescue effort.

In light of this, the German commander Guderian had clearly begun to realize the mistake he'd made by not pursuing the defeated Allied armies when he'd first bottled them up at Dunkirk. Now, determined to stop the flow of troops reaching safety in England, the Luftwaffe had stepped up their bombing and strafing runs, and at the radio Sigerson was getting word of more and more casualties every few minutes.

As if the German advance and the stepped-up air attacks weren't enough to presage disaster, the inshore winds at Dunkirk this morning—which had been atypically calm throughout the operation until now—were playing havoc with smaller boats such as the *Doll*. From across the Channel, Sigerson was busy fielding distress signals and trying to coordinate the rescue of several that had been blown onto either sand bars or the beach itself.

He was also picking up occasional chatter from the German command, reporting on the advance of Panzer divisions well into the ten-kilometer perimeter around Dunkirk. At the present rate, the city and its harbor and beaches would fall within a couple of days at most, dooming Dynamo and the thousands of men still waiting on the beaches.

Sigerson's only contact with the outside world was the radio that Duffy's brother-in-law had installed a few years back. It was a simple and rather primitive shortwave with a limited range that they'd moved to the relatively greater safety of the hold and off the bridge when they'd stripped the boat down for action. With the high winds and with the growing swell on the water, Sigerson's reception was often spotty at best, but he had his charts spread out on his lap and could at least take note of the position of distressed vessels—he had spoken to six of them already—so that when they got closer, they could possibly direct other boats to the disabled crews. It was little enough, but at least he was doing something, although exhaustion struggled to claim him.

The *Doll* fell heavily into a deep trough. Its hull slammed into the water under them with a bone-shattering force and the radio cut out with a last squawk in the middle of a transmission from another boat that had been beached on the mainland by the wind.

While Sigerson had been working with the radio, both boys had been sleeping in bedrolls on the bench-like seats built into the hull. With the impact, George, the younger, rolled over and moaned, but remained sleeping. On the other side of the lower cabin, Harry, fifteen, sat up. "What was that? Are we hit?"

"We fell off a wave."

The boy stretched around to look out the portholes at the pitching sea. Coming back to his surroundings here below, he yawned extravagantly, then pointed. "Is the radio bollixed?"

"For the moment." Sigerson turned it off, then on, off then on. "A fuse must have come loose, although getting to it might be tricky until we're a little more stable. Did you get some sleep?"

Harry broke a wide and weary grin. "What's that?"

Sigerson smiled, too. "Yes." Then made a joke. "At least we're dry."

"This is dry, then?"

All of their clothes, even the changes, were damp through and through from their days on the water. After the third pickup, Sigerson stopped going overboard to guide the men. They saw what they needed to do and had no problem utilizing the ladder. Beyond that, order and discipline took care of the actual boarding.

Now Harry stood, stretched, walked back the four steps to the deck and on up. Sigerson slapped at the radio a few times. For a moment, his eyes closed. He'd almost dozed when he heard a thump—Harry jumping down from the deck. The boy was smoking a cigarette, no doubt a present from Uncle Duffy, and the smell of it nearly made Sigerson swoon. Harry took a drag, inhaled deeply, held it out for Sigerson. "Bit of fag?"

"Don't mind if I do. Thanks." Sigerson sucked in the welcome smoke and immediately felt the charge of the nicotine. Harry had dug a screwdriver out of his pocket and now peered around the back of the radio. Sigerson backed away, exchanged a puff of cigarette with the boy again, then sat down to watch.

"Uncle's got some tools up top," Harry said. "I feel better when everything's working."

"I do, too. I see you know about radios."

"A little."

In their days together, Harry had also told Sigerson that he knew "a little" about boats, and reading sea charts, and repairing engines, and navigation by both night and day. If you listened to the boy, you would guess that "a little" was a general level of knowledge, and you would be wrong. Sigerson thought back to the young London street urchins he'd often used to excellent effect in his regular work when he'd been young. If Harry knew a little about radios, Sigerson would let him get it running again.

Now Harry removed the back of the radio and started reaching in, checking connections. "Uncle says we're fifteen minutes out, give or take. Doesn't see no fighters yet. Probably the wind's keepin' them grounded, too."

"Devoutly to be hoped," Sigerson said. It was his turn with the cigarette and he took a last drag, then handed the butt over to Harry. "I've heard reports that Jerry's made it to the beach in places already."

"Bloody sods. How long do you reckon we got until they take the whole place?"

"A day, day and a half."

"And how many men are left?"

"No one knows exactly. The radio transmissions are urging every available craft to keep coming. Perhaps as many as two hundred thousand men are still stranded."

Abruptly, Harry turned from the radio. His mouth hung open in shock. "Two hundred thousand *more*?"

Sober, Sigerson nodded. "That's what I have heard."

"God's teeth," Harry said. "And here I was thinking we'd done some good."

"We have."

Harry shook the impossible number out of his head and went back to his work at the radio. Suddenly there was a squawk and then, quite clearly, a voice intermingled with the sound of weapons firing. ". . . under continuous attack since about two hours after dawn. I repeat, this is Colonel Bryce Hagin, with the 14th Highland Regiment, and we are pinned by German patrols. . ."

Sigerson was around at the front of the unit, working the controls. Hagin's dispatch was one of the clearest he'd heard so far, and he flicked his "send" switch. "This is the *Dover Doll*. State your position, over?"

"We're at the southern extremity of the Dunkirk strand."

Sigerson turned to Harry. "Run up and ask your uncle how good we look to hit the southernmost beach." Into his microphone, he said, "How many men are you?"

"Maybe sixty left. We're pinned down in the ruins of an old fort where the sand juts out a bit. There's a pleasant little brook."

"I see it!" Harry was already coming back and yelled up from the doorway to the cabin. "Two o'clock, Uncle."

"We're coming in," Sigerson said. "You should see us now. Try to get your men down into the water."

"Are you serious? That would be suicide."

"Have you another option?"

A pause, then Hagin said, "Bloody hell."

⬦

Bloody hell was what it was.

Hagin had ordered a contingent of his men to stay behind among the walls of the fort and cover the rest of the unit's retreat against the near constant barrage of the German infantry battalion dug into the sand only a dune away. Duffy, cautious of the inshore gale and the heavy surf, was only able to get the *Doll* to about forty meters of where the waves were breaking on the sand, breakers with enough power to slow the men down considerably.

From the back of the boat by the ladder, Sigerson watched as Hagin's unit—in a crisp, double-time line—broke into the water, guns held over their heads, and struggled to make headway in the shifting sand on the bottom, through the heavy chop. It was very tough going, and their weapons didn't make it any easier. Most of the other troops they'd picked up over the past few days had abandoned their ordnance, but this group seemed determined to keep it with them, carrying Bren guns and boxes of ammunition, rifles, Mills bombs, artillery belts slung over their shoulders.

The first man had just reached the boat, was reaching for Sigerson's hand, when a line of machine gun fire from out of the dunes dappled the waves. He and the next three men behind him spun and fell as the water churned into shades of red.

"Down! Get down!" Sigerson yelled to his boys. "Below decks! Now!"

The next hand he gripped made it to the ladder and aboard, then spun on the boat, took a position behind the bulkhead, and began firing back at the enemy. Perhaps ten men made it aboard before another volley took a couple more in the close water, then another two.

The dead bodies were floating now, tossed by the chop, and the men had to negotiate them as they tried to reach the safety of the boat. Two more of Hagin's men had mounted the bridge of the *Doll* and were returning fire from there, and for some minutes there seemed to be a lull in the German's attack.

Hagin's men took full advantage, breaking from their cover now behind the fort and into the water, still in organized lines.

Sigerson couldn't help but admire the discipline.

Now, on the *Doll*, Hagin's men were firing from three or four locations. But the boat was also beginning to take concerted return fire from the shore. Ironically, this seemed to be good for the men in the water, and perhaps it had been Hagin's orders—to draw fire from the men who couldn't defend themselves as they tried to gain the boat.

Most of the men aboard had crammed themselves down below, and when that area had filled, they hunched low on the deck, taking some measure of safety from the hull. Even so, at least five men had been wounded and lay moaning or screaming in pain and shock on the deck. As Sigerson glanced over, a bullet took off half the head of the shooter on the stern next to him. The man pitched overboard, his place immediately taken by another of Hagin's troops.

A machine gun volley raked the lower structure of the bridge and Duffy yelled down. "We've got to get out, Sigerson, or we're all gone."

In desperation, Sigerson saw that the last of the men, maybe fifteen of them, had left the fort. And a hundred and fifty meters behind them, a row of German troops broke from the shelter of the dunes and began a charge, firing as they came. "Give me two minutes!" he yelled. "We'll get them on board."

The German charge, it turned out, was the Brit's salvation. The advancing lines of Panzer troops blocked the shooting angle of the machine guns that had been inflicting such devastation on Hagin's men. All of the last group but one made it to the ladder and then aboard. As the last man came over, soaked and bloody from an arm wound, he straightened up and saluted. "Colonel Bryce Hagin," he said. "Thanks so much for stopping by."

Then Duffy revved the engine. They jerked forward, and Sigerson grabbed Hagin to keep him from flipping out of the boat, into the chopped up and bloody sea.

⊸◆⊸

Though they continued to take sporadic fire from shore, most of the men lay either on the deck, protected by the hull, or in the lower cabin, and they took no further casualties—although the *Doll* was peppered at the bridge and the waterline—until they were blessedly, finally, out of range. Riding low in the water with the load of human cargo and the heavy seas, the *Doll* was regularly taking water over the bow at the way Duffy was pushing her, and now he pulled back on the throttle and brought the craft down to a more reasonable cruising speed.

Despite his wounded arm, Hagin himself had mounted the bridge and remained standing up there next to Duffy, staring back toward the shore. The man who'd taken over the stern firing from the soldier who'd been killed was sheltering next to Sigerson on the deck. Now he sat up, glanced back behind them, turned to Sigerson. "We owe you, grandpa. Thanks." He smiled and put out his hand. "Wilkes."

"Sigerson."

Both men got to their feet. Beyond them, other men were starting to move, and Wilkes immediately fell into a leadership role. "I want the wounded men brought down below out of this weather and made as comfortable as possible." He turned to Sigerson, asked with a quiet efficiency. "Have you any medical supplies on board? Drugs? Blankets? Anything at all like that?"

"Afraid not. All gone long ago. We're ferrying, that's all."

"That's plenty, don't get me wrong." He went back to his men, grabbed the one nearest to hand. "Roger, first thing we'll need some makeshift tourniquets. See to that, would you?" Roger nodded, stepped back to the cabin entrance and disappeared down into it. Wilkes came back to Sigerson. "How long do these crossings take?"

Sigerson had noted the slowdown as the boat strained for stability in the rough water and he kept his voice low. It wasn't the best news he could be delivering, especially for the seriously wounded. "At this speed, about four hours. If the wind drops," he added, "it could be quicker."

Wilkes nodded and raised his voice to his troops. "Below decks for the wounded and those helping them, please. Everyone else, up here, find some comfortable patch of deck and curl up for a bit of a kip. Tea in Dover at sixteen hundred hours, give or take."

Breaking a grin at the badinage, Sigerson was just turning when he heard the engines cut to dead slow. His brow clouded and he looked first up to the bridge, then—the memory of diving and strafing Stukas still fresh—back toward the receding shoreline. He heard a crisp voice from above. "Wilkes."

Wilkes stepped out from the cabin doorway, looked up squinting into the bridge, saluted. "Sir?"

"How many men have we left?"

The young lieutenant didn't even need to count. "Thirty-two able bodied, sir. Five wounded, not including yourself."

"And our supplies?"

"Supplies, sir?"

Hagin's voice sharpened. "Guns, man. Pistols, rifles, ammunition, grenades. I know bloody well we left the radio on the beach. But what else have we got?"

"I'll need a minute, sir."

"All right, then. Take one. Just."

Wilkes's face mirrored Sigerson's own reaction over the peremptory tone—impatience, frustration, even a flash of anger. Then his expression softened into one of tolerant good humor. Wilkes had undoubtedly grown used to his commander, though he took him very seriously indeed. Immediately, he went below to take the measure of their firepower, although Sigerson couldn't imagine what they could need it for now.

For his part, he made sure that Harry and George were both unhurt, up and moving, then he mounted the ladder to the bridge. In the minute or so since Duffy had cut the engines, they'd stopped making any forward progress whatsoever, and now the *Doll* hung bobbing in the turbulent chop. Looking up as he mounted, Sigerson saw blue in the sky again— many, many dark scudding clouds, but also traces of blue between them.

A moment of unsullied bright sunlight washed the deck. At the top of the ladder, Sigerson stepped onto the bridge. "Are we all right?"

"We're fine."

Sigerson said, "We seem to have slowed down on our rush to Dover. Some of the men down below are anxious to get home."

Duffy eyes were gray and distant. "Talk to the colonel."

Sigerson nodded, turned and saluted. "Colonel Hagin. How's your arm?"

"Useless. But it's merely a flesh wound. It doesn't matter a whit."

"Sir, we're beginning to treat the wounded down below," Sigerson said. "They're putting together some makeshift bandages as well as they can. You might want to stop down there and have somebody look at you, get you fixed up."

"I'm fixed up, as you put it, well enough. To the contrary, Mr. Sigerson, is it? You might want to refrain from giving orders to superior officers who've got serious work to do."

Sigerson's eyes narrowed, his nostrils flared. "That was a suggestion, sir. Not an order. You are of course free to do as you please."

"I'm aware of that. And you need to be, as well."

Churchill may not have stood upon rank or lack of it for any of the mission's volunteers, but Sigerson had no illusions about whether a genuine British colonel outranked an old man like himself culled from the rolls of the retired, and Hagin seemed to harbor none either. If Sigerson were going to question the legitimacy of Hagin's takeover of the craft, he'd have to shoot him, and though he was angry and appalled at the colonel's attitude, he wasn't prepared to do that. So he merely nodded. "Of course, sir. Apologies."

Duffy turned in his seat. Maybe the fatigue, tension, gunfire, and mayhem of the last rescue had finally pushed him beyond his threshold, but he now appeared to be physically ill, green-tinged and enervated. "Colonel Hagin," he intoned without inflection, "would like to have a look at our charts, Sigerson. Would you please go get them and bring them up?"

"Our charts?"

"Our navigation charts."

Sigerson knew what charts he'd meant—there weren't any others. "Yes, sir," he said. "I'll be right back."

Below, the boys and Wilkes had gotten both the wounded and the other men arranged for the journey, and already a modicum of order had been restored. Miraculously—they must have packed them under their hats or helmets—some of the men still had dry cigarettes and most of them were smoking. As Sigerson dug around near the radio for their charts, he heard Wilkes behind him on the deck, reporting to Hagin on the bridge. "We've got nineteen carbine rifles, sir, with sixteen boxes of ammunition. Twenty-four pistols with about a hundred rounds each. Six Bren machine guns with four boxes of ammunition, no heavier guns, no mountings. Forty Mills bombs. Nothing dry."

"I didn't suppose anything could be dry, Lieutenant Wilkes. My concern is that things work. Please have the men inspect, test, and ready their weapons."

Wilkes didn't ask any questions, but merely saluted. "Yes, sir."

Still inside the lower cabin, unseen from the deck, Sigerson whispered. "Is the man mad?"

Wilkes shook his head quickly—*don't ask!*—and turned to convey his latest order from above to the men. He moved aside from the door, whispered to Sigerson. "If you're fetching something for him, you'd better be moving."

Sigerson took his charts and ascended back to the bridge.

There, Hagin used his good arm to take them from him without any thanks or ceremony. Holding down the bottom corner with the elbow of his injured arm, he unrolled the charts in the lee of the bridge's wind-shield and after asking Duffy for their current position, he leaned over to study them.

The *Doll* remained in neutral, rising and falling on the chop, as Hagin perused the documents. On deck below them, the test shots from the men's weapons began to sound. Sigerson and Duffy exchanged a glance, but mostly they both just waited. It was late May. The sun was beginning to shine more steadily, and the chuffing air had suddenly lost some of its distinct chill.

Finally, Hagin cleared his throat and straightened up. "Captain," he said to Duffy, "if I'm reading this correctly, and I believe I am, we are about twelve kilometers from the Aa Canal, is that right?"

Duffy went over to the chart and looked down. "Yes, sir, very close."

"So we could be there, at the canal's mouth, in say half an hour?"

"Yes."

"All right, then, set your course accordingly. That's where we'll make our attack."

Duffy couldn't help himself. "Attack, sir?"

"Yes, Captain. Attack. Strike a blow for the king and dirty the Bosch nose a bit." Hagin turned to include Sigerson. "To say nothing of the strategic value of a rearguard action. If the Germans think we're coming at them from behind, it can't help but postpone their advance into Dunkirk. We may give our dear brothers on the beach another day, or perhaps two."

"Excuse me, sir," Duffy said, "but with respect you've only got thirty men and all of 'em are done in."

Hagin bristled. His back went straight as he pulled himself to his full height. "I'll forgive your question, Captain, because the service you're rendering now with the *Dover Doll* is both heroic and invaluable. That said, you should know that I have the privilege to command, and you are currently transporting, one of *the* best fighting units, if not the best fighting unit, in the entire BEF. The Fourteenth exists and only exists to go into battle for the glory of England.

"And again, for your information, I am not so foolish as to contemplate an extended campaign on the Aa. My Lieutenant Wilkes speaks Kraut well, you know, and before we were attacked at our last bivouac, he managed to monitor regular German radio transmissions between their advancing units. It seems that all of the tanks now converging on Dunkirk have crossed the Aa, which is only thirty meters wide, by means of two pontoon bridges. Now they've abandoned those bridges to small auxiliary forces to protect their tanks' return. I don't suppose my men and I will have much trouble taking out one or both of the bridges." He allowed the trace of a smile. "Even with one hand tied behind our backs, so to speak."

⌘

Though Sigerson considered Hagin arrogant and ill-advised, he couldn't deny that the colonel had bravery to burn. He also had a way with the leadership of his troops.

Soon after he'd conceived of his plan to "liberate" the Aa Canal pontoons, he called Wilkes up to the bridge, where he described the operation he had in mind in some detail. Despite his haste to make the mouth of the Aa, he intended to get there not out of a bloodthirsty and possibly foolish desire to encounter unsuspecting German troops, but so that his men would have a more comfortable resting place—out of the wind and surge of the Channel—for several hours before they again went into battle. They might even get an opportunity to sleep. They would also be hungry, of course, and he told Wilkes that though that worried him, there was nothing he could do about it until they got back ashore, when they would send a couple of teams into the countryside to nearby farms or villages. The locals, he reasoned, would probably be sympathetic after the ferocity of the *blitzkrieg*.

While Duffy pushed the *Doll* back in toward the coastline, Hagin and Wilkes descended to the deck, assembled the men, and went over the plan again with them. There was no cheering—these troops had after all seen what German soldiers could do—but neither was there any sign of discontent. The men had already field-tested their weapons, and now Hagin told them to find a comfortable spot if they could. They should try to get some sleep. He had no intention of exposing them in broad daylight to Germans who might be patrolling either or both sides of the canal. They would anchor in the shelter of the levee, in calm water.

Hagin then asked for volunteers to leave the boat in search of food when they got to shore, and Sigerson took the opportunity to step forward.

He noted the look of both surprise and approval in Hagin's eyes, but then the colonel said, "Good show, Mr. Sigerson, but we're going to need you to help get us out after we've destroyed the pontoons. Besides, as a civilian, if you were captured you would be treated as a spy, and undoubtedly shot. But we all of us appreciate the gesture. Thank you."

Suddenly Sigerson had a new understanding of why Hagin's men had such loyalty to him.

Twenty minutes later, Duffy cut the engines back again. While all the men except Hagin and Wilkes hunched below the level of the hull, the *Doll* crossed unhindered through the mouth of a breakwater, and then into a small bay. There were no houses, no commercial buildings, and most importantly, apparently no Germans. Duffy pushed the boat through a kilometer of harbor and then into the mouth of a wide, low-sided canal—the Aa.

After about another three hundred meters, Hagin gave the brisk, evenly-toned order to kill the engines. When they'd gone still, a profound silence hung in the air. They anchored against the north shore—green fields with livestock, horses, and houses far in the distance. They'd barely come to a stop when four men, two teams of volunteers, Wilkes among them—left the boat and scrambled up over the levee.

Hagin ordered Sigerson and even Duffy below with the boys and the wounded and ordered them to lie down and close their eyes. He himself would keep a lookout from the bridge and would wake them if they were needed. Meanwhile, he announced to his men, the mission was to rest.

It wasn't yet noon.

⊷◈⊶

Sigerson suddenly was aware of sounds—the slight creaking of the boat, snores and moans of the men around him, crickets. He opened his eyes and knew immediately that he'd slept for a good portion of the day. The sun had eventually broken through the cloud cover and now painted the bow wall of the cabin a bright orange. He realized that he wasn't cold anymore, either. The temperature had risen dramatically.

Then, suddenly, he knew what it was that had awakened him. The sound of horse hooves. Horses!

Captain Duffy was out cold, flush up against him on the floor, but Sigerson was careful to leave him undisturbed as he sat up slowly, then got to his feet. Out on the deck, the troops were littered like matchsticks, covering almost every inch of space. Every one of them slept, most with their rifles in their arms. The sky in the east was just beginning to turn a deeper blue, presaging dusk and a warm and still night.

Stepping around the men on the deck, and their clothes where they'd spread them to dry, Sigerson got to the bridge's ladder in time to see two men bareback on horses appear as they crested the levee. Wilkes was one of them. He'd ridden up on a fine black Arabian stallion. He gave a general thumbs up as he dismounted and pulled the *ficelles*—sacks made of heavy string, loaded with food—from his horse's neck.

Bread, at least, Sigerson thought, his mouth suddenly watering at the thought of it. He could see the thick baguettes sticking out of the top of the sacks, and also bottles—apparently milk and even wine—and greens, and other items wrapped in paper or cloth. Above him, Sigerson heard the creak of the pilot's seat. He looked up to see Colonel Hagin standing at the top of the ladder. The colonel looked down at him and motioned with his good hand that he should join him on the bridge.

"Did you sleep?" Hagin asked when he reached the top.

"Yes, sir. Thank you."

"Are you hungry?"

"No, sir."

"Don't be a martyr, Mr. Sigerson. Of course you're hungry. We've continued to be fortunate. Both search parties seem to have found sympathetic locals and some victuals." He pointed to four more *ficelles* stuffed under the pilot's seat. "The other team made it back an hour ago with these supplies, but I wanted to wait to see if Wilkes had some success as well before anyone tore into this batch. Now it seems he has, so break yourself off a piece of bread and some cheese. There. There's my man! There's some milk in the bottom, too, a bit warm now I'd imagine, but drinkable."

It was thick-crusted, chewy bread, freshly made. The cheese was pure white, hard and pungent, and the milk was in fact warm and thick with cream. Over his long life, Sigerson had eaten at some of the finest restaurants in the world, but he thought he'd never tasted anything so delicious.

While Sigerson chewed, Wilkes and his partner made their way down to the *Doll* and on board, laden with their goods. From the pilot's chair, Hagin consulted his watch, turned to look at the position of the sun low in the sky, made his decision. He stood up and leaned over to Wilkes. "It's time to wake the men, Lieutenant Wilkes, and there's more food up here."

⬦

Before it was full dark, the well-rested men had been fed with bread, cheeses, milk, wine, sausages, ham, lettuces, even chocolate. They had held a brief religious service for the one wounded man who had died, and whose body they elected to leave on the boat and return to England for burial on his native shore.

Now they were moving slowly up the canal, their running lights out, the *Doll*'s modest engine noise reverberating like the scream and clank of a steam locomotive. Sigerson was on the point of the bow with Wilkes, watching for the first sign of lights from the pontoon bridges, which were out somewhere in front of them.

"The Boche must be hearing this bucket of bolts," Wilkes said.

In his young manhood, Sigerson had often been impatient to the point of rudeness when he needed to explain the obvious to people who did not see it. Time had softened his approach. "Yes, well, we are, after all, on a canal, are we not, Wilkes? You'd expect to hear a boat from time to time, wouldn't you?"

"You're right. I'm just nervous, I think."

"Perfectly understandable."

After a pause, Wilkes asked, "How many runs have you made?"

"I couldn't tell you exactly without stopping to count. Perhaps twenty."

"Round the clock?"

"Very much so."

"The boat's been raked pretty bad."

"It's had its moments."

"Well, I'm grateful you picked us."

"You can thank yourself if that was you running the radio. We just happened to be in the area."

"Still, though. When I think of all those other poor blokes still waiting . . ."

They fell silent. Sigerson peered into the night over the bow. A low half moon reflected off the water. On either side, he could still see fields stretching out to the horizon. To the north—Dunkirk. A dull orange glow hung in the sky and every now and again they would hear, or feel, a deep thud—heavy artillery or bombs—even over the noise of the *Doll*'s motor.

But for the moment, the fields and the moon were closer, and Sigerson was on still water on a suddenly, unexpectedly warm night. He was well-fed and rested. He might almost have been home on the South Downs.

He surprised himself when he spoke. "I did not expect you to show up on that stallion. And bareback."

In the darkness, Wilkes asked. "You know horses?"

"For a time when I was a boy, they were my life. I still love them, though I don't own one anymore. But I'll ride every chance I get."

"Me, too. That boy today was a treat."

"He just let you mount him?"

"I'd already gotten some sugar. I tricked him. But once I was up, he was in my hand. He was a beauty. Ran like the wind."

"Makes me wish Hagin would have let me volunteer to go out for food."

"It was a bonus, I'll give you that."

Hagin rasped out from the bridge. "Lieutenant Wilkes, if that is you and Mr. Sigerson making all that racket down there, button it up, would you please?"

"Yes, sir."

⬩◈⬩

It was close to ten o'clock when the men went over the boat's side and up the levee. Ahead of them, Hagin had seen lights indicating what he thought was a town, and he'd ordered Duffy to stop the boat and pull up at the water's edge. For fifteen minutes or more after they'd gone, Duffy and the boys waited in growing suspense on the *Doll*'s bridge.

Sigerson was below decks with the sleeping and suffering wounded. He was at the radio, trying to intercept what might be relevant reports of German troop movements, listening to chatter from the ships that were still involved in Dynamo.

Hagin's plan, he knew, wasn't complex. His idea was to "strike a blow for the king," and hopefully divert some of the Panzer troops now closing the circle around Dunkirk. But nobody—including the colonel—gave much credence to the idea that they would succeed in destroying even one pontoon bridge. The object was to make enough noise so that they might in fact be able to slow some part of the enemy's inexorable advance. Then they would return to the boat and, if they could, make their getaway to the Channel.

The battle began with a series of small explosions—the handheld British Mills bombs or grenades. Next came a series of sharp pops that carried down to them over the surface of the canal. Within only a couple of minutes, it grew to what sounded like a substantial firefight. The sky before them lit up with mortar fire as the distinctive crack of the Brit's Bren submachine guns gave way to the deeper staccato rumblings of heavier mounted guns, the return fire of the Germans.

It was clear to Sigerson that even if Hagin had achieved the element of surprise for which he'd hoped, he had miscalculated the rearguard strength of the Panzers. Either that or he'd stumbled upon several platoons or more that had been moving to the front. He came up the steps to the deck and stood in the darkness, listening. The firing was almost constant now. Out at the horizon, he could make out some steadier source of what appeared to be significant light—perhaps searchlights or automobiles being assembled with their headlights trained on what Sigerson thought had to be Hagin's men.

He could picture them dug into the slope of the low levee. If that were the case, any German troops out on the pontoons or, worse, on the opposite shore, would find them easy targets, unprotected. When at last the steady barrage let up slightly, and Sigerson took the opportunity to mount halfway up the ladder to the bridge. "They're taking a lot of fire, Duffy."

"Sounds like."

"We might try to go in and get them."

"We'd be sittin' ducks, Mr. Sigerson. Middle of the canal, Jerry on both sides." His face, lit up by the glow of his cigarette, was set in worry. "Besides, his majesty ordered me to wait here. At least that way they'll know where they need to get to."

Sigerson looked out over the bow to where the fighting was taking place. A concerted volley of what sounded almost like anti-aircraft fire pierced the night—high-caliber, rapid fire weapons that far surpassed anything Hagin's men had managed to carry onto the boat. As he watched, there was another flash, then another, then the by-now-familiar *whump* of each percussion. More mortars. "We can't just wait here, Duffy. They're being slaughtered."

There was a harshness to Duffy's voice that Sigerson hadn't heard before. "If they're trying to retreat and get to us here and they make it here and we're gone, what happens to them then? What happens to us?"

But just at that moment—Sigerson could not believe his ears, but the sound was unmistakable—he heard the steady pulse of horse's hooves again, this time at full gallop. Close by, and then—"Don't shoot! It's me, lads." Here was Wilkes, astride another horse at the top of the levee. He dismounted and half-stumbled, half-fell down to the water's edge. Breathing hard, he could barely get the words out. "They've got us pinned down by the first pontoon. There must be half a division on the roads. Hagin says you've got to come up. There's no getting out."

"You just got out," Duffy said.

"Yeah. My two mates didn't, though, and I wouldn't have made it myself if I hadn't seen that nag on the way in and remembered where it was." A fresh round of heavy artillery drowned his next words. ". . . not much time."

"No, I don't expect there is."

Sigerson looked up and saw Duffy turn, then in another second heard the muffled roar of the boat's engines. "Are you coming aboard?"

"It would be quicker, I'd expect." He boosted himself up and over the hull. "There's slight cover if the Bosch haven't come around behind us yet."

"Beautiful," Duffy said. "How far is it?"

"Five hundred meters, maybe a bit more. You'll see it."

"I don't doubt I will." But he'd already put the boat into gear.

❖

Running dark, the *Doll* came around a slight bend and suddenly the noise of battle was all but deafening. A pontoon bridge crossed the entire canal in front of it—this was as far as the boat could go. Hagin's men had dug in on this side of the thing, but the Germans now had them pinned down and had begun to concentrate a withering fire on the steeply banked levee where they huddled in the partial shelter of the bridge.

The sound of gunfire was coming from the opposite side of the canal as well, which Duffy Black, on the bridge, read correctly as a bad omen.

It meant the enemy now had Hagin's men effectively surrounded, with the only possible escape now by water they way he'd come in. But the *Doll* itself presented a huge, slow and absolutely defenseless target. Once the Germans made any concerted movement across the pontoon from the opposite side—and Duffy thought he saw crouching forms advancing in the darkness even now—Hagin's men would be done. They would either have to surrender or die, and from what he'd seen so far of Hagin and his men, Duffy didn't doubt which option they'd choose.

But all wasn't lost yet. In their intense concentration on Hagin's position, the Germans hadn't yet noticed the *Doll*'s approach—either that or they had not yet identified it in the dark as an enemy vessel. In either event, so far Duffy wasn't taking any fire as he eased the boat though the still, dark water. In about a hundred meters, he'd be to the pontoon, where he would turn the *Doll* around and try to get the men to board.

Still, he hesitated for one last minute. Say what he would about his plans to help the men escape, he knew that as soon as he committed to the rescue from this point, he and Wilkes and the wonderful crew of three that had done such heroic work over the past days—Sigerson and the boys—were in all probability going to be dead. Certainly they would at least be captured. The Germans controlled the levee on both sides and the pontoon directly ahead. Three out of four compass points. As soon as the Germans identified the *Doll*, it would be over.

He decided to turn the boat around here where he had greater maneuverability. Maybe the Germans would even take the gesture as if not exactly friendly, then not hostile either—a local boat running into a firefight and turning around to get away from it. Duffy knew that at this remove, the *Doll* was at most a black shape in the water. And neither he nor Wilkes nor anyone below had fired a weapon yet.

They still had a few more moments.

He turned the boat around and put it into reverse. Now it really was only a matter of time until their intent would become clear and the Germans would commence firing at them. Wilkes was directing him to Hagin's men's exact position and they were quickly closing the gap. To seventy-five meters, sixty, fifty.

And then suddenly, they clearly heard commands being screamed out in German—it seemed as though it was all around them—and just as suddenly, the noise of the barrage fell by a half, then half again. This time, from close enough to see now, there was no mistaking the forms—it looked like an entire platoon or two—double-timing across the pontoon.

But astoundingly, Duffy thought, even though the German troops on the bridge continued to take small arms fire from Hagin's men, they did not stop to finish the small job right underneath them. Instead, they kept moving rapidly back toward the town. Thirty seconds later, as the *Doll* nudged into the levee's bank, nearly all the firing had stopped. All they heard was the occasional spurt of submachine gun fire from back over the levee wall, toward the town. Wilkes and the boys were down on the deck, everyone screaming to Hagin's men—"Move! Move! Come on, now! Move!"—to get aboard.

Duffy wondered briefly where Sigerson was, thinking with a pang that he must have been hit, but there was no time for contemplation. He didn't know the cause of this blessed hiatus nor its possible duration. All he wanted to do was get the men aboard and get out. With what he recognized as typical *esprit* from Hagin's men, they had passed the living wounded aboard first, and now the last of the men were hoisting themselves up and over onto the deck.

"Get down! Stay low! Go below!" The boys were getting the wounded down on board. At first glance, Duffy thought there might be as many as ten of them. As the able men came aboard, Wilkes had several of them take up defensive firing positions up at the bow and on the stern. Then Duffy heard him cry out, "All right, Duffy! Everybody's on. Take us out."

"Where's Hagin?"

"Dead."

Duffy threw the throttle forward and the *Doll* responded with a roar of her engines and clouds of exhaust. But she was moving now, on her way at top speed down the canal back to the safety of the Channel.

Wilkes was back up on the bridge next to him. "What happened back there? Why did they stop?"

"No idea, mate. The hand of God, maybe. How many men made it?"

"Eighteen, half of 'em hit."

"What about Sigerson?"

"Haven't seen him."

"Damn." He brought his hand up to his eyes. "God damn."

"Yes, sir. My thoughts exactly."

From behind them near the pontoon, a German machine gun opened fire again, its tracer rounds striping the night. The men at the stern, guided by the reverse trajectories, returned the fire steadily, but to no apparent effect. Duffy, keeping as close as he could to the precise center of the channel, guided the *Doll* around the bend and finally out of the sight lines of the scene of the battle. Half a minute after that, there was no other sound but the throaty roar of the boat's engines and the occasional groan or cry of agony from one or another of the wounded men below.

Wilkes knew that the below decks cabin was filled to overflowing with the wounded, so along with the rest of the survivors, he sat on the deck. Not only was he an officer, but he'd been the man who'd risked his own life to get back to the *Doll*, so the men had left him a spot on one of the stowage lockers, with the bulkhead behind him to lean against. He sat exhausted but in modest comfort, his knees up with his arms wrapped around them for some warmth. He'd gotten wet again—he'd never completely dried out since the morning—during the events of the night, and now he put his head down and tried to let the engine's vibrations lull him into something approaching rest.

"Give your poor ancient grandpa some room, would you?"

The old man's voice seemed to come from far away—maybe Wilkes had dozed a little after all and was imagining it—and now he looked up and even in the darkness could recognize Sigerson's weary face. "Am I dead, too?" he asked.

"What do you mean? Too?"

Wilkes shook some of the cobwebs out. He could see that they'd crossed the breakwater and were now somewhere out in the Channel. He sat up and stretched. "Duffy and I lost track of you. We thought you'd been cashiered."

"No such luck. I was just now up on the bridge with him. He says in a couple of hours we should be dockside at Dover."

"Where were you back there?"

"Stuck below."

"And how are the men down there?" he asked.

"We've lost three more. The rest are holding up. At least they'll make it home."

"Not to speak ill of the dead, but damn the colonel! It was a suicide mission from the start. We're all of us lucky to be alive at all. Thirty men striking a blow for the bloody king against three hundred Krauts, maybe even three thousand for all it seemed! That's not striking a blow. That's walking into a death trap."

Sigerson was silent a moment, then said, "Actually, it was a hundred and twenty."

"What was?"

"The garrison left behind to rearguard the pontoons. A hundred and twenty men."

"Still," Wilkes said, "four to one against isn't . . ." He stopped in mid-sentence. "How do you know that? The number of men they had?"

Sigerson gestured back behind him. "The radio. I said I was stuck below. Just before we headed upstream, I tapped into their frequency. When I realized that they were guarding the pontoons outside of Arquez, I knew it had to be the group we were holding against, so I established contact."

"You *talked* to them?"

"*Ich bin Hauptmann Braun, Offizier im Stab von General Guderian. Dies ist eine Angelegenheit der höchster Priorität.*" He broke a tight smile.

Wilkes translated. "I am Major Braun with Guderian's staff. This is a matter of the highest priority."

Sigerson's teeth showed his grin in the dark. "I asked them to report their strength and position."

"And they did?"

"Jerry is an efficient boy."

"So then what?"

"Then I'm afraid as Major Braun I must have given them the impression that an immense, highly mobile and unexpected counterattack of nearly a full division of Allied troops who'd somehow evaded our pincer movement was moving through the town, their objective being to take control of the bridges. The few skirmishers at the pontoon were undoubtedly decoys deployed to draw our fire and keep our rearguard occupied until their main force had moved through Arquez without resistance. Major Braun's orders—*my* orders," Sigerson said with a satisfied chuckle, "direct from Guderian himself, were to abandon the bridges immediately—*immediately*—and try to hold the town against the Allied assault. It looks like it worked."

"Worked? I'd say it worked. You bloody well saved us all."

Sigerson waved that off. "I should have told them to blow the bridges, too. That would have iced the cake."

"Forget the cake, man. What a plan! Duffy thought it was an actual bloody miracle. Hand of God, was what he said."

Sigerson shook his head. "Hardly that. Mostly a bit of luck when we needed it."

"What was the luck, then?"

"Stumbling on their radio channel."

"Thinking to look for it, more like. No luck about it."

"Well, the important thing is it got us out of there."

"That may be the important thing, but you ought to get a medal for it."

"That's nonsense, Wilkes. Right now I'd settle for a little space on this locker. I'm about done in."

In five minutes, Sigerson was snoring, an old man finally taking a bit of a rest.

⊷◈⊶

After nine days, Operation Dynamo, the Dunkirk evacuation, concluded on June 4, 1940. Approximately 800 British boats, pressed into emergency service as the *Dover Doll* had been, managed to rescue and return to England a total of 338,226 soldiers. The *Doll* itself ran a total of thirty-eight missions, eighteen of them after the attack on the Aa Canal pontoons.

Mostly because Frank Duffy returned to his daily job at the War Office and told everyone he encountered about it, news of the heroism and brilliance shown by the oldest member of the *Doll*'s crew, a civilian known only by the name of Sigerson, gained a nearly legendary status— apparently it was true that the pontoon skirmish on the Aa had led to a substantive German retreat that had delayed the Bosch's final assault on Dunkirk by at least a couple of days, saving countless lives.

Eventually, the story reached all the way to the top of the British High Command. Winston Churchill launched an investigation into the incident, corroborating the actual events, and verifying their strategic results. But even after an exhaustive search for the hero of the encounter, the old man was never further identified or located. No one by that name lived in or around the Sussex Downs, and that was all that Frank Duffy had known about him or his history.

Nevertheless, in October, 1940, Churchill awarded Britain's highest military decoration, the Victoria Cross, for valor "in the face of the enemy," *in absentia* to an unknown volunteer seaman surnamed Sigerson.

That medal was never claimed.

THE PROBLEM OF THE EMPTY SLIPPER

Script by Leah Moore and John Reppion

Illustrations by

Chris Doherty and Adam Cadwell

LEAH MOORE and JOHN REPPION with illustrations by CHRIS DOHERTY and ADAM CADWELL

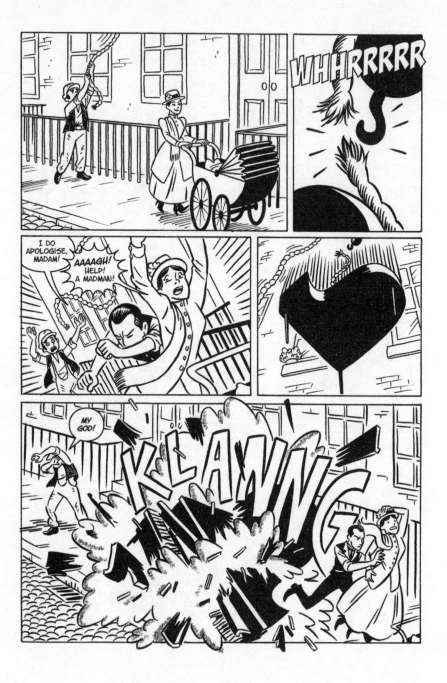

LOST BOYS

by *Cornelia Funke*

❖

Dear Holmes,

You always took care to hide your past under a cloak of mystery. No man is more aware of how dangerous a weapon it can be in the hands of an enemy. Only one case lifted this cloak for moments and I followed your wish—one may even call it an order—to destroy everything we gathered or wrote down on it. But I know you well enough (though you don't make it easy to gain such knowledge, my dear friend, as I dare to call you by now) to be sure that one day you'll wish to look back at what I am going to preserve with this letter: the shadow of a past that made you the man you are.

I often wondered whether you unveil the crimes and secrets of others so passionately because they remind you of secrets you hide from the world. This case—let's call it "The Case of the Lost Boy"—proved that suspicion more than any other. It made me understand that my best friend covers his emotions with layers of frost because he is haunted by memories that are only bearable in such a frozen, lifeless state. The demons the great Sherlock Holmes fears live all within himself, and his best-kept secret is the place from which they hatched.

"I felt a foreboding the moment I cast eyes on him." How often we use this phrase knowing that we only project onto the past what we learned from the future. But yes. I felt a foreboding the moment I set eyes on the boy, who at first introduced himself as Nicholas Hawkins. It is and remains the truth.

Even Mrs. Hudson who, bless her heart, is not the most perceptive of women, couldn't take her eyes off him.

But this is not the beginning. I try too hastily to get to the core of the story.

It began with one of the meals that you so graciously grant to the Baker Street Irregulars whenever they bring useful information for a case. Sometimes 221B Baker Street hosts more than twenty of the dirty little rascals. At most of these occasions Mrs. Hudson needs my assistance at some point, because she caught their dirty fingers on far too many things dear to her. You, in contrast, always loved the company of these underaged criminals. Along with your passion for outrageous disguises and your ability to think in a more organized fashion than your fellow men—even when surrounded by self-created domestic chaos—this affection is by far the strongest proof for your true Inner Self, which despises authority. You would probably add: of doubtable foundation. But I suspect it includes any authority, especially the religious and political kind.

Sherlock Holmes believes in the necessity of rules and is the fiercest fighter for the principle of justice, but he rarely sees it reflected in human laws. Therefore, he feels free to ignore or even break them, whenever he considers them to be in the way of true justice.

The boys who call themselves, with considerable pride, the Baker Street Irregulars share these views—they probably understand them much better than our adult collaborators on the quest for justice. Life taught these boys at an early age that human laws protect property far more efficiently than their health and well-being. The Irregulars never had the chance to build trust in the justice of the world and you respect them for their grim perception of the world while around them grown-ups wear the comforting glasses of illusion.

It was not the first time Billie Leaside, the leader of the gang, brought a new boy to participate in the Baker Street Feast as they call it. The Irregulars constantly recruit new members on the streets or amongst the garbage of the river banks. I know of several boys whom they saved from abusive fathers. Sometimes they even free them from the workhouses. Billie always brings them to me to make sure their bruises don't hide broken bones or damaged organs. For most of the Baker Street Irregulars, "family" means danger and "home" translates to battlefield. In fact, I think the violence they encountered did even more harm to their young souls than to those of uniformed soldiers, as there is no cause to be fought for on the domestic battlefield, no comrades to shield their backs, just helpless fear of the ones who are supposed to love and protect them.

It was not the clothes that gave Nicholas Hawkins away. The Irregulars often wear fashion of suspiciously well-tailored origin. After all, they are very talented thieves, as they prove regularly when we send them out to acquire an evidence we cannot get in more respected ways. Yes, the new boy's clothes were very well tailored. All the stains and dirt couldn't hide that. But I also noticed that the expensive shoes were neither too large nor too small, as so many of the shoes the other boys were wearing. (After all, you didn't teach me your methods of deduction in vain.) The skin under the grime was pale, but not working-house-bad-nourishment-pale. It had the paleness of a rich boy's sheltered skin. The hands that took the plate Mrs. Hudson offered him were lean and soft, and when I asked for his name, every vowel and consonant betrayed a privileged upbringing, though I didn't hear the distinct accent of Eton or Westminster.

It was not so much the lean face that reminded me of you, my friend, though there was a slight resemblance. No, it was the boy's gaze. Both rebellious and fearless, though scarred by fear: passionate emotion, shielded by intelligence and frozen by pain. And then the way he held himself—so upright, so proud . . . fighting everything in himself that was weak . . . young . . . vulnerable. It all felt so familiar.

Of course you saw it, too. The Irregulars had brought a younger version of yourself, though the boy's hair was blond, not dark, and the eyes, guarded like yours, were brown.

Nicholas Hawkins did not utter a word, while the others were as always so noisy that Mrs. Hudson cast me a gloomy glance each time she filled their plates once again with gravy and mashed potatoes.

No, he didn't say a word and he barely ate. But he stole a fork of the old family silver that you allow the Irregulars to use, despite Mrs. Hudson's protests.

I cast you a glance.

Yes, you had noticed the theft.

The boy tried his best to hide the silver under his dirty shirt, but he clearly wasn't as practiced a thief as the others.

You signaled me to stay in my chair when I was just preparing to rise from it. We know each other so well, that we rarely need words to communicate about matters like that. A slight raise of your left eyebrow, your lean finger trailing the arc of your nose, a slight touch of the upper lip or just a hand on the knee . . . our wordless vocabulary is very reliable by now.

There is an unwritten rule the Baker Street Irregulars obey as strictly as if they signed it with blood (a ritual they perform quite regularly, as we know, for other forms of contracts): The lodgings of Sherlock Holmes are sacred ground and therefore not stained with theft, swearing, spitting, or the disposal of lice and other unpleasant creatures housed in their hair and clothes.

Nicholas Hawkins had no doubt been informed about this rule. But despair breaks even the most strictly enforced law and despair nested in his eyes, blacker than any I have seen in the eyes of any adult seeking your help at Baker Street 221B.

With a quick movement of your gray eyes you drew my gaze to the mug of lemonade, that Mrs. Hudson had brought in as reluctantly as she had the food.

I have become quite a good actor in your service (not as good as you, perhaps: Sherlock Holmes could probably make me believe he is one of the cats Mrs. Hudson feeds at the back door.) I managed to spill most of the lemonade over Nicholas Hawkins without raising any suspicions in the notoriously suspicious minds of our rascal guests, and thanks to my obvious clumsiness and Mrs. Hudson's extremely sticky lemonade, Nicholas Hawkins (I was quite touched when I found out that he had stolen the last name from a favourite book) had to stay behind while the other boys stampeded down the stairs to shadow a well-known banker whom you (rightfully) suspected to have financed some of the late Moriarty's endeavors.

Nicholas betrayed his good upbringing once again when he mumbled excuses while putting on the dry clothes Mrs. Hudson brought from the well-filled wardrobe we keep for the Irregulars. The boy had managed to hold on to the fork. It was by now hidden in his left sleeve, but he was clearly embarrassed about it.

You sat in your chair puffing your pipe when I brought the boy back to the living room. You looked at him with the silent gaze you use on both clients and future victims, a gaze as cold and detached as that of a snake ready to strike. But there was something else in your face, a hint of the compassion I detect there only on very few occasions—and usually not at such an early stage of acquaintance.

"I think you underestimate your current companions," you said without taking your eyes off the boy. "They have an astonishing capacity for sympathy. I am sure they would have raised the money for the ticket if you had informed them about your situation."

Nicholas Hawkins' face was almost as expressionless a mask as Sherlock Holmes likes to wear. But he was too young to erase all hints of shame, fear, and wounded pride. A winter like that which you impose on your own emotions was coming for this young boy, but the spring of youth still found its way through the frozen surface.

"I don't know what you are talking about, Sir."

"Well, you certainly don't know much about the criminal trade in this city. A fork like the one you hide in your sleeve will never pay for a train ticket to . . . shall I guess . . . York? Scarborough? The silver is barely fifty years old and shows strong traces of wear. Apart from the fact that it sadly shows an inferior hallmark. As it does have some sentimental value for me, though, I must ask you to return it."

The boy hesitated, as if he still hoped to keep the pose of the innocent, but then he opened his sleeve and brought the fork forth. He had tears in his eyes when he dropped it into your outstretched hand. His look of injured pride . . . you show it rarely, but I have seen it.

"How did you know what I need it for?"

You put the fork on the table. "You weren't especially hungry while the others were eating. I don't see symptoms of any addiction you have to feed. You are obviously not from London, though your accent is covered by a good teacher's efforts, and the state of your clothes suggests you haven't been home for at least two weeks. You wear a locket that you touch quite often. Considering your age, I assume it doesn't bear witness to a romantic attachment, so that leaves a son who is tenderly fond of his mother."

I still cannot say who was paler when you uttered these words, my friend, the unfortunate boy or you yourself.

"I need to get back. It was wrong to run away."

"Yes. And no," you replied. "Yes, you will have to go back, or you may never forgive yourself. But this return has to be prepared, or it may prove dangerous. Which leads to the 'No'. No, it was not wrong at all to run away, because it brought you here and I will do my very best to help you."

You nodded at the boy's chest. "Would you mind opening your shirt to show Dr. Watson the traces I am sure you wear on your chest and back?"

The boy just looked at you, as white as a corpse.

"There are certain rushed movements that betray you. The fear of physical pain does amazing things to us. We become as alert as a deer. Not that it helps, for the hunter is our master. Isn't he?"

The boy bit his lip so firmly that it turned even whiter than his face. "I see what he is doing."

"Yes, you do. And he knows."

And there they were, my friend. On your face. Memories. Not the boy's, but yours. And I write them down, as I have been the scribe of your memories for so long. The paper is a safer place to preserve them than your mind, where you decided to turn them into ice. In my days of war I sometimes asked men who had been traumatized by the events on the battlefield to write down the memories that haunted them and then burn the paper. I fill these pages only for that purpose. But you'll have to burn them at the right time . . . when the words are ready to take the memories with them. Sadly this method doesn't always work.

"There is one thing I can do," you continued. "As I suspect you don't want me to involve the police."

The boy shook his head vigorously.

"Well, let's leave that option aside for now." You straightened the fabric of your trousers, as if straightening your thoughts. "In fact, I fear you are right. Domestic situations like this are seldom improved by the police."

You got up and stepped to the window, something you often do when your emotions threaten to escape the corset you forced them to wear.

"Please promise you won't go back without my letter," you said without turning your head.

The boy nodded, but I saw that all he wanted was to get away from this man who read his heart and mind like his own. You would have done the same. And of course you were aware of it.

"The letter will also protect your mother," you added.

The boy just stared at your back. He didn't believe you. He was past believing that anything could protect her.

You sent me after him, when he left.

To make it short, although it is one of the heaviest burdens on my heart: I lost the boy.

I have never seen you angrier.

You went yourself to find Billie, but Hawkins, as he called himself, hadn't gone back to the Irregulars.

You had them search for him. You paid them to guard all the main stations. And stayed up all night, the letter you'd written waiting on your desk.

The boy could not be found.

Two days later the *Times* reported that Beatrice Beauchamp, wife of Richard Beauchamp, a rich merchant with vast estates near York, had committed suicide. She left a son behind. An only child called Nicholas.

When I still heard your steps at three in the morning, pacing the living room, I knocked at the door. You called me in, my friend. I am still grateful for that. This night explained so much and I never received a greater proof of trust from you.

"He didn't have a brother. I found that to be the most worrying detail." You stood by the window and stared into the night, as if trying to penetrate a different kind of darkness with your gaze. "I would never have been able to stop it without Mycroft. At that young age my brother was even more my superior when it came to deduction and logic unblurred by emotion. I would have drowned in my emotions without him."

The hoarse voice of a coachman rose from the street, as if to remind us of the violence that lurks under the surface of our world. And that it sometimes doesn't pass by the places we call home.

"We stopped our father with blackmail. We found proof of several petty crimes he had arranged in order to threaten a business partner—nothing that compared in our eyes to what he did to our mother, but which would have ruined him if the police had found out. We were scared he would kill us when he realized we had sent the letters, or have one of his men do it. But he decided to escape to the colonies, taking most of the money and leaving a highly indebted estate behind. My mother never quite forgave us. Though Mycroft still believes that her strongest emotion towards us is the embarrassment she feels about her own weakness and the fact that she still loved him."

You turned and looked at me. "I had forgotten how it feels to be so young, Watson," you said. "And how such a father teaches us to not trust anyone. I feel quite embarrassed about my ignorance. Please find out where the boy is. I still want his father to get my letter."

I found him. At the terrible school his father had sent him to, half mad with grief. Holmes' letter made sure that Nicholas Beauchamp was sent to the best school in the country—I delivered it in person—and that he was never forced to leave for home visits.

He didn't have a brother, my friend. But he found Sherlock Holmes.

THE THINKING MACHINE

by *Denise Hamilton*

❖

Bill Gleason was eating lunch at his computer and running some consumer analytics when his eyes wandered to a picture frame at his desk. Pondering the sublime geometry of its crisp angles and parallel lines, Bill sank into a mathematical trance.

But something nagged at him.

Slowly, the numbers receded, the image *inside* the frame swam into focus and Bill beheld his older daughter Portia, smiling as she accepted a trophy at the Science Olympiad.

Bill examined the beloved face. Soon Portia would be off to college, and only Samantha, whom Bill called daughter number two, or "Dos," would remain. He envisioned packing up the Volvo station wagon and driving Portia off to her dorm at some. . . .

Suddenly, Bill made a strangled sound and sat up straight.

What if he could muster up enough data to determine which families had kids leaving for college? Those kids would need lamps, bedding, pillows, shelves, and tech. And Landmart, the national chain of big-box stores where Bill toiled in R&D, could target those families with strategically placed coupons and ads.

For several weeks, Bill kept his thoughts to himself. Because having an idea was different from explaining it to a room of people and requesting money to pursue it. At such times, his childhood stutter returned with a vengeance, along with a facial tic to deflect the stares of his colleagues.

Bill often felt like the resident alien at the Landmart Corporation. After earning a Ph.D in mathematics while barely out of his teens, he'd spent the next decade at a research university dwelling happily in a world of pure numbers. It was a comfortable world where he felt at home. Numbers were precise and did exactly what they were supposed to. They never let him down, unlike the human world, with its messy emotions and unpredictable behavior. A world Bill was so bad at navigating.

But then math got sexy and guys like Bill who knew analytics and data forecasting were suddenly in high demand. After years of turning down overtures from Silicon Valley and corporate America, Bill said a reluctant goodbye to university life when Landmart dangled a salary that was 4.256864 times higher than what he earned at his cash-starved institution.

Because by then there was Lisa.

Somehow, Lisa had found him and unlike most humans of the female persuasion, she refused to be scared away by what she diplomatically referred to as his "quirks." And now they had Portia and Dos, who were an endless source of marvel.

Bill had been nervous about fatherhood. He knew he got along better with pixels than people. But to his great relief, Bill discovered that he loved his daughters with a ferocity he hadn't known he possessed. With a trembling finger, he traced the Fibonacci spirals of their pink seashell ears as they slept. He spent hours testing diaper absorbency to find the best brand for his waddling darlings. He hunched dutifully over the cereal box, making elf sandwiches of Cheerios, cheese and turkey.

And if he was halting and clumsy with them, and rather wooden in his hugs (though he'd gotten better), they still hurled their small bodies at him when he arrived home from work and demanded that he read bedtime stories with proper drama instead of a mumbling monotone.

And as *Little House on the Prairie* gave way to *Twilight*, Bill learned not to argue about the biological impossibility of vampires or question the attractiveness of certain hairstyles and outfits because of the statistical probability of outrage (21.7%) and tears (17.6%). And then one day when the girls were fifteen and seventeen, Lisa announced she wanted another child.

At her age, that meant fertility doctors, invasive tests, and painful shots. They decided not to tell the girls until things "took," a decision whose wisdom was confirmed when Lisa suffered two miscarriages.

Bill hoped that might be the end of it, but Lisa channeled her grief by redoubling their efforts. She insisted he drive home at lunch when she was ovulating and once he even flew back two days early from a Data Analytics Conference in San Francisco. Bill loathed these "dates" because they turned the best thing ever into a mechanical act and brought back taunts from his childhood:

> *Ro-bot*
> *Ro-bot*
> *Billy's just a Robot!*

The lunchtime rendezvous also distracted him at work when he could least afford it. When Landmart hired him, Bill had built a computer database to analyze the buying patterns of the firm's customers, which Landmart called "guests."

Since then, he'd sliced and diced the data in every conceivable way, amassing a frighteningly large pile of information. For instance, guests with credit cards emblazoned with photos of their children kept up payments better. So Landmart launched an aggressive campaign of free credit cards with personalized photos and the store's delinquency rate fell 3.2%.

For Bill, whose social intelligence hovered near negative googleplex, this was proof that cold hard numbers concealed—but could also reveal—unassailable emotional truths.

Despite the corporate praise that followed, Bill was far from content. Staring at his gleaming pillars of data, he saw only a pale ghost of the statistical portrait he *really* wanted.

And then came that eureka moment in his office.

The following month, Bill bragged to his bosses that he'd soon be able to identify Landmart guests with college-bound kids. He just needed more data.

"I believe there are numerical patterns hidden in the data that can be revealed using forensic modeling," he told the bosses. "This would be nothing like those morons in marketing endlessly focus-testing which color headers and fonts work best for e-coupons. It would be revolutionary."

Landmart declined to buy the expensive consumer data Bill wanted, saying he already had plenty to work with. And when it came time for his annual review, his evaluation mentioned a "caustic and abrasive" manner with colleagues.

"You need to sugar-coat things a little more," the HR manager said.

"But their ideas are stupid and they don't work."

The HR manager flinched.

"Look, Bill. We all know you're a brainiac. You've done great work here. But there's book smarts and there's people smarts. The people who get ahead in this world are the ones who have both. Who know how to navigate the system."

Maybe I don't want to navigate the system, Bill thought mutinously. *Maybe I should just go back to the university where I belong.*

The next time his department met, there was a new person with blinding teeth and fancy shoes at the conference table. A vice president for research and development. He introduced himself as Moriarty.

And this time, when Bill finished his usual pitch about data mining, Moriarty stared thoughtfully and didn't complain about Bill's lack of people skills. Later, Moriarty glided into Bill's office, sleek and silent as a shark.

He picked a half-eaten protein bar off a chair, dusted the seat and sat down.

"I think you're on to something, Bill. Psychologists say people are most vulnerable and open to suggestion when they're going through life changes. Can your data predict things like marriage, divorce, and home ownership? If so, we can hit our guests with targeted ads."

Bill's eyes goggled. His Adam's apple moved up and down. In his excitement, he could barely speak, but then he did, for five minutes, until Moriarty cut him off.

"I don't need the details. Just tell me how much you want and we'll draw up a budget,"

Bill trembled as he named a figure.

Moriarty said he'd see what he could do.

Then he stared at Bill, narrowing his eyes in a way that made Bill nervous. Despite himself, Bill's foot began to tap

"This has to stay top secret," Moriarty said. "If our competitors get wind of what we're doing, it's all over. We'll have the lawyers draw up a non-disclosure statement for you to sign. Just pro forma, of course."

"No problem," Bill said, grimacing because he was tapping away at Beethoven's Ninth with his sneakers and Moriarty had interrupted his rhythm.

"You can't even tell your wife and family. And no talking to friends at dinner parties."

"Right," said Bill, who didn't get invited to dinner parties.

"How long before you get me some preliminary results?"

Bill said he didn't know. He hated estimating, it was imprecise and unscientific. So he threw out some technical jargon and kept tapping. He couldn't stop until he'd finished the chord progression. Any second now, Moriarty was going to ask what the hell that noise was.

But Moriarty leaned back in his chair, his eyes glassy and far away.

"Imagine being able to peer inside people's souls and tap into their deepest desires. To sell them tons of product almost before they know they need it," he said. "It would be like finding the Holy Grail."

⬧

That night, Bill went home with his usual pile of work.

He'd been putting in extra hours lately, and the new project Moriarty had green-lighted would gobble up even more. It bothered Bill that he saw so little of his family now that they'd outgrown soccer games and Girl Scouts. He missed those rituals. He missed being needed.

Portia was so self-sufficient it was almost like living with another adult. He'd watched her almost clinically as she grew, always looking for—and fearing to find—signs that she might be like him. But Portia had inherited the best of both of them—his analytical brain and Lisa's emotional intelligence.

"Hey Dad," she said, bounding down the stairs, her long chestnut hair whipping behind her, smelling of lemons and honey. She hugged him and he forced his limbs to relax and hug her back. She'd been a late bloomer, but recently she'd begun to show signs of Lisa's curves. Bill thought she'd looked good with a few more pounds, but he'd seen her shredding lettuce and cutting tomatoes for school lunches and knew she worried about her figure.

"More letters came today," Portia announced, smiling. "Brown, Swarthmore, University of Alabama."

Since the PSAT test results had arrived, Portia had been bombarded with brochures from colleges.

"They all want you, daughter of mine," Bill said. "Keep up your grades and you can write your own ticket."

Bill looked forward to making a cup of tea. He'd sit with Portia at the kitchen table and she'd tell him all about her week.

But Portia was shrugging into her coat.

"Got a hot date?" he asked, hiding his disappointment.

Already, he sensed the emptiness that lay ahead when Portia, then Dos, left for college. Although she never spoke of it, Bill knew this was why Lisa wanted another child.

"Don't be silly, Bill," Lisa said, emerging from the kitchen. "It's not like when we were growing up. These high-achieving kids travel in packs, they're too busy to date. I'm dropping her at the mall to see a movie with her friends and you've got pick-up duty at midnight."

Clutching the car keys, Lisa explained that the pizza was still warm.

"Where's Dos?" Bill said.

Lisa's nose wrinkled.

"Upstairs. And isn't it time you stop calling her that? It's going to give her an inferiority complex."

"But she *is* daughter number two," Bill said mildly. "Besides, mathematically speaking, two is double the value of one. So really it's Portia who should have the inferiority complex."

"Oh honestly, Bill," said Lisa.

A blast of cold air as the door opened, and they were gone.

Bill put two slices of pizza on a plate, poured a glass of milk and ambled upstairs, marveling at the maturity and drive of his older daughter. At seventeen, Bill had been ditching school to hang out with a slightly sinister high-school dropout with only eight fingers who shared his love of rocket launchers, muscle cars, and explosive chemicals.

At Dos's room, he knocked on the door that said KEEP OUT, waited, then pushed it open.

Dos wore earbuds and moved sinuously in front of the mirror. She'd tied the tails of her shirt above her midriff and rolled the waistband of her skirt down to her hips to expose her stomach, which was ground zero in a recent war over the installation of a belly ring.

"That one will bear watching," Bill's aunt said with pursed lips when they visited Los Angeles and Dos flirted with all the surfers and begged to visit the cemetery and take a picture at Marilyn Monroe's grave.

Suddenly, Dos saw him and gave a startled scream.

"You could knock, you know."

"I did knock."

He pointed to her earbuds, then stared at his feet.

"I'm home," he mumbled.

Dos's face grew soft. She pulled out her buds and ran to him.

"Silly Daddy," she said, laying her head against his chest and hugging him. But just as he put his arms around her, she slid out of his grasp like an eel and resumed dancing.

"When will you and Mom let me date?" she said.

Bill felt a twinge of panic. He wished Lisa was here. After trying and failing to calculate the right answer, he said:

"Is this a theoretical question? Or has a boy asked you out?"

Bill took his glasses off, cleaned them with a chamois cloth he kept especially for that purpose, then put them back on and peered at her.

"I just want to be prepared," Dos said.

Bill let out his breath. "Your mother and I will have to discuss it."

Dos scowled.

"Why does everything have to be a democracy in this house?"

"Because that's the best kind of government."

"Then why don't I get a vote?"

"Because you are not of age," he said gravely.

But his mind was already wandering to his work, and Dos had her earbuds back in, dancing to the unheard music.

Bill backed out of the room and shut the door, filled with the sense of inadequacy and bewilderment he often felt with his younger daughter.

❖

In the following months, Bill bought reams of data from banks, credit card companies, retailers, e-tailers, mortgage firms and online sites that tracked customer purchases, then he cross-referenced them with Landmart's data and searched for patterns.

Because all secret projects need a nickname, Bill and Moriarty christened theirs "Sherlock." As a kid, Bill had devoured the stories of Arthur Conan Doyle and harbored a secret fantasy that Holmes, with his flat affect, his devotion to logic, and his brusque, sometimes superior manner, might be just like him. Maybe when his creator wasn't looking, Holmes put down his pipe, fled into the bathroom and flapped his arms madly behind locked doors the way Bill did to relieve the tension brought on by work.

While psychologists had long believed that most purchases were driven by emotion, Bill's data-crunching showed they were actually quite logical. Project Sherlock, like its namesake, relied on reason, deduction, data clues, previous patterns of behavior, and inference to winkle out those reasons, then manipulate Landmart's guests into buying more things.

It was elementary.

Moriarty's first assignment for Bill was a test balloon: Build a database of all Landmart guests with pets who would then receive holiday catalogs crammed with ads for animal-related products. By January when they crunched the figures, pet accessory sales had jumped 17%—even with the weak economy.

Bill got a modest raise.

He was pleased, but it was the work that absorbed him.

All day he swam through streams of pure data, probing, exploring, mapping an entire new universe. With credit card statements, job histories and online activity—he built magic windows to peer inside the hearts and minds of Landmart shoppers. He became an electronic voyeur, dizzy with the power and secret knowledge he wielded over thousands of people he'd never met.

If Mr. and Mrs. Smith spent $572 on marriage counseling and $350 to appraise their house, Bill knew they might be headed for divorce. If the Jones family bought a secondhand car, IKEA extra-long Twin sized bedding and SAT workbooks, they might soon send a child off to college. If they lived in Los Angeles and bought a winter coat, that kid was headed to a cold climate and would probably need mittens and thermal underwear too, and plane tickets home for Thanksgiving.

"You're like an alchemist, turning raw data into gold," Moriarty gloated as they settled into a booth at St. Louis's fanciest steakhouse for their monthly lunch meeting. "For years we've searched for a wormhole, a path into people's brains. And you're the guy who's making it happen."

Bill muttered something about patterns being easy to spot, and began to shred his napkin into half-inch strips under the table.

No matter what they ordered, Bill picked at his meal, cutting off all the gristle, slicing everything into precise cubes, then inspecting each one for uniformity of size, color and texture before putting it into his mouth.

"Picky eater?" Moriarty said, attacking his steak with the same gusto he mustered for Power Point presentations.

"Not really," Bill said, squirming.

Moriarty nodded sagely. "I know. Cholesterol. I only allow myself red meat once a month."

"It's not that . . ." Bill said, scraping mashed potatoes off a green bean. He hated when one food touched another on his plate.

Moriarty patted his abs. "You can say it. My six-pack needs some work. Gonna hit the gym extra hard tomorrow."

Bill put his fork down, put his head in his hands.

"No, no, no," he said. "That's not what I meant at all."

The Italian restaurant wasn't much better, and the Chinese, with all those gloppy sauces and unidentifiable vegetables, made Bill so nervous he ate bowl after bowl of steamed rice.

"My girlfriend's favorite restaurant," Moriarty said, deftly deploying his chopsticks on the kung pao chicken.

Bill was fishing cashews out of the kung pao and wiping them carefully on his napkin before eating them. They were good that way. Nice and dry. At Moriarty's words, he looked up, startled.

"I thought you were married."

"I am," Moriarty said.

Bill stared at his plate and his face flushed bright red.

"You really are one of life's innocents, aren't you?" Moriarty said.

Bill was silent. He thought about how to write a program to detect adultery among Landmart guests. He'd look for spikes in purchases of jewelry, florists, hotel rooms, restaurant meals, perfume, Viagra. On secondary credit cards, of course. Whose monthly bill went to a different address.

Moriarty folded his napkin and tucked it under his plate.

"You just keep doing your job, and I'll do mine."

⋘◆⋙

Things were going well at work. Moriarty put him on a team with a specialty sales manager, a marketing whiz, a psychologist, and a neuroscientist Landmart had hired away from MIT. They held "blue sky" meetings to talk about ideas.

One day, Moriarty came in all fired up.

"If we wanted to find out if a Landmart guest was pregnant, even if she didn't want us to know, could you do that?" he asked.

"I can try," Bill said.

"At the hospital, they get coupons for disposable diapers and formula," Moriarty said. "By that time, the whole world knows they've had a baby. We want to find out before our competitors."

The specialty sales lady nodded. "We have a baby registry at Landmart, and lots of women sign up for it so friends and family know what to buy."

"I like it," said the psychologist. "In terms of buying patterns, pregnancy is the biggest life change out there. They're emotional and more open to trying new things. If we can hook them, we have them for life."

Moriarty turned to Bill.

"I want you to crunch the data of every woman on that baby registry, as far back as you can go. Find out what they have in common."

Bill's first move was to analyze what women bought the nine months before they gave birth. He ran analytics for each trimester, then each month, then each two week period. He also ran it for six months prior to conception.

At the next meeting, Bill brought charts and some answers.

"Home pregnancy kits are often the first marker," he said. "By the fourth month, we see purchases of bulk vitamins, unscented lotion, and cocoa butter. By the sixth, it's area rugs, babycare books, soothing music."

"How accurate are these predictors? Forty, fifty percent?" Moriarty asked.

Even though the answer was seared into his brain, Bill pretended to flip through his notes so he wouldn't have to meet anyone's eyes.

"Eighty-seven percent," he mumbled.

The room was silent.

"Holy cannoli," the neuroscientist said.

"That figure does *not* leave this room," Moriarty said hoarsely. "If what Bill says is true, it's going to revolutionize the baby business."

Bill slumped in his chair.

Babies, babies, babies.

He was surrounded by real and theoretical babies. Thanks to Moriarty, the entire Landmart team was obsessed with conception, gestation, and birth, which was almost unbearable to Bill, considering what was going on at home.

Each month, the rollercoaster of emotion. Was Lisa pregnant or wasn't she? And then the inevitable letdown. Last month, Bill had kissed Lisa's damp face and pulled out some colorful graphs and flow charts he'd drawn up, hoping they would provide solace.

The charts showed that since the big pregnancy push, Bill's work efficiency was down 14% and Lisa's freelance consulting earnings had dropped 28.2%.

Bill had also written a program to calculate the cost of a baby over eighteen years, including number of calories expended per day, hours of sleep lost, and the cost of clothing, food, extra-curricular activities, medical care, and university education. He'd charted how their own physical prowess, muscle mass, energy level, memory, and endurance would begin to decline exactly when the child reached adolescence.

Bill was gratified to see that his bright colors and attractive fonts stopped Lisa's tears. But when he began to explain, Lisa screamed and slapped the graphs away.

Stunned, Bill fell silent.

Then to his great relief, Lisa hugged him.

"I know you mean well, Bill, but not everything can be reduced to charts and numbers. Life doesn't work that way."

Bill stared at the floor and bit the inside of his mouth until it bled.

But it does.

I'm proving it day by day with my analytics.

Instead, he smoothed her hair, dried her tears, and petted her like a cat. Lisa had fine golden hairs on her forearm and he stroked downward, so the hairs lay flat. It was irritating if you did it the other way. Even the cat howled and ran off. He stroked her right arm thirty times, then moved to the left for thirty more, the rhythmic feel of skin on skin soothing them both, until he felt the tension in her body dissolve and she leaned her head into the crook of his neck and said, "Oh Bill, I love you but sometimes I wish you wouldn't be so damned rational."

"I can't help it," he mumbled, inhaling the dear, familiar scent of her hair.

"I know."

Recalling this at the meeting, Bill's shoulders grew heavy. He was tired of not being able to tell anyone at work. Of pretending to the girls that everything was fine, Mom was just tired or having one of her spells. But Lisa wasn't the only one. Sometimes Bill felt the top of his head might blow off. Several times a day, he locked himself into the handicapped stall to flap his arms madly just to calm down.

"What if the couple having a baby wants to keep it a secret?" Bill thought, then was horrified to realize he'd spoken aloud.

Moriarty gave a sinister grin. "Thanks to you, Bill, there are no secrets anymore. Landmark has the ability to peer inside your brain, your bedroom, even your womb."

The head of the art department said:

"We already send out glossy catalogs targeted to our guests' needs, so we can certainly create baby-centric ones. Our pregnant guests don't need to know their neighbor got a different one. All they see is, 'here's a coupon for something I can use.'"

Bill thought of how concerned he and Lisa were about keeping a potential pregnancy private until it proved viable.

"But won't women get creeped out if they get a catalog that says 'congrats on the impending birth of your child' when they haven't even told anyone yet? I know Lisa and I would."

He reddened, afraid that his colleagues might guess his secret. "I mean . . . it could be a public relations disaster. Corporate big brother breathing down the necks of unsuspecting citizens. And what if a um . . . country like, eh . . . China got a hold of these programs and used it to spy on pregnant women and force them to have abortions?"

"I don't give a flying fuck about China," said Moriarty, "except how to sell them more diapers and car seats."

"Bill raises a good point," the psychologist interjected. "We shouldn't send pregnant guests catalogs full of baby products. That *would* freak them out and it might backfire. Subtlety is key here. Let's scatter baby ads throughout the catalog so they have no clue we've got them in our crosshairs."

"Bring me a mock-up in two weeks," Moriarty said. He stood up and held out his hand to Bill. "Well done, man. I'm putting you up for a promotion."

Bill forced his face to crease into a smile as they shook. It still wasn't automatic, but years of practicing in front of the mirror had made it easier. A nod and quick glance at Moriarty, then away, because men don't sustain eye contact unless they're after something else.

He'd learned that the hard way, too.

After the meeting broke up, Bill went to the bathroom and washed his hands. He did it twenty times. When he caught his reflection in the mirror, he looked away, unable to bear the eyes of the man with thinning hair and a creased brow who stared back.

⬦

Things weren't so good at home. Lisa's ever more desperate efforts to jump-start a life had drained and hollowed her out and some days she found it hard to get out of bed. The rest of them chipped in to shop, walk the dog, and run errands. Portia, who'd just gotten her driver's license, was especially solicitous, even driving across town to get Lisa's favorite Lebanese food.

Bill told Lisa about his raise. He was glad Moriarty had sworn him to secrecy. Lisa wouldn't want to hear about him analyzing the buying patterns of thousands of pregnant women across America when her womb remained empty.

Helpless to make things right for Lisa, Bill turned to what he could control.

Project Sherlock's 87% success rate might be high enough for Moriarty, but that meant 13% of their pregnant guests slipped through the cracks. Bill began to stay later at work, manipulating variables, writing new programs, casting a wider net. The work was painstaking, meticulous and exhausting and Bill envied the real Sherlock his 7% solution, "so transcendently stimulating and clarifying to the mind."

One night when he'd knocked off early at 10 p.m., Bill was opening a bottle of zinfandel when Lisa walked in, looking glum. He got another glass down and poured them each one.

"I shouldn't," Lisa said, twirling the stem and sniffing the ruby liquid longingly.

Why not? Unless there's something you're not telling me, it's not like you'd be harming a fetus, Bill thought.

But Bill knew it was part of her regimen to encourage procreation: no booze, very little caffeine. Healthy eating. Exercise.

"Oh, I might as well," Lisa said, lifting her glass. "You know, sometimes I think . . ."

Then she stopped, because Bill had fled the kitchen and was hurrying upstairs, muttering to himself.

"For heaven's sake, Bill, I can't even talk to you anymore, you're always working. Hello! This is your wife, your family calling. Wake up, Bill."

But Bill was already at his desk, feverishly sketching out a new algorithm. Alcohol! Caffeine! Consumption of both would drop among pregnant women. But conversely, they might buy more decaf coffee and herbal tea. Bill worked into the night, integrating these new markers.

When he ran the numbers again, his prediction rate rose seven-tenths of one percent.

He began to scrutinize his own family.

When he commented on the gray lace mantilla spreading across the crown of Lisa's usually glossy black hair, she frowned and said that hair dyes could be absorbed through the bloodstream. A week later, he saw a bottle of henna in the bathroom. After reading the ingredients, he googled "natural hair coloring" and tinkered more with his calculations.

Watching Portia "like" a band on Facebook, he realized that tracking the "likes" and sites visited by newly pregnant women would give him more pieces of the puzzle.

Bill's prediction rate inched up, but perfection eluded him.

He yearned for a program as pristine as Fermat's Theorem, as all-encompassing as $E = MC$ squared. He sought no less than the golden ratio of pregnancy prediction.

He became a man obsessed, staying at the office til midnight, working at home all weekend. And the number kept rising: 95%, 97%, until he hit 99.3%. Try as he might, he couldn't crack that last seven-tenths of one percent. At last, he decided that further refinements were probably impossible, not to mention statistically insignificant.

He had to stop before he made himself crazy.

More crazy, that is.

⌖

Soon thereafter, Moriarty called him in and told him that Landmart had created a new position for him—Director of Analytics & Forecasting. With it came a fat promotion, a corner office, and his own staff.

Bill hurried home, elated to tell Lisa. They'd be able to go to Europe this summer and put aside money for each girl's college tuition. They'd be able to afford another round of fertility treatments.

In the foyer, he stopped to look through the mail. A few bills, more college brochures for Portia. The usual circulars, junk mail, and catalogs. His eye caught the familiar Landmart logo. Because of course, the Gleasons were Landmart guests too. A feeling of pride suffused him at what he and the team had accomplished. And how much he enjoyed his job. He made a good living, and even if it meant long hours, it allowed him to provide for his family. He might have trouble communicating his affection for them, but he loved them. He'd do anything for them.

Bill picked up the Landmart catalog and leafed through it. Its hotshot art director had won awards for bold design and ad copy that invoked deep subconscious anxieties but also reassurances that buying these products would propel you into the luxury lifestyle depicted in the catalog.

Bill saw an ad for a tractor lawnmower and one for a kitty condo. In between was an ad for a baby crib.

He turned the page. Next to ads for bookshelves and potting soil was an ad for prenatal vitamins.

Something flickered in his heart and he flipped the pages faster.

A crock pot, a pup tent, skis, and a baby monitor.

Paper towels, brightly colored throw rugs, scented candles, and disposable diapers.

Every couple of pages, subtle as hell but also clear as a bell if you'd been in on the conception, if you'd sat through the gestation at endless design meetings, arguing about color and font size and how to manipulate a pregnant woman's subconscious.

Duvets, toasters, and baby strollers.

Bill heard a ringing in his ears.

It couldn't be.

"Hi hon," Lisa said.

She walked up to kiss him and he grabbed her.

"Lisa! You didn't tell me."

"Tell you what?"

"The good news!"

She disengaged herself and stepped back. "What news? What's wrong, Bill? You sound really agitated."

She began to pat his shoulder in a way that usually calmed him down.

He couldn't look at her. Instead, he addressed the vase of tiger lilies on the entryway table.

"How long have you known? Was it that day it was storming outside, with all the lightning and the thunder? There was something special about . . ."

"Known what?"

"I can see why you wouldn't want to say anything to get our hopes up after the mis . . ."

He caught himself.

"Oh, honey," Bill said, "I know how badly you wanted this. I'm so happy."

He picked up her up and twirled her around.

"Bill," she squirmed. "Put me down."

He tried to speak but the words locked up inside and made him hyperventilate.

"Are you having some kind of fit?"

The tenor of Lisa's voice caused Portia, who was at the dining room table studying with a friend, to look up from her AP Physics book.

Bill got ahold of himself. He had to respect Lisa's wishes to keep the news quiet. So he hugged her again and whispered in her ear.

"How far along are we?"

Hand across her mouth, Lisa backed away in horror.

"What gave you? . . . I would have told . . . I'm not . . . pregnant," she hissed out the last word between clenched teeth.

Stunned, Bill looked from his wife's agonized face to the brochure on the foyer table.

Project Sherlock predicted pregnancy in Landmart guests with 99.3% accuracy. It extrapolated based solely on facts, on logic. It was impeccable. He, Bill, had made it so.

Snatching the brochure off the table, he stabbed at the images.

"L-l-l ook! . . . Ads for b-b-baby things. That's what I've been working on. The top-secret program I couldn't talk about. The raise. It's . . ."

Lisa was shaking her head and whispering "no" over and over.

Upstairs, a door slammed.

Bill's head jerked up.

Dos.

Fifteen years old going on twenty-three. Always posing and voguing in the mirror, obsessed with boys.

If Lisa wasn't pregnant, was it possible that Dos, his boy-crazy little girl, had gone and gotten herself . . .

No!

Bill refused to follow this line of reasoning to its logical conclusion.

And yet, the data didn't lie. He knew that. Though there was that pesky 7%. Yes that's what it had to be. His family fell into the statistically insignificant minority.

Bill almost cried with relief.

In the dining room, Portia and her classmate were somehow managing to study. Funny how life went on, despite the complete meltdown of his orderly, logical life.

But what if Project Sherlock wasn't as sound he had claimed? With his swagger and his hubris. His haughty dismissal of those peons in art and marketing. His insistence that only numbers told the truth. Was Project Sherlock flawed in some basic way? Was Landmart funneling huge amounts of money into something that would never pay off? In which case, maybe his career was about to go down the drain.

Bill had to go upstairs immediately and review Sherlock's analytics, piece by infinitesimal piece. It might take weeks, but if there was a flaw in the program, by God, he'd find it. He'd fix it, then he'd run diagnostics. He'd correct the error.

But first, he owed Lisa an apology. Lisa, his beautiful wife, who looked like she was about to cry.

Unable to look into her eyes, Bill focused on the two heads in the next room bent over their textbook. How the streetlight shining through the window—at a 75 degree angle, he calculated—caught the red highlights in Portia's hair and turned the short tousled blond hair of her companion to gold. Bill searched his memory for the boy's name. He'd seen this particular boy before, but he was so bad at matching up faces and names. He'd have to ask Lisa.

Lisa, whose voice broke through his reverie:

"Bill? Are you even listening? Have you been *drinking?*"

She reached for the catalog but fumbled. The catalog hit the floor, falling open to reveal a plump, photogenic baby sitting in an ergonomically correct high chair.

And as Bill stooped to pick it up, he suddenly remembered the name of the boy sitting next to Portia. It was Zach. He was on the swim team. He was one of the gang that Portia hung out with.

Then he noticed something else.

Under the table, where no one could see, Portia and Zach were holding hands.

Bill straightened and stood there, swaying.

He rewound his memory and saw Portia coming home after doing the marketing, Landmart bags dangling from each hand. Good, conscientious Portia, who volunteered to shop for her mother who was ill in bed after a fertility treatment. Or more recently, with depression. Portia, who always did her schoolwork, who managed her time wisely, who planned ahead, who was destined for a wonderful college.

They'd added her to their Landmart credit card this year so she could shop for what she needed.

What she needed.

Bill began to sprint up the stairs like a madman, leaving his wife in the foyer, thinking he'd lost his mind.

Upstairs, he slapped the computer out of hibernation and began to tap out the Ride of the Valkyries on the desk.

Lisa came up behind him. She leaned into him, placed her hands on his shoulders.

"Talk to me, hon," she said, her voice soft and pleading. "You're scaring me."

Bill whirled in his chair.

"Oh, Lisa!"

And then in a calm voice, he sketched out the entire project. How he'd slaved at improving his prediction models for pregnancy. The catalog on the floor of their foyer. How he'd seen Portia's hand under the table, gripped tightly with the boy's. And above it, the curve of a belly that hadn't been there before, that he and Lisa had been too busy and obsessed with their own problems to notice.

"Portia? Do you really think it's possible?" Lisa said wonderingly.

"Of course not. There's a mistake somewhere," Bill muttered. "I must be wrong. I have to be wrong."

He paused.

"Because if I'm wrong, then everything is still all right."

"What if she really is pregnant?" Lisa said.

Her voice was thick and dreamy and her eyes were suffused with the warm memory of cradling soft mewling helpless mammals. "Portia's baby! Our grandchild. We could raise it here. She could still go off to college. It's not an ideal situation. But it could work. We'd make it work. People do it all the time."

Bill groaned.

"Lisa, how can you be so calm and rational about this?"

He turned back to the screen, which was taking forever to boot up, and in the pauses between flickering images, he saw the two of them silhouetted against the dark screen, him slumped in his chair, and Lisa behind him, hands resting on his shoulders, her face uplifted, radiant and beautiful. Expectant.

The image was so dramatic, so strange, and yet familiar, that he thought he'd seen it in a dream, his wife's yearning for a child suddenly answered, but in this most statistically improbable of ways. He saw himself stumbling out of bed at 3 a.m. to answer hungry cries, changing diapers, wiping pureed peas off a tiny chin, and the entire tumultuous experience roared through him, filling him with horror and love and confusion and exhaustion. He couldn't do it again. But then Lisa pressed against him, her limbs warm and pliant. His heart swelled with love for his wife and his family. Whatever form that family might take. And as they leaned into each other, the space between them dissolved, and he felt more connected to her than he had in years and he knew that somehow it would be all right. Then Lisa shifted and the cold air rushed between them. The safe feeling vanished. Bill felt the stable, orderly life he'd worked so hard for rise up like the chimera it had always been and leave his body.

And as he waited for the pillars of gleaming data to scroll across the screen, Bill put his head down on the keyboard and cried:

"Please Lord, just this one time, let Sherlock be wrong."

BY ANY OTHER NAME

by Michael Dirda

"How could you? Just how could you?"

Jean Leckie looked up at Arthur Conan Doyle, the tears streaming down her cheeks. The couple were seated in a quiet corner of an ABC Tea shop in Camden Town. Her companion, dressed in handsome tweeds, appeared perplexed.

"Dearest, sweetest love. Please don't cry."

"It's easy enough for you to say. Don't you care about my feelings?"

"I adore you."

"Save that for Touie, you hypocrite. You clearly adored *her* enough to make your marriage, your happy marriage the subject of this!" Jean brought out a book from her capacious handbag and slammed it on the table.

Arthur quietly picked up the small volume and looked at the cover: *A Duet*, by A. Conan Doyle. The pretty but distraught young woman continued:

"Nothing to say for yourself? You look as though you'd never seen it before."

"Darling, *A Duet* came out years ago. I can hardly remember anything about the book."

"Really? And I suppose you don't remember this either."

She reached into her bag again and tugged out a thick bundle of paper, each page covered with neat handwriting.

"What's that?"

"So soon they forget. You gave this to me as a gift. It's the manuscript to that charming portrait of the happy marriage of you and Touie, and of your domestic bliss together, a bliss suddenly threatened by"—another round of sobs—"a scheming Other Woman. Now who, you might ask, could that female demon, that evil succubus, that Lilith be? Could it just possibly be Miss Jean Leckie, the unhappiest woman in England? And to think I believed all your declarations of love, to think how long I've been waiting . . ."

"Uh, Jean."

"What? You . . . you toad, you viper. What?"

"This is all ancient history, sweetheart. Why are you bringing it up now?"

"Well, darling," replied Jean coldly. "I finally read the book. I was afraid to earlier, but felt that I should if we were going to. . . ."

"Jean, please don't cry."

"Arthur, this book makes it impossible for us to marry."

"What!"

"Yes, Arthur, I would always live in the shadow of the love you depict so tenderly in these pages. I couldn't bear it. And who knows, Touie's spirit could be watching us right now. Her invisible presence could be hovering nearby." She glanced around the tea shop.

Arthur Conan Doyle slumped resignedly in his chair, then seemed to pull himself together and finally said: "Jean, I ought to have told you this long ago. I don't know whose marriage that book portrays but it has nothing to do with me or Touie—or us."

Jean began to laugh, then stopped.

"What are you saying? Next, you'll be claiming that you aren't the well-known author A. Conan Doyle."

"Actually, I'm not."

"Liar."

"No, really, I'm not. And I didn't write *A Duet*, my dove."

"Your name is on the title page."

"My name is on lots of title pages. While I'm not absolutely positive, I think *A Duet* is actually by Grant Allen, the chap who brought out *The Woman Who Did*."

"But what about this manuscript?"

"You may have noticed that there aren't any corrections, erasures, or revisions to any of the pages."

"Yes."

"That's because I simply copied it out from the book."

Three months later:

"So A. Conan Doyle is a *Strand* house name. I should have guessed."

Zebulon Dene—clubman, journalist, and occasional consultant to Mr. Sherlock Holmes—blew smoke from his cigarette and leaned back into his favorite red leather settee. Outside the bow window of the Amnesiacs' Club—where anything could be said and nothing would ever be remembered, not even in a court of law—he watched the passersby hurrying to the nearby underground station.

"Yes," he continued, "I should have guessed long ago. Nobody could write that much, in so many different styles. But how did it come about?"

Herbert Greenhough Smith, editor of the *Strand Magazine*, took a sip of brandy. "I suppose it was because of Watson. He came to me with these wonderful accounts of his adventures with Holmes, yet was clearly uneasy about using his own name on them. It wouldn't do, he said, for a medical man to be scribbling fiction, not if he was to be taken seriously as a doctor."

"Does anyone take John seriously as a doctor?"

Greenhough Smith smiled. "Touché. But Watson's a good man and a damn good writer. Besides, he'd already used 'A. Conan Doyle' for a pair of cases about Holmes in *Beeton's* and that American magazine, *Lippincott's*."

"The one where Wilde's *Dorian Gray* first appeared?"

"Yes, that's the one." Greenhough Smith drained his glass. "At all events, I suggested it was time to retire the pen name and that John H. Watson should appear as the 'onlie begetter' of 'A Scandal in Bohemia.' But Watson wouldn't hear of it. Holmes, I daresay, felt literary celebrity would bring an unwelcome attention to 221B. Personally, though, I think Mary was the chief reason. She grasped immediately how infatuated some women can become with writers and, wise woman, knew her husband could never resist a pretty face or ankle. No, for Holmes's sake and for marital serenity, it finally seemed sensible just to stick with A. Conan Doyle."

Dene signaled the waiter. "Another brandy, for my guest." When they were again alone, he added, "While all this is mildly interesting, just ten minutes ago you hinted at something more, that Watson hasn't been the only one using the A. Conan Doyle *nom de plume*."

The *Strand*'s editor looked a bit shame-faced. "I suppose it's really my fault. One night E. W. Hornung and I met at Emmuska Orczy's for dinner. You know how Hornung's always coming up with puns? Well, that night he made some remark about the author of 'The Red-Headed League' being *a* Conan Doyle rather than *the* Conan Doyle. Of course, he knew that his brother-in-law couldn't write a prescription, let alone a short story."

"But his dedication of *The Amateur Cracksman*—'To ACD, this form of flattery'?"

"Just irony or another gentle poke. That crook Raffles isn't the upright gentleman he appears to be; A. Conan Doyle isn't the author he appears to be. Both present fake facades to the world."

Greenhough Smith paused, took a swallow of his brandy and began again. "The whole business really goes back to the 1880s. John H. Watson and Arthur Conan Doyle are longtime friends, and even look enough alike to be taken for brothers. As young medical graduates, they came to know each other in Switzerland when they were both studying with some famous eye specialist there."

Greenhough Smith eyed his nearly empty glass, then continued. "About the time he was finishing up *A Study in Scarlet*, John learned that his old chum was going through a rough patch while trying to establish a practice in some provincial town. Portsmouth or Southsea, I think. In fact, Conan Doyle had no patients to speak of. As Holmes will be the first to testify,

John's a good-hearted soul and knew from first-hand experience what it was like to be alone and desperate in a strange city. To tell you the truth, I don't think he's ever fully got over what he went through at Maiwand or even during those first months back in London. Holmes can tell you about the nightmares. . . . But I digress.

"The long and the short of it is, Watson cut a deal: He would pay his friend Arthur a percentage of his literary earnings in return for the use of his name. Of course, Conan Doyle would also need to pretend that he was the author of first one, then two, and now numerous 'Adventures of Sherlock Holmes.' Confused readers did and still do complain: Is Holmes real or fictitious? Were his cases being written up by Watson or being made up by Conan Doyle? Either way, the mystery has been good for publicity, and I've made sure such riddles remain unsolved even by Sherlock Holmes."

Greenhough Smith finished his second brandy.

"As time went by, Conan Doyle readily fell in with a literary crowd, though he still found plenty of opportunity to indulge his real passions—cricket and billiards—and to travel back to Switzerland for skiing holidays. Would you believe he even boxes? There are times the man quite reminds me of Jack London, though London can actually write."

Dene sniffed, "Conan Doyle has always seemed too much the hearty for my taste. Alfred Douglas once told me that he actually served on a whaling ship. Did you know that? I can just picture him with a harpoon instead of a ski pole in his hand. As for Jack London, please. Let's just say I've spent half my life fleeing from these Wild West, he-man types. Some of my own worst nightmares are about my unhappy time in the Guards. Now Henry James—there's a writer after my own heart."

"Can't bear him myself. What is it poor Clover Adams said? 'Henry James chews more than he bites off.' If you ask me, that stout pseudo-Englishman has simply no idea how to tell a story. Was the governess in that novelette of his insane or not? I never could tell. Give me Saki any day." Greenhough Smith reflected a moment, swirled the fresh brandy in his now refilled glass and, with a sigh, went on with his story.

"Watson didn't think the arrangement would last long. Just a year or two. In fact, after the doctor moved his practice to the Sussex Downs, the Holmes adventures stopped appearing altogether for several years. The Watsons were happy, busy, and didn't need much money living the simple country life. But after the baby died and poor Mary killed herself, John started to spiral downhill. Drink, gambling losses at the track, the old nightmares about Afghanistan, then the Jezail bullet wounds started acting up again, and, finally, one night he picked up his old service revolver, resolved to blow his brains out. What was there to live for? Well, it was Holmes who really saved him, first by inviting him back to 221B and then by urging him to write up more of their cases."

"And so," Dene interjected, "Watson slipped back into harness with *The Hound of the Baskervilles*."

"Well, not exactly," said Greenhough Smith. "Watson only took up recording the Holmes cases again with 'The Adventure of the Empty House.' But long before that *Strand* readers had been clamoring for another exploit of the great detective and, so far as I knew at the time, Watson never intended to write another word about him. So I asked Fletcher Robinson to take on that sinister Baskerville affair. John, generous as always, was happy to lend his notes and scrapbooks. As a thank you, Robinson quite beefed up Watson's own role in the whole business. He might have even gone a bit overboard. Still, Robinson knew Dartmoor like a native and he proved a dab hand at all those eerie touches readers like so much. To my mind, Dene, nothing comparably spooky could really touch *The Hound* until Monty James started bringing out his ghost stories. Still, it was rather cheeky of Robinson to dedicate the book to himself."

"Through your editorial machinations then, Fletcher Robinson, using Conan Doyle's name and Watson's notes, became the actual author of *The Hound of the Baskervilles*. And I thought Mycroft was Machiavellian."

"Dene, you're a journalist, at least of sorts. You know what editors are like. When Holmes mentioned the Baskerville mystery late one November night, it lodged in my memory. How could I let such good copy go to waste?"

"So, if I have this straight, at that point there were two writers behind the Conan Doyle name?"

"Oh, more than that. I was utterly shameless. After Hornung made his pun, it led me to think of Watson as just 'a' Conan Doyle. Why couldn't there be others? The name was already famous and people would buy just about any tosh bearing the words 'By A. Conan Doyle.' One afternoon I was talking with Stanley Weyman when I found myself suddenly asking if he might be willing to write a swashbuckler under a pen name. Weyman was just starting out then—I think he'd only published *The House of the Wolf* and one or two other books—so he jumped at the chance to do *The White Company*. Alas, we had a falling out and *The Cornhill* serialized it. Not long ago, though, I managed to entice our friend Emmuska into taking on *Sir Nigel*. The gypsy in her was deeply pleased to have a secret identity, much like her own Sir Percy Blakeney, better known as—"

Dene exclaimed, "Please, don't," but it was too late.

"—as The Scarlet Pimpernel! 'They seek him here, they seek him there, those Frenchies seek him everywhere. . . .'" By this time Greenhough Smith had leapt to his feet and was brandishing an imaginary sword, assuming so heroic and noble a stance that Fred Terry himself, or even Sir Henry Irving, would have envied it. Dene, however, was stricken with embarrassment.

"That's really quite enough, my good sir," he commanded, "please remember where you are and do sit down. I'd rather not have a guest of mine removed from the club for excessive exuberance."

Greenhough Smith reluctantly lowered his sword arm and returned to his seat, muttering softly "Is he in heaven? Or is he in hell? That damned elusive Pimpernel." Zebulon Dene lit another cigarette.

"So how many Conan Doyles are there?"

"Hard to say, just offhand," answered the out-of-breath editor. "Let's see. I gave Stoker the germ—so to speak—of *The Parasite*. Vampires and what not. Anstey simply reworked *Vice-Versa* into 'The Great Keinplatz Experiment.' *Beyond the City*, the comical one about the emancipated woman, was actually written by Shaw. I'll never work with him again. Ouida, you won't be surprised, suggested the kidnapping novel set in the Middle East. *The Tragedy of the Korosko* may actually be my favorite Conan Doyle novel. As it happens, a few of these assignments I ended up rejecting, but lesser periodicals were always eager to take them. I've worked hard, Dene, so that the *Strand* has never gone for too long without the name Conan Doyle on its contents page."

"This ghost-writing continues then?"

"Yes, but I'm not sure for how much longer. Why do you ask? Would you care to try a Conan Doyle? I've an idea for a kind of Battle of Dorking tale about submarines destroying English sea power. No? Ever been up in an airplane? A shocker about creatures living in the clouds just might"—chuckle—"fly."

"I'm afraid such fancies are more in the line of Wells or M. P. Shiel. I prefer to deal with facts and actual, living people. I am a journalist."

"Oh, don't be so high and mighty, Dene. All sorts of people have written under the Conan Doyle name. You didn't see the hand of Jerome K. Jerome in *The Stark-Munro Letters*? That combination of humor and religiosity, I thought, would give the game away. Mrs. Bland brought me 'The Leather Funnel' and that piece of Grand Guignol about Lady Sannox. They were, she said, relief from all those E. Nesbit children's books. And I'm sure that working up Captain Sharkey stories provided Barrie with the first inkling for Captain Hook. Anyway, it became all the rage to write a Conan Doyle. But the public, of course, was kept entirely in the dark. Nobody suspected, not even you."

"I heard rumors."

"But nothing more than that."

"Yes, that's quite true. Which leads me to ask again why you're telling me all this now. What precisely is the problem? And why do you need my help?"

Meanwhile at 221B Baker Street:

"So, Watson, what do you make of it?"

Holmes strode cross the sitting room and dropped the latest issue of the *Strand* into his friend's lap. The good doctor picked it up gingerly.

"Well, Holmes, to all appearances this is the latest issue of the *Strand Magazine*."

"Precisely, my dear fellow. But do you remark nothing more?"

Watson carefully scanned the cover, which depicted a bustling street scene. He opened to the contents page. Pictures of the royal family at home. A scientific romance called "The Hollow Earth," by H. G. Wells. An article on spiritualism by A. Conan Doyle. . . .

"I don't see anything."

"You never do, Watson. You never do."

"Except, I was going to add, this Conan Doyle piece called 'The Coming Revelation.' Complete balderdash, if you ask me."

"You didn't write the article yourself?"

"Lord, no, Holmes. I only do up your cases. I may heighten the atmosphere somewhat, add a little color and dialogue for dramatic effect, but I'm careful to stick to the facts."

"Can you, my dear Watson, deduce who did write this article?"

"I haven't the foggiest notion. Greenhough Smith—quite on the hush-hush—has been working the A. Conan Doyle name pretty hard in recent years. Employs a whole stable of authors to crank out swashbucklers, romances, every sort of thrilling wonder tale. Anthony Hope, if I'm not mistaken, produced those witty Brigadier Gerard stories—wish I had his talent. . . ."

"Watson, comparisons are invidious and you have a knack for describing our cases that imbues them with quite the air of romance. As it happens, I know beyond doubt that neither you nor the author of *The Prisoner of Zenda* produced this fatuous article. You have evidently forgotten that I once undertook a stylometric analysis of all the major contributors to the *Strand, Pearson's, Chambers'* and a dozen other periodicals. The frequency of certain turns of phrase, the pet adjective, the length of paragraphs—all these may be used by the trained mind to establish the identity of an unknown author. This essay lying before us, this glorification of a so-called astral realm, is certainly not the work of any magazine writer known to me. I will admit that for a moment, however, I suspected it could be from the pen of that Blackwood fellow."

"Do you mean Algernon Blackwood? Greenhough Smith tells me he's now at work on some stories about an 'occult' investigator named John Silence, still another of these so-called fictional 'rivals of Sherlock Holmes.' Yet if you'd never become a consulting detective, I doubt we would have ever heard of Martin Hewitt, Romney Pringle and Professor S.F.X. Van Dusen."

"Did you say rivals, Watson? I presume this is another example of your pawky humor. But pray let us not be distracted from the matter at hand. I initially thought the article might be Blackwood's in part because of his membership in the so-called Hermetic Order of the Golden Dawn. More puerile and distasteful mumbo-jumbo! It offends the scientist in me. But this isn't the work of Blackwood, or even that Welsh mystic friend of his, Arthur Machen. I now know the true identity of the article's author."

"Who is it?"

"Conan Doyle."

"Yes, yes, that's what the byline says, but which one?"

"You dolt! I mean your friend Arthur Conan Doyle, who has, for reasons yet to be discovered, suddenly taken to writing under his own name."

"But that's ridiculous, Holmes. The man doesn't care about anything except sport—and, if I'm not mistaken, a comely young woman by the name of Leckie." Watson paused, reflectively. "Do you think that explains why he's been so active in divorce law reform? I wonder . . . But frankly, Holmes, Conan Doyle as a writer—it's ridiculous. Next you'll be telling me that you want to record your own cases! I'd like to see you write up that business of the lion's mane." Watson began to chuckle. "Laughable even to think of it."

"Laughable indeed," replied Holmes. "But not for the reason you think, Watson. I concur with the astute Thomas Carlyle that magazine work is below street-cleaning as a trade." Nonetheless, the great detective looked thoughtful for a moment, as if he had just had a singular idea, albeit one for which the world was not yet prepared.

"Please, Holmes," responded Watson, interrupting his friend's reverie. "Don't denigrate my Grub Street labors. After all, my scribbling for the *Strand* pays half our rent. Besides"—and for a moment the doctor's usual bonhomie fell away—"writing helps me through the long nights."

"All right, Watson. I withdraw my rude comment. It was ungracious of me. But you do recognize, old fellow, what this means? I fear that your literary career may be at an end. Still, unless I very much underestimate my man, Greenhough Smith is probably at this very moment on his way to see a certain journalist—and I don't mean Langdale Pike. Yes, Watson, this is a case for Zebulon Dene."

Three days later, at the Amnesiacs' Club:

"This business is already replete with too many Conan Doyles. May I call you by your given name?" said Zebulon Dene. "I trust you will excuse my presumption. Being christened Zebulon Andrew Dene—after an American explorer and my mother's cousin, the author of *The Blue Fairy Book*—I am rather sensitive about names myself. But forgive me. These genealogical details can be of little interest to you."

The handsome, mustachioed sportsman attempted a wan smile. He was beginning to wish he'd never listened to Jean.

"Yes, you may call me Arthur."

Dene continued, "You and John here are, I am assured, well acquainted. Later we may be joined by the editor of the *Strand*, Mr. Greenhough Smith. Alas, Sherlock Holmes is currently en route to the island of Uffa, about some business there involving underground phenomena. There are rumors, apparently, of something similar to that Blue John Gap cave-monster. In my own opinion, however, I rather suspect he has simply fled London until this whole matter is settled. He is, after all, the *fons et origo* of this . . . tumult."

Arthur Conan Doyle and John H. Watson pulled their armchairs closer to Zebulon Dene, who lounged on his usual red leather settee. He continued:

"As your fellow physician Dr. Thorndyke might say, let us review the facts. Fact number one: Many years ago, John persuaded Arthur, who was then in financial straits, to allow him to use the pen name A. Conan Doyle for what are commonly referred to as the adventures of Sherlock Holmes. I say commonly called thus, because I know how much Holmes cringes at that penny-dreadful word 'adventures.'

"Fact number two: Over time Herbert Greenhough Smith, the editor of the *Strand Magazine*, gradually began to employ, in a somewhat careless fashion, the name A. Conan Doyle for every sort of fiction, from historical romances to accounts of contemporary life to novels of manners.

"Fact number three: From private communication with Miss Jean Leckie, I have learned that she was deeply distressed after reading A. Conan Doyle's *A Duet*. It is, to all appearances, a largely autobiographical portrait of a happy marriage, one that she believed mirrored that of Arthur and his late wife Louise, usually known as Touie.

"Fact number four: Arthur remonstrated with Miss Leckie that he had not written *A Duet* and that its author was, in fact, Grant Allen. That supposition, by the way, is incorrect. Greenhough Smith informed me that the actual author is Marie Corelli. No matter. Upon further questioning, Miss Leckie learned that her, eh, friend had, in fact, never written any of the books bearing his name.

"Fact number five: Miss Leckie, who is a young person of considerable moral rectitude, was shocked to discover that a gentleman for whom she entertained a high regard was living a lie. She could only respect a man, she informed me, who was, in her colorful phrase, 'steel true, blade straight.' In short, Miss Leckie threatened, I don't think that word is too strong, to break off all social relations with Mr. Arthur Conan Doyle unless he 'set things right.' Above all, she meant that the promiscuous, and to her mind mendacious, use of the A. Conan Doyle name must come to an immediate halt.

"Here we approach the crux of the matter and, if you will permit me, I will merely summarize subsequent events. But, first, may I offer you a brandy? No? A glass of port? Sherry?"

"Just get on with it, Zeb," said Watson.

"Now, Arthur—" Here Dene glanced at the burly sportsman. "—obviously had a serious problem. Not only his social status, but much of his income derives from the various works published under the A. Conan Doyle brand, to borrow a useful term from the cattle ranchers of the American West. Going public with the truth would lead to ridicule and even penury. So he offered a radical counter-proposal to Miss Leckie. Would you share it with us, Arthur?"

Conan Doyle looked even more uncomfortable. "Words aren't really my strong suit, but in essence I promised Jean, Miss Leckie, that from now on nobody but I myself would write as A. Conan Doyle. The past is past, I told her, and it can't be changed. But I pledged that in the future the A. Conan Doyle name would be used for good."

"For good? What do you mean by that, Arthur?" asked Watson.

"I intend, John, to defend those wrongly accused of crimes, to support legal and civic reforms, and, most of all, to promote the cause that Jean has taught me to believe in."

"And that, I gather, is spiritualism?" interrupted Watson. "How can you credit such nonsense, Arthur? You, an educated man, a graduate of Edinburgh, a physician . . ."

"Yes, I knew you were going to mock me, John, and you won't be the last, but I've seen things and heard things that have convinced me that there is an Other World, that spirit communication is possible, that that—"

"If you say so, Arthur, if you say so. But in my opinion when A. Conan Doyle signs his name to psychical tracts, he will simply be continuing to write fiction by another name."

Just then a door quietly opened and an elderly waiter ushered a slightly unsteady Greenhough Smith into the room. "Hello, lads. I see he's told you the bad news. Henceforth, the proud A. Conan Doyle name, once that of the greatest storyteller of the age, will grace polemics and apologias and histories of spiritualism and, I don't doubt, books about the edge of the unknown and, who knows, maybe even fairies and the little people."

"Come, come," said Watson. "That's a little harsh, Herbert. You've already stretched the Conan Doyle name pretty far by commissioning what are little better than shilling shockers. Now, don't look so disingenuous. There's that revived mummy story, for instance. 'Lot No. 249,' if I've got the right number. But fairies, really! I'm sure Arthur won't go to quite that extreme."

If possible, Conan Doyle looked even more uncomfortable, as he pretended to glance casually out the club window.

"Well, perhaps you're right," answered the *Strand*'s editor. "We'll just have to see. At all events," Greenhough Smith continued, "I spoke with Miss Leckie and she allowed that those Professor Challenger stories we've been stock-piling could still appear. You know the ones, John, the three or four that Kipling and Haggard wrote as a lark on their golfing holidays in Scotland. But Miss Leckie did insist that her future husband would eventually show Challenger coming around to the truth of spiritualism. Having a scientist, even a fictional one, join the movement would apparently give it a great boost. 'If only,' she said, 'Challenger were actually real like Captain Scott or Sir Harry Flashman.'"

"But what about me?" protested Watson. "What about my own accounts of Holmes's exploits?"

"Well, John," replied Conan Doyle with a smile, "since you were good enough to share your earnings with me for the cases you wrote up, it's only fair that you receive the same percentage in return—if you'll let me continue the chronicles of Baker Street. My writing won't be a patch on yours, I admit, but lend me your notes for, say, the Mazarin Stone case and that Three Gables affair and I'll do my very best to make them as thrilling as 'The Speckled Band' or 'Silver Blaze.'"

"But, Arthur, I say this as an old friend, you don't realize how much effort I expend on those *Strand* pieces."

"Come now, John, you certainly make it look as if they wrote themselves. I'll bet almost anyone, given the facts in a case, could scribble out a Sherlock Holmes adventure. 'It was a wet October night in the year 1892, but Holmes and I were snug in our sitting-room when Mrs. Hudson announced a visitor.' Nothing to it, see? But now I must take my leave. Miss Leckie awaits in the vestibule. After tea, we're going on to a séance—Aleister Crowley has introduced us to our very own spirit guide. Such knowledge! Such ancient wisdom! Pheneas might actually make a wonderful subject for a book some day and I've already got the title, *Pheneas Speaks.*"

After Conan Doyle left, there was a visible sigh of relief. "Oh, Lord," groaned Dene, "I dread to imagine what kind of third-rate sermons and tedious propaganda will now issue from the pen of A. Conan Doyle. I exerted all my powers to persuade him and the Leckie woman to maintain the status quo, but to little avail. Is there nothing more to be done?"

"Nothing," said Greenhough Smith. "It's a pity, but there you are. Still, the *Strand* will soldier on. And I'm beginning to feel it may have been time for some changes anyway. Out with the old, in with the new, so to speak. Would you, for instance, care to write a 'spy' thriller, John? In my view, *The Riddle of the Sands* has opened up some fresh possibilities in storytelling. What do you say?"

"It's kind of you to offer, Herbert, but I think not. I enjoyed Childers' book, but then you know how fond I am of any sea story, not just Clark Russell's. Still, fiction itself is rather beyond me. I've simply no imagination whatsoever. No, John H. Watson retired once before from writing and this time it's probably for good. But I have squirreled away a few of Holmes's investigations in my box at Cox's Bank, including that long one involving the Valley of Fear, so I may slip our poor deluded friend the occasional manuscript. I will, that is, if I can escape the gimlet eye of the future Mrs. Arthur Conan Doyle. With luck, then, and I say this without any false modesty, there should still be a few good Baker Street adventures even in the future. Overall, though, I suspect that readers will detect a certain falling off. Spiritualism—oh, Arthur!"

Greenhough Smith shrugged. "As you wish, John. Well, how about you, Dene? Surely, you can be persuaded to take on a thriller—could be good money here."

"You editors never give up. As I said before, fiction isn't my line either."

"Oh, come on. It's not that different from writing for newspapers. Besides, you do dabble in detection, from time to time. There was that crime wave at Blandings and the mystery of Lord Strathmorlick's courtship and, of course, it was none other than Zebulon Dene who first suggested that it could be Jill the Ripper. Since you'll be using a pen name, there would be absolutely no risk to your reputation as a, uh, distinguished journalist. Besides, I've already done the hard work, coming up with the plots and titles. Now A.E.W. Mason has already signed on to write *The Power-House*, but you'd be perfect for *The Thirty-Nine Steps*. Here's my basic idea: An innocent man, wrongly accused of murder, goes on the run from both the police and ruthless enemy agents. Sounds good, doesn't it? Do say yes, Dene, otherwise Chesterton could end up writing it and, if that happens, he and Mason might take the whole enterprise over to my dreaded competitor *Blackwood's*. Please? For a friend? I predict that 'John Buchan' could become almost as popular and prolific as 'A. Conan Doyle.'"

HE WHO GREW UP READING SHERLOCK HOLMES

by *Harlan Ellison*®

A bad thing had happened. No, a "Bad Thing" had happened. A man in Fremont, Nebraska cheated an honest old lady, and no one seemed able to make him retract his deed to set things right. It went on helplessly for the old lady for more than forty years. Then, one day, she told a friend. Now I will tell you a story. Or a true anecdote. For those who wish this to be "a story I never wrote," have at it; for those who choose to believe that I am recounting a Real Life Anecdote, I'm down with that, equally: your choice.

Once upon a time, not so long ago . . .

A man in an 8th floor apartment in New York City lay in his bed, asleep. The telephone beside him rang. It was a standard 20th Century instrument, not a hand-held device. It was very late at night, almost morning, but the sun had not yet risen over the decoupage skyline of Manhattan. The telephone rang again.

He reached across from under the sheet and picked up the phone. A deep male voice at the other end said, very slowly and distinctly, "Are you awake?"

"Huh?"

"Are you awake enough to hear me?"

"Whuh? Whozizz?"

"Are your bedroom windows open . . . or shut?"

"Whuh?"

"Look at the curtains!"

"Whuh . . . whaddaya . . ."

"Sit up and *look* at the curtains. Are they moving?"

"I . . . uh . . ."

"*Look*!"

The man's three-room apartment was on an airshaft in mid-Manhattan. It was in the Fall, and cold. The windows in his bedroom were tightly closed to shutter out the noises from the lower apartments and the street below. The curtains were drawn. He slumped up slightly, and looked at the curtain nearest him. It was swaying slightly. There was no breeze.

He said nothing into the phone. Silence came across the wire to him. Dark silence.

A man, more a shadow, stepped out from behind the swaying curtain and moved toward the man in the bed. There was just enough light in the room for the man holding the phone in his hand to see that the man in black was holding a large raw potato, with a double-edged razor blade protruding from its end. He was wearing gloves, and at the end of the gloves, at the wrists, just slightly outstanding, the man in the bed could see the slippery shine of thin plastic food-server gloves. The man in black came to the bed, stood over the half-risen sleeper, and reached for the phone. Keeping the slicing-edge of the razor blade well close to the neck, he took the receiver in his free hand.

From across the line: "Just say yes or no."

"Yes, okay."

"Is he sitting up?"

"Yes."

"Can he see you . . . and whatever you have at his throat?"

"Yeah."

"Give him back the phone. Do nothing till I tell you otherwise."

"Okay." He handed the receiver back to the man quivering beneath the razor blade. The eyes of the man were wide and wet.

Across the line: "Do you believe he's serious?"

"Huh?

"All I want from you is *yes* or *no*."

"Who're . . ."

"Give him the phone." Pause. Again: "*Give* him the phone!"

The frightened man handed back the instrument.

"I've told him to say yes or no. If he says anything else, any filler, any kind of uh-huh-wha . . . can you cut him?"

"Yes."

"Not seriously, the first time. Let him see his own blood. Make it where he can suck it and taste it." The man in black said nothing, but handed the receiver back, laying it tight to the other man's ear. "Now," came the motionless voice out of nowhere, "are you convinced he's serious and can do you harm? Yes or no?"

"Listen, whoever the hell you are . . ."

The potato swept down across the back of the man's hand, from little finger to thumb. Blood began to ooze in a neat, slim line, but long, almost five inches. He dropped the phone on the bed; blood made an outline on the top sheet. He whined. It may have been the sound of a stray dog sideswiped by a taxi in the street far below, faint but plangent. The man with the razor-in-a-potato reached toward the pale white throbbing throat and nodded at the dropped phone. All else was silence.

Sucking on his knuckles, he lifted the instrument with a trembling, slightly-bleeding hand; and he listened. Intently.

"Now. Listen carefully. If you say anything but yes or no, if you alibi or try to drift in anything but a direct, straight answer, I have told him to get a thick towel and jam it into your mouth so no one will hear you scream as he slices you up slowly. And your brother Billy. And your mother. Do you understand?"

He began to say, ". . . uh . . ." The potato moved slightly. "Yes," he said quickly, in a husky voice, "yes. Yes, I understand."

The level, determined voice off in the distance said, "Very nice. Now we can get down to it."

The man in the bed, with morning light now glinting through the curtains and shining off the razor blade poised quivering near his throat said, "Yes."

"You hold a painting by a nearly-forgotten pulp magazine artist named Robert Gibson Jones . . ." The voice paused, but the man beneath the razor blade knew it was merely a lub-dub, a caesura, a space in which, if he said the *no* or *I don't know what you're talking about* or *it's at my cousin's house in Queens* or *I sold it years ago* or *I don't know who bought it* or any other lie, his body would be opened like a lobster and he would lie in his own entrails, holding his still-beating heart in his fingertipless hands. Throat cut ear to ear. Immediately.

He said nothing, and in a moment the voice at the other end continued, "You have been offered three purchase prices by four bidders. Each of them is eminently fair. You will take the middle bid, take the painting in perfect condition, and sell it this morning, Is that clear?"

The man holding the phone, whose blood was now pulsing onto the bedspread, said nothing. The voice from Out There commanded, "Give the phone to . . ." He held the instrument out to the dark figure poised above him. The potato-blade man took the phone and listened for a few seconds. Then he leaned close enough to the other so the man snugged in his pillow could see only the slightly less-black line where the knit watch-cap covering the potato-man's head gave evidence he had eyes. No color discernible. "Is that clear?" Then he said into the phone, "Says he understands," and he listened for a few more moments. There was moisture at the temples of one of the men in the bedroom. The connection was severed; the razor blade sliced through the cord of the telephone receiver: the man in the bed was swiping at the back of his left hand, sucking up the slim tracery of blood. The figure all in black said, "Now close your eyes and don't open them till I tell you to."

When the bleeding man finally opened his eyes, a minute or two after total silence, even though he thought he'd heard a bump of the apartment door to the hall closing . . . he was alone.

An *haute couture* newsletter editor on *le Rue Montaigne dans le huite arrondissement*, greatly hacked-off at her Third Editorial Secretary, demanded an appearance, *en masse*, of all her "verticals," the 21st Century Big Business electronic word for "serfs," "minions," "toadies," "gofers," "vassals," "water-carriers," "servants." Slanguage today. She fired five of them. The wind blew insanely near the northern summit of Mt. Erebus in Antarctica.

Within the hour, one of two thin-leather driving gloves, black in color, had been weighted with stones from the East River and sealed with a piece of stray wire from a gutter, and had been tossed far out into the Hudson. Another glove, same color, filled with marbles from a gimcrack store on Madison Avenue, sealed with duct tape, went into the Gowanus Canal in Brooklyn. Items were dropped in dumpsters in New Jersey; a pair of common, everyday, available-everywhere disposable gloves used by food-handlers were shredded, along with five heads of cabbage, in an In-Sink-Erator in a private home in Rehoboth, Massachusetts. One of a pair of undistinguished off-brand sneakers was thrown from a car on the New Jersey Turnpike into the mucky deep sedge forty feet from the roadway. The other piece of footwear was buried two feet under a garbage dump in Saranac Lake. A day and a half later. But quickly.

But only three hours and twenty-one minutes after the closing of a door in mid-Manhattan, a man in an 8th floor apartment called a woman in McLean, Virginia, who said, "It's a little early to be calling so unexpectedly after what you said last time we talked, don't you think?" The conversation went on for almost forty minutes, with many question marks hindering its progress to an inevitable conclusion. Finally, the woman said, "It's a deal. But you know you can *never* hang it or display it, is that okay with you?" The man said he understood, and they agreed at what time to meet on the third stairwell of the Flatiron Building to exchange butcher-paper-wrapped parcels.

In a second-floor flat in London, a man removed one of three hard-backed books from a stylish slipcase. He took the book to a large Morris chair and sat down beneath the gooseneck reading lamp. He glanced to the wall where the overflow of light illuminated a large and detailed painting of a long-extinct prehistoric *Lepidopteran*. He smiled, addressed his attention back to the book, turned a few pages, and began reading. In a shipping office in Kowloon, a young woman, badly trained for her simple tasks, placed a sheet of paper from a contract in the wrong manila folder, and for days, across three continents, "verticals" raged at one another.

Sixty-five minutes after the exchange of parcels at the Flatiron Building in New York, a 70 lb. triangular concrete cornice block from a construction pile did not somehow unpredictably come loose while being hoisted on pulleys above Wabash Avenue in Chicago, but a white man whose collar fit too snugly did not, also, go to his office at the international corporate office where he was a highly-paid Assessment Officer: instead, he made a dental appointment, and later in the day he removed his daughter from the private pre-school she had been attending. Nothing whatever happened in the Gibson Desert in west central Australia; nothing out of the ordinary.

In London, a man sat reading under a painting of a butterfly. For every action . . .

However inconsequential it may seem . . .

There is an equal and opposite reaction in the River of Time that flows endlessly through the universe. However unseen and utterly disconnected it may seem.

Every day, in Rio de Janeiro, late in the afternoon, there occurs a torrential downpour. It only lasts a few minutes, but the wet, like bullets, spangs off the tin roofs of the *favellas* beneath the statue of Christ the Redeemer. On *this* day, at the moment nothing was happening in the Gibson Desert, the rain did *not* fall; the Avenida Atlantica was dry and reflective. Pernambuco had hail.

Later that day, a trumpet player in a fusion-rock band in Cleveland, Ohio heard from a distant cousin in Oberlin, who had borrowed fifty dollars for a down payment on a Honda Civic ten years earlier and had never bothered to repay him. She said she was sending a check immediately. He was pleased and told the story to his friend, the lead guitarist in the group. Four hours later, during a break in that night's gig, sitting in just a club, y'know, a woman unknown to either of them drifted up between them, smiled and inquired, "How are ya?" And in the course of a few minutes' conversation both the guitarist and the trumpet player recounted the unexpected windfall of the stale fifty dollar repayment. They never saw her again. Never.

Even later that day, a hanging ornament from a 4th Century BCE Dagoba stupa originally from Sri Lanka, missing from a museum in Amsterdam since 1964, was mailed to a general post office box in Geneva, Switzerland stamped STOLEN PROPERTY ADVISE INTERPOL. Stamped in red. Hand-stamped. At the Elephant Bar of the Bangkok Marriott, a Thai businessman was approached by the bartender, extending a red telephone. "Are you Mr. Mandapa?" The gentleman looked up from his gin sling, nodded, and took the receiver. "Hello yes; this is Michael Mandapa . . ." and he listened for a few seconds, smiling at first. "I don't think that's possible," he said, softly, no longer smiling. Listened, then: "Not so soon. I'll need at least a week, ten days, I have to . . ." He went silent, listened, his face drew taut, he ran the back of his free hand across his lips, then said, "If it's raining there, and it's monsoon, you will do what you have to do. I'll try my best."

He listened, sighed deeply, then put the phone back in its cradle on the bartop. The bartender noticed, came, and picked up the red telephone. "Everything o-kay?" he said, reading the strictures of Mr. Mandapa's face. "Fine, yes, fine," Mr. Mandapa replied, and left the Elephant Bar without tipping the man who had unknowingly saved his life.

Somewhere, much earlier, a man stepped on, and crushed beneath his boot, a dragonfly, a Meganeura.

The next morning, at eight a.m., four cars pulled up in front of a badly-tended old house in Fremont, Nebraska. Weeds and sawgrass were prevalent. The day was heavily overcast, even for a month that usually shone brightly. From the first car, a Fremont police cruiser, stepped a man wearing a Borsalino, and from beside and behind him, three uniformed officers of the local police force. The second car bore two Nebraska State Troopers; and in the third car were a man and a woman in dark black suits, each carrying an attaché case. The fourth car's doors opened quickly, wings spread, and four large men of several colors emerged, went around and opened the trunk, and took out large spades and shovels. The group advanced on the house, the Sheriff of Fremont, Nebraska leading the phalanx.

He knocked on the sagging screen door three times.

No one came to the closed inner door. He knocked again, three times. An elderly white woman, stooped and halting and gray, dusted with the weariness of difficult years, opened the inner door a crack and peered at the assemblage beyond the screen door. Her tone was midway between startled and concerned: "Yes?"

"Miz Brahm?"

"Uh, yeah . . ."

"We're here with a search warrant and some legal folks, that lady and gentleman there." He nodded over his shoulder at the pair of black suits. "They've been okay'd by the Court to go through your propitty, lookin' for some books your son took to sell on eBay or whatever, for a lady back East in New York. Is Billy here?"

"Billy don't live here no more." She started to close the door. The Sheriff pushed his palm against the screen door, making an oval depression. "I asked you if Billy was here, Ma'am."

"Nuh-uh."

"May we come in, please?"

"You g'wan, get offa my property!"

At the same moment Miz Brahm was ordering the Sheriff of Fremont, Nebraska off her porch, in Mbuji-Mayi, near the Southern border between the Democratic Republic of the Congo and Zambia, a representative of Doctors Without Borders found his way to a small vegetable garden outside three hut-residences beyond a wan potato field. He carried two linen-wrapped packages, and when a nut-brown old man appeared at the entrance to the largest hut, he extended the small parcels, made the usual obeisance, and backed away quietly. Miz Brahm was still arguing with the Nebraska State Troopers and the men with shovels, and the duo in black suits, but mostly with the Sheriff of Fremont, Nebraska, nowhere near Zambia. There was, however, thunder in the near-distance and darkening clouds. The air whipped frenziedly. A drop of rain spattered on a windshield.

The argument would not end. Inevitably, the officers of the law grew impatient with diversionary answers, and yanked the screen door away from its rusted latch. It fell on the porch, Miz Brahm tried to push the front door closed on the men, but they staved her back, and rushed in. Shouts, screaming ensued.

A hairy, unshaven man with three pot-bellies charged out of a back hall, a tire iron doubled-fisted behind his head; he was yowling. One of the state troopers clotheslined him, sending him sprawling onto his back in the passageway. Miz Brahm kept up a strident shrieking in the background; one of the attorneys–when attention was elsewhere–chopped her across the throat, and she settled lumpily against a baseboard.

"That ain't Billy," Miz Brahm managed to gargle, phlegm and spittle serving as consonants. "Thas his *broth*-er!"

One of the troopers yelled, "Let's get 'em *both*!" He pulled his sidearm and snarled at the downed tri-belly, "Where's yer brother?"

"You ain't gonna take *neither* of 'em!" screamed the old lady: a foundry noon-whistle shriek; she was pulling a rusty hatchet out from behind a chifferobe. The trooper kneecapped her. The hatchet hit the linoleum.

Four hours later two of the men with shovels, who had been stacking and restacking magazines, digging out rat nests and spading up rotted floorboards, found Billy hiding in the back corner of the last storage quonset behind the property. He tried to break through the wall, and one of the laborers slammed the spade across the back of his head. The search went on for the rest of that day, into the next, before the attorneys were satisfied. The weed-overgrown property was a labyrinth filled with tumbling-down shelves and closets, bookcases, cardboard boxes piled so high that the ones on the bottom had been crushed in: vintage pulp fiction magazines, comic books in Mylar sleeves, corded sheaves of newspapers, and the forty-seven pieces Billy had cozened out of the old woman Back East.

The next day, the entire family was in custody. At the same time, but eight hours later by the clock, Greenwich Mean Time, the man in London who had been reading "The Red-Headed League" closed the book, looked long at the wonderful painting of an ancient butterfly above the mantel, smiled and said, "Ah, so *that's* how it all comes together. '*Omne ignotum pro magnifico.*' Clever."

This story is dedicated to the memory of my friend, Ray Bradbury.

THE ADVENTURE OF MY IGNOBLE ANCESTRESS

by Nancy Holder

It is a truth universally acknowledged . . .

. . . that sometimes mysteries can't be solved.

My parents were killed on a vacation to Rome to celebrate their fortieth wedding anniversary. They'd been so excited. "Still in love," my mother told me on the phone. "I wish that you . . ."

And then she'd trailed off, because I'd already told her that somehow the love gene had skipped a generation. I had my work. I was a *New York Times* bestselling author, and that was enough.

They were shot in an alley on the way back from a nice meal. Robbed. They had invited me along to Rome (I am—I was—their only child, and we were close) but I didn't go because I had a book deadline, and I had waited too long to get started. Procrastination probably saved my life.

After my parents were murdered, I dropped everything and devoted myself to their case. I spent an incredible amount of money on private detectives and false leads. I got scammed a dozen times. A year passed, two, three. I never finished that book. My editor stopped asking about my progress. My literary agent suggested that a break would be good for both of us. I still had some cash left at that point, and I decided to make it last until I woke from this terrible nightmare. Money from royalties would come in the way it always had.

While that was true up to a point, the amount I received decreased every year as readers moved on. But I could not move on. Nothing I did made a difference. No one came forward with a name or a reason. No case-breaking clues were found. Still, I didn't give up. I badgered the Roman police, I exploited all forms of social media, and I kept up the heat.

That was how Blackfield Carpenter, an English law firm, linked me, Nancy Holder the horror writer, to a Victorian-era banker named Alexander Holder. It turns out that I'm a descendant of this man, the closest one, in fact.

And Alexander Holder was a client of Sherlock Holmes.

Dr. Watson described Alexander's case in "The Adventure of the Beryl Coronet." I had never heard of it, but as soon as I was contacted, I read it right away. It was riveting stuff, and I wished there were a Sherlock Holmes in my time. Surely he would have solved my parents' murders by then.

Blackfield Carpenter explained that, while there was little cash included in the inheritance, I was now the owner of "Fairbank," Alexander's large Victorian house. Unfortunately (from their point of view), it was the subject of a court case. Five years previous, Fair Estates, a housing development company, had bought up a vast tract of land in southern London. Fairbank sat inside the perimeter, and the developer argued that they owned the house as well and had every right to demolish it, which they planned to do.

A group called the Holmes Trust, dedicated to preserving buildings and memorabilia connected to the Great Detective, had filed a lawsuit to stop them. During the bitter legal battle, Fairbank had been set on fire—arson was proven—and although the stone house had been saved from complete destruction, it was in bad shape. Ironically, around then the British economy had tanked and the developer walked away from the project altogether.

Now the Trust wanted to meet with me to discuss various "schemes" to restore the house. I figured they didn't realize I was nearly broke, and I didn't tell them otherwise. I didn't exactly want the world to know that the happy-looking woman in the photograph on the dust jackets of my (aging) novels was no longer the "wildly successfully bestselling author" she had once had been. So I responded vaguely and diffidently, but they were happy that I had responded at all. As far as they were concerned, the game was afoot.

My British lawyers wanted me to come to England to take possession of the house. The Holmes Trust was even more eager to meet me in person. Nothing was happening in Rome–nothing had happened, ever–but it was still very hard for me to leave. I had a panic attack just thinking about it. I knew I wasn't being rational. I knew I had put everything on hold, allowed this single event to take over my entire life. I had lost friends, my career. I just couldn't seem to move on because of my obsession—the awful feeling that if I didn't remain vigilant, justice would never be served. I wrote horror; I wrote about terrible things—or I had—and I knew that sometimes, the monster wins.

Then it dawned on me that the Holmes Trust might be interested in purchasing Fairbank from me. That would mean more money for the battle. I flew to London and rented a car, and from there drove through bucketing rain to Streatham, in South London, and found myself in a wasteland of moved earth and concrete foundations, all that was left of Fair Estates. And there stood Fairbank itself, a blackened heap surrounded by a chain link fence and forbidding KEEP OUT signs.

Sections of the two-story structure stood intact, and as I waited for the security guard to answer my text and let me in, my imagination wandered through the rooms, replaying the crime that had taken place inside those very walls.

I'd already signed a million forms and taken legal possession of the property, and the representative from Blackfield Carpenter and a security guard were happy to see me as they drove up and found me waiting for them in my car. The rain was pouring so hard I could barely make out their faces.

The cold was bone-chilling. I began to rethink my romantic idea of spending the night in the house as I gathered up my sleeping bag and suitcase. My black umbrella collided with that of the lawyer from Blackfield Carpenter as he took my suitcase. I could see my breath.

"It's haunted, y'know." The guard grinned as he unlocked the padlock on the front door. "You can hear footsteps. Crying sometimes."

"I see," I said, and despite Rome, I actually managed a faint smile. It would be nice to be haunted by something else.

"Some say it's Alexander Holder, grieving for his lost niece, Mary," he continued. He looked at me expectantly.

"I know the story," I replied. "Mary conspired with her lover to steal the Beryl Coronet from Alexander. It was being held as collateral for a loan."

"Yes. Sir George Burnwell was the paramour. Sherlock Holmes set everything to rights," said the young solicitor from Blackfield Carpenter. "The coronet was returned to the 'highest in the land', assumed to be the Prince of Wales. The bank received the prince's loan payment of fifty thousand pounds plus interest, and Holder's honor remained intact."

I said, "And Alexander reconciled with Arthur, his son, whom he had falsely accused of the theft."

"And Mary and Burnwell were never seen nor heard from again," the solicitor added.

"Hence the ghostly grieving," I said.

"Hence," he replied, and the door creaked open.

We three entered Fairbank. The Holmes Trust had gone to some effort to make the place habitable—mostly cleaning—and they had purchased some flashlights, a battery-powered lantern, and a heater for me. On a hexagonal inlaid table, they had placed a crystal vase filled with red roses and beside it, a fruit basket. I offered an apple to the lawyer and the guard but both turned me down. There was no other furniture; the Trust had lent me the table. What had been retrievable had been taken to the Sherlock Holmes wing of the British Museum, although I could request the return of any items I wanted.

I literally walked through Dr. Watson's narration of the crime as we explored the dank old house. There was the window where naive Mary Holder had passed the beautiful coronet to the evil and dashing Sir George Burnwell. There, the kitchen door where Lucy Parr, the maid whom Mary had half-heartedly tried to pin the crime on, had snuck out to see her sweetheart, Francis Prosper, the one-legged greengrocer. Upstairs, I inspected the ruins of Mary's room, which she had fled as soon as she realized that Sherlock Holmes would find her out. Next, the equally decrepit room of Arthur, son of the house, falsely accused of the crime. Because he was deeply in love with the real thief, his cousin Mary, he had refused to defend himself. Chivalry had landed him—temporarily—in irons.

And then there was the blackened, smoky chamber of the mercurial Alexander Holder himself, who had nearly given himself a stroke during the affair.

Sections of the ceiling were draped with plastic sheeting, not too effective against the downpour. The house was charred, damp, and moldy; I wondered how on earth Fairbank could ever be restored to its former glory.

We discovered that below-stairs had the driest rooms, although plenty of walls were wet and mildewed. During Mary Holder's time, the house had a typically large staff: four maids had slept in the house; the two male servants, groom and page, had lived elsewhere. With the help of "my" two men, I arranged my heater and lights and unrolled my sleeping bag. After I assured them I'd be fine, and promised to call if I needed anything, they left.

Rome to London is a short flight, but emotionally, I had traveled leagues. I kept panicking. I just knew that because of my absence, a clue would be overlooked, a confession, ignored. I was aware that I had post-traumatic stress disorder, and I was obsessive. I had strong sleeping pills that I hardly ever took because I was afraid I would miss a call. It was the middle of the night in all of Europe, so I dry-swallowed a pill and crossed my fingers. Sometimes they worked, and sometimes they didn't. As I drifted off, I told my parents good night. I always did. And then I cried.

I always did that, too.

So when I woke up to the sound of sobbing, I wasn't surprised. But after a few seconds of coming out of my medicated hangover, I realized that this crying wasn't coming from me.

Thunder and lighting crashed over an echoic, low moaning. The sound was grief-stricken, a keening; then across the room, by the glowing orange light of my ceramic heater, I saw the profile of a woman cut out against the wall. It wasn't my shadow. I caught my breath and lifted my flashlight into the dark corners. There was no one else in the room to cast the silhouette.

The crying grew louder.

My heart pumped. My hand shook. I blinked and my lips formed the same soundless words when I first heard that my parents had been murdered: This isn't really happening.

Then the shadow vanished, and in its place, the outline of a small hand with thin, tapered fingers appeared on the wall.

I let out an icy breath. I was crackling with fear.

After my parents died, I had waited, hoped for something like this to happen. Something supernatural. Something like what I wrote about in my books: *Possessions; Witch; Damned.* Messages from beyond the grave. The name of their killer, whispered in my ear. Assurance that they were in a better place. I had visited mediums and gone to séances. But I'd done too much research into the "business," and I saw all the tricks. A couple of times I let myself be scammed just in case there was a grain of truth mixed in with all the BS, but eventually I gave up the hunt and concentrated on Italian police procedure, Roman forensics. Science. But this was not science. This was the provenance of my obsession. So I told myself that I was imagining it. That I was still asleep.

The hand remained on the wall, not so much a shadow as an imprint, very dark and clear. Very real.

It had to be a prank set up by my law firm or the Holmes people. "Hello?" I said loudly. "Nicely done." No response. So I unzipped my sleeping bag and went hunting for a projector, or a scrim instead of a plaster wall. I found none.

Then I tripped on an apple that had not been on the floor when I had gone to bed, and fell forward. I put out my hand to catch myself, right against the hand on the wall, and with a scream I fell through sodden, pliant plaster. There was a space behind it; I jerked my hand away and looked up at the watermark on the ceiling. The rain was coming in through the wall.

But the rain had not left an apple on the floor.

My hair stood on end. I grabbed my phone to call the police but I wasn't actually sure how to. Somehow I remembered that the UK number was different from Italy's, but the only thing that came to mind was "666." I told myself that the apple had been accidentally gathered up in my things as we moved me downstairs. That the crying and the images had been part of a dream.

But I was shaking as I did a cursory search of the house. The windows and doors were boarded up, and there was no sign that anyone else was inside. I went back downstairs and looked inside the hole my hand had punched. There were so many cobwebs behind the plaster wall that at first I thought they were fiberglass. I spotted something at the bottom, and it was a simple matter to push my way through the mushy wall down to the baseboard.

It was a small, rotted wooden box.

"Okay, then, the game's afoot," I murmured, shivering with fear and maybe a dollop of excitement.

I opened it.

3 April, 1890

My dear Lucy,

Your letter of 6 February arrived, and I thanked heaven on my knees for the mercy it contained. How kind you are to forgive me and to help me after I attempted to cast you into a criminal light, the better to hide in the shadows of my own guilt when I took the coronet! I was wild with fear when my uncle engaged the services of Mr. Sherlock Holmes, he of the sharp and spiderlike countenance, for I perceived that his brilliant mind should unravel the tangled web that I had woven. It was with the terror of one drowning that I suggested you and the greengrocer, Mr. Prosper, (newly your husband, you tell me! I wish you joy!)

as potential partners in crime. I am wholly undeserving of your charity.

For myself, I doubt I shall ever feel joy again. You know what my uncle is, but as temperamental as he can be, I see only now how he strives to act gently toward his own. After my father died of his lingering illness and Uncle Alexander took me in, I thought I should live the life I had only dreamed of. Balls, concerts, plays, frivolities! My youth had been spent in the sickroom, but I thrilled that I should pass young womanhood in gay company, enjoying the delights of society! But all too soon I saw that my uncle wished me to stand in as the lady of the house, and not as its indulged young daughter. Imagine my dismay!

I thought to turn to his son, my cousin Arthur, to serve as my guide into society, but as he loved me, it was impossible to separate his feelings from my purpose. To allow him to be my escort would be to accede to his request for my hand. Additionally, I detected in my dear cousin a nervous tendency to please those he believed to be his betters—the wealthy dandies of his club—and I sensed that I would be trading one prison for another: married life beside a young, agitated man who would eventually judge me lacking, as he judged himself, because I was with him.

It was so bitter to watch the last roses fading in my cheeks as I made my rounds throughout our house— ordering our provisions, supervising our staff, always an organizer and observer of life. Then into that life Sir George Burnwell rode like a knight upon a charger. He was urbane, sophisticated, worldly, and so brilliant! He had been everywhere, done everything. Knew everyone. He promised to share such a life with me. I was utterly mad with happiness!

Once I was completely besotted, Sir George told me a complicated tale of heaps of debts he had paid on my cousin Arthur's behalf—which, he said, Arthur had concealed from his father. I quite believed him, as Arthur was always asking Uncle Alexander for advances on his allowance. Sir George allowed that because of his protection of my cousin's good name at the club, he had fallen into distress himself. I, in my intemperate and sheltered way, thought to even that score by giving him the coronet. As I write these lines, it is all so ridiculous, but I was caught up in the drama and excitement. It happened so fast—the arrival of the coronet, the plan to sell it to make good on all those crushing debts—that at the time it did not seem like madness. As you are well aware, I left my uncle's home in the dead of night like the thief I was, and presented myself to Sir George.

But he informed me that he had changed his mind and had already returned the coronet to my uncle. Yet my fate was cast! I could not go back to Fairbank. I had already admitted my guilt. And that is when Sir George married me—rue the day!

I know that your lot is not easy, Lucy, even though you now retain the happy title of wife, and I am sure you are shaking your head in disbelief as you read these lines. Yet this very moment, had I the power to change my station, I would beg for employment as a scullery maid at Fairbank!

I must be as frank as I must be brief. Fear of discovery informs every word I write to you. We live on a small island, cut off from all society, though we are not so distant from London as one might think. Still we are a world away. Sir George is . . . unkind, and as short of money as he professed to be. Yet he spends what little we have on drink. Also, I fear, worse things. I am uncertain of all his weaknesses, as he banished me when I was with child to a separate wing of the house. Such as the house is: a mansion crumbling and falling into the waters that isolate us from the mainland. I must depend on a small ferry, oared by a good man whose occupation it is to move islanders to town and vice versa. We have become friends . . . but friends only, I assure you.

The only reason Sir George has not gambled away our island home is that he can't; it's entailed. It must be passed down to his eldest son. But we cannot leave because we have nowhere else to go. His fair-weather friends have deserted him, or perhaps word has gotten 'round what a bounder he truly is. Not one word of congratulation reached his ears upon the birth of his child, our son, dear Charles George Alexander.

Little Charles is a beautiful, sunny child, and I do not deserve him. He is my sole reason for continuing. Without him I fear I would plunge myself into the waters off our island, no matter the consequences to my soul. Lucy, I fear for my baby's well-being. Despite our continued habitation in the most distant wing of the house, Sir George says that Charles's incessant crying is driving him mad. He is only bitter and cruel in regards to his heir. I think that he would abandon us here, if only he dared. I am legally bound to him body and soul, as is our child, but I cannot subject Charles to Sir George's frightful temper. George has twenty times the ferocity of my uncle at his wildest moments. And so . . . I plan. I wonder if I may depend upon your aid?

With thanks for your Christian charity, I am,
Mary Burnwell, née Holder

I was stunned. The Trust would go wild when they read the letter. No one had ever known what had happened to Mary Holder, and it appeared as though we were all about to find out.

There was another letter:

5 May
Dear Lucy,
I have found increasing sympathy and kindness in the form of the boatman who sends our letters back and forth. (Although I hasten to assure you that nothing untoward has

transpired between us—he is married, as am I). He and his dear wife have waited nigh these six years for a child of their own, and so he reminds me that while there is much about my situation that does not engender envy, in this one area he counts me most fortunate. He himself has given me the courage to attempt my escape, and for this I am sincerely grateful.

I am ever so grateful, and at your service always,

Mary Burnwell, née Holder

❖

And then another:

19 May

Dear Lucy,

I have had an interview with someone whom I previously thought my enemy. Our talk has come to a sad conclusion and therefore, I must change my hopes. I had thought simply to leave on a steamer, arrive in London, and make my way to my uncle with my babe in my arms. There I would plead for sanctuary. But it has been explained to me that the law is quite on my husband's side. He can take my baby from me, and I am sure that he would.

With this great person as my ally, I have arranged with my friend the boatman to fake my death, and that of my tiny boy. Once hope has fled, I will board the Hampstead *under the name of Mrs. Able Brown, and reunite with you at the London Docks. My ally has arranged for my trunk to be sent on to you, aboard the* Hampstead *on its usual route Tuesday next.*

Of my child . . . for the time, he will be with two who love him dearly; and if the situation looks to be against me, they shall raise and love little Charles as their own. With assistance from my previous supposed foe, I have made arrangements that they shall not suffer for their kindness. I dare not print their names even here, but will tell all when the time is right.

Therefore, look for me, on 10 June, at the docks. Not one word,
I beg you, not one, to either my uncle or to Arthur, my cousin. I
must see how I fare before I take them on. And then, God willing,
we shall find a way to reunite my son with his true family.
On your discretion hangs my happiness.
M.

❖

The next item was a newspaper article dated 10 June, 1890:

THE *HAMPSTEAD* SINKS
All lives lost!

I read the article with a cold, heavy heart: steaming down the Thames Estuary from Kent, the *Hampstead* foundered, then quickly took on water. She listed to starboard, and sank. It happened in mere minutes, and all crew and passengers were lost. Holding my breath, my eyes ran down the passenger manifest.

Mrs. Able Brown.

I took a moment to feel the death. Grief was so familiar to me; it was a comfortable, known feeling. An old companion, if not a friend.

Mary Holder hadn't made it. After everything she'd gone through, she'd died a tragic, random death.

There was writing in the margin of the article: *We decided not to tell Mr. Holder any of it, nor to give him the trunk. It would only break his heart. Lucy Parr Prosper.*

❖

There was nothing else in the box.

I became aware that the crying had stopped, and my own cheeks were wet with tears.

And that someone was knocking hard on the front door and calling out, "Ms. Holder? Ms. Nancy Holder?"

It was ten in the morning. I had no memory of sitting there all night long, but I had to compose myself before I could go upstairs and answer the door. I wiped my face and blew my nose. Apparently I had had a very long cry.

My visitor was Kim Jones, from the Trust. He was a nice-looking guy around my age, and he was very apologetic about coming by without receiving a callback confirming that it was convenient. He'd been afraid that I'd had no cell reception and so had been unable to reply. I checked my phone. He'd called an hour before.

I was alarmed. Since the night of the murders, I had never missed a single phone call. I took them all, even the come-ons and the scams, in case it was the one that somehow, through whatever convoluted means, broke my parents' case. I woke up even if I had taken something to help me sleep. But I hadn't heard his call.

It frightened me. It made me want to fly back to Rome immediately.

I didn't tell him about the box, not then, although I put it in my over-sized purse. I wanted to think the story through. I hadn't had any coffee, or a shower, or even brushed my teeth. It was frigid in the house and I didn't have any running water. I knew Brits were generally polite and oblique, but I asked him straight out, American style, if he could help me. He took me to the Holmes Trust office, which wasn't far from the British Museum. The place was furnished with Holmes's own furniture, a Victorian settee and overstuffed chairs, and he told me that if I wished, they could make a room up for me to stay in furnished with Holmes's own bed. Everyone there made much of me. No one there mentioned my parents, and I wondered if they knew.

After a croissant and some coffee, I finally showed them the box. They were jubilant.

"We have to let Shipley have a look," they kept saying over and over. Finally Kim explained to me that Will Shipley was one of the curators at the Holmes wing of the museum, and he had made it something of a hobby to investigate what had happened to Mary Holder. He was already on the list of people they wanted me to meet.

A coterie of Trust employees joined Kim and me for the walk to the museum. It was much more modern than I had expected. The Holmes

Wing was enormous, containing carriages, interiors of rooms, opera capes and top hats, deerstalker caps, pistols, a walking stick concealing a wicked blade, a Stradivarius violin, a myriad of magnifying lenses, tiny glass vials and bottles, a doctor's bag with the initials JHW, a tin box, pipes, syringes, and the Persian slipper where Holmes kept his tobacco.

Kim knocked on a door marked WILL SHIPLEY ASS'T CURATOR, and soon I was showing the box and its contents to an older but still handsome man in a nubby gray sweater and black wool trousers. His blue eyes gleamed as he examined what I had brought. I didn't tell him about the weeping or the apparitions. I still didn't know if they had really happened. I kept telling myself that they had to have been real, because we had the box, but why this? Why now? Why not all the thousands of times I had begged the universe to tell me what had happened to my parents?

I put my trembling hands in my pockets and said yes, I was cold, and Kim assured me there would be tea.

Will Shipley put on white cloth gloves and picked up each letter and the newspaper article with both hands, as if they were fragile pieces of glass. I imagined the Roman police sifting through the debris they had collected from the alley where my parents were murdered with as much reverence. I had gone down to their labs. I had looked at their photographs. I called them constantly. They were never offended. They looked at me with their soulful Italian eyes, like Caravaggio paintings, and told me how sorry they were that they had nothing new to tell me.

"A trunk," Shipley marveled. "Lucy Parr Prosper collected Mary Holder's trunk."

When my parents had been murdered, I'd had to go public with my pleas for information, for clues: there had been none. But the Trust had prodigious databases and worldwide connections. Sherlock Holmes was much beloved.

A week passed, with no more weeping, or shadows, but still I stayed at Fairbank every night. . Waiting, hoping, in the same stasis in which I had spent years of my life. Kim, Will, and their colleagues were galvanized, as merry as Holmes ever was on their treasure hunt. I also sensed deep hope on their part; they were waiting for me to make some kind of announcement regarding my plans for the house. They still didn't know that I was living off pennies.

There were no developments in Rome. One of my favorite police detectives left the force to open a clothing store in Milan.

❖

On my ninth day in England, a lead seemed to come in. There was a trunk in a farmhouse, but it turned out to be from the 1940's. Will and Kim were disappointed, but scrupulously polite.

"I'm still convinced that the 'ally' was Holmes himself," Will said one night. "You know, when Dr. Watson wrote about your family's case, he made mention that Sherlock Holmes pocketed a one-thousand-pound reward. I like to think he gave the thousand pounds to Mary Holder." He smiled at me. "To fund the shipping of the trunk, and pay for the passage on the *Hampstead*. And to compensate 'the two' for her son's care."

"She didn't say anything about that in her letters," I pointed out.

"No, but it may have been discussed in a previous letter. Or perhaps she wanted to be discreet on the subject. Victorians were weird about money."

Unlike us, I thought. I was pretty sure he knew by then that I had no money; more often than not, he offered to pay for dinner. And though I didn't want to let him, I did. I had begun to ponder the notion of subletting my apartment in Rome. But then the old panic set in: I had to be there to watch over my parents' case.

"She had to have money to set her plan in motion," he said. "I doubt Sir George was giving her any. So unless she stole it out of his pockets, I would imagine she got it by other means."

I almost said then that the Trust would have to fix Fairbank by other means. But I looked into his eyes and I thought about—maybe not wedding anniversaries, but possibilities. His dreams. His hopes. The Holmes Trust. A wider world than a grubby alley.

"What do *you* think happened to the trunk?" he asked. "Do you think the Prospers gave it to Holmes? What if there was something *amazing* in it, that helped him solve some other case?"

He was so excited. I realized that I spent my nights at Fairbank listening for tears; I was focused on dashed hopes and death. He saw clues and puzzles and excitement.

There was a second lead, and a third. A possible fourth.

Three weeks after I had taken possession of Fairbank, it dawned on me that I couldn't remember the last time I had phoned the Roman police, or turned over the clues of my parents' murder in my mind. I caught myself waiting for word on the fourth lead.

"What happened to your son?" I asked the damp air of Fairbank. There could be another line of Holders. Relatives I didn't even know about.

The fourth lead was a bust. Will told me that the funds allocated for the search of the trunk were nearly gone, and there was talk of giving up. That would be a loss, such a loss, and I couldn't bear the thought. I stayed up all night walking through Fairbank, and I heard gentle crying. There were tears on my cheeks. When the sun rose, I dried them. Or maybe Mary did it for me.

Once New York was up and running, I placed a call. There were several beats of silence after my erstwhile editor picked up. I knew I had to grovel. I had to apologize. I had made her look bad at the publishing company; I was her author, and I had screwed up.

"I'm ready to get back to work," I swore. "I want to write a Sherlock Holmes homage. It's about someone I'm related to. Her uncle—*my* several-times-great-uncle—was a client of Holmes, and she turned out to be the guilty party in the case."

"Really." She sounded warmer. Intrigued. "Run it down for me."

I told her the story of Mary Holder and her trunk, leaving out the haunting. I didn't want her to think I was still crazy. I said, "But I don't know how it ends yet."

"Well, you're a horror writer. You could leave it open-ended. You could say that some mysteries aren't meant to be solved."

"Yes. Absolutely. We'll let the readers write the ending."

"Love it." She was excited. Our game was afoot.

"And we'll shoot my house for the cover," I added. "It will be beautiful by then."

It's beautiful now, I heard Mary whisper. Or maybe that was me. I didn't know, and it didn't matter, not one jot.

THE CLOSING

by Leslie S. Klinger

◅◆▻

McParland pulled into the empty parking spot in the Santa Monica strip mall, turned off the car, and got out, taking the folder of papers from the front seat. The escrow company's small office was a few doors down, but he could see through the windows that Rachel was already there, seated in an office in the corner. He opened the door and spoke to the woman at the front desk.

"James McParland, for the Arizona Avenue escrow closing. Betty is handling it."

The receptionist didn't look up from her monitor but waved in the direction of the back of the office. "She's in the conference room."

McParland circled her desk and walked to the small conference room. It was sparsely furnished, with glass walls, thin blinds that could be closed for privacy, if needed, and a cheap table and eight chairs. Rachel sat on one side, pen in hand, while another woman—evidently Betty—passed her papers to sign. They both looked up as he entered.

"Mr. McParland?" Betty said. "Mrs. Lund is almost done. I'll help you sign the papers next."

"Fine," said McParland, taking a seat opposite Rachel. He looked through the window behind her at the parking lot outside, seeing little but dazzle from the mid-afternoon sun.

Rachel finished the last few documents, put down her pen, and looked at McParland. His heart thumped, as it always did.

"How are you?" she said. "Charlotte says you've been on the road."

He shrugged. "Yeah, had to go to New York for a client. Just a few days, though. How are you?"

Rachel smiled. "Great. Great." McParland loved her smile. "How's Sherlock?"

McParland smiled back. This had been a running joke with them, ever since law school, when she'd bought him an annotated edition of Conan Doyle's stories and he'd gotten hooked. He'd been especially thrilled when he learned that his great-great-grand-uncle was the real-life model for a Pinkerton agent who appeared in one of the stories. His bizarre fascination with Holmes and his world had always amused Rachel, he thought, especially the Sherlockian "game" of pretending that Holmes and Watson weren't fictional.

He turned to Betty. "You know, could you give us a few minutes, before you go through these with me?" he said, gesturing at the pile of legal documents.

"Sure," said Betty, and stood up. "I'll be at my desk." She closed the glass door behind her.

Rachel shifted in her chair. She was wearing a track suit, McParland noticed, but as always, she made it look like *haut couture*. A small diamond pendant sparkled at her neck. She frowned slightly. "You know, I never thought you'd want to sell the building."

McParland shrugged again. "Didn't have a choice. UCLA said sell or they'd force us to sell it. We got a fair price. Remember when we bought it?"

"Thirteen years ago," said Rachel. "I remember being pretty nervous. It seemed like an awful lot of money, with a new baby to pay for. It took a lot of our cash, but you believed in it."

"I told you it would be a good thing," said McParland. "Here we are now, selling it for three times what we paid for it. And no taxes either, at least not for you." Rachel looked momentarily confused. "Bill's death, you know," McParland continued, embarrassed now. "Remember? I explained about the tax rules? Because you put it in both names?"

Rachel nodded. "Oh, yes. That was good advice you gave us. When Bill got sick. Thank you." She gave him a small smile.

McParland felt his face get hot. Was he actually blushing? "The benefit of having an ex-husband who's a tax lawyer. The only benefit, I guess." Time to change the topic. "How's Charlotte?"

Rachel frowned. "She's fourteen, what do you expect? She's deep into her 'please-God-don't-let-me-turn-out-like-my-mother' stage. It'll pass, I'm told, but for now, everything's a fight. Maybe you could take her somewhere for a weekend? I'd really like a break from the battle."

McParland smiled. "I'd love to. She hasn't figured out yet that I'm uncool, so we might have a good time. Maybe I'll take her up to San Francisco. She hasn't been there since she was little. I could show her the Sherlock Holmes sitting room model they have there."

"Bill and I took her to the Bay Area for her twelfth birthday," said Rachel. She added quickly, "But it's still a good idea. Take her shopping—she wasn't much interested at twelve. And maybe the art galleries. She seems to be enjoying her art history class at school. And sure, show her your friend Sherlock's room ."

McParland nodded. "Sounds good. I forgot you and Bill took her. Charlotte looks great. More like you every day. When she's eighteen, she'll be your twin."

"In my dreams of eighteen, maybe."

"No, really." McParland frowned.

Rachel looked at him closely. "Are you OK?"

McParland took a deep breath. "I was excited to do this," he admitted. "Spend a few minutes with you. Actually see you, not just talk on the phone. Sorry."

Rachel reached across the table and put her hand on his.

"How did we get here?" McParland said. "Meeting at an *escrow company*?"

"You know," she said.

"Last week was our 16th anniversary. But I'm sure you know that."

Rachel pulled her hand back. "Jimmy . . ."

"Sixteen years ago, we went out for pizza. A year later, and you were pregnant. Two months after that, we were married. And then we lived happily ever after," he said bitterly.

"I tried," said Rachel, her voice thick with emotion. "I really did."

McParland was quiet. "I know," he finally said. "But I just wasn't the one."

"No," Rachel said quietly. "I couldn't love you the way you loved me. It was my fault."

"It was no one's fault," said McParland. "I know we don't get to choose who we love. I didn't choose you, the lightning just hit me. We were good together, though."

"You mean the sex?" Rachel asked. "It was great. And we made a beautiful girl! But I was lying to you all the time. Lying that I loved you. I thought you were great, a little weird with your invisible friends, but smart, kind, romantic, devoted—but I could tell. I could tell right away. I wanted to love you because you loved me so much. So I lied, and then I just couldn't anymore."

"I just wasn't the one."

"No."

McParland hesitated. "Can I ask you something?"

"Sure."

"Was Bill the one?"

Rachel closed her eyes and didn't speak for a minute. When she opened her eyes, they were shining. "Yes he was. When I first met him, I couldn't breathe. That happened a lot. Even with the cancer. Even that last day at the hospital." Tears welled up in her eyes. "I'm sorry."

McParland was silent. That last day . . .

Bill Lund lay shriveled on the hospital bed, his face and skin a disturbing yellow. Charlotte was in the cafeteria, Rachel off on some errand. McParland sat next to the bed, wondering awkwardly why he was here. Lund spoke in a rasping voice.

"Are they gone? Are we alone?"

McParland nodded, then said "Yes."

"I need you to do something for me. For Rachel and Charlotte. You're the only one. I'm too weak to get up now." His voice sounded like it was tearing his throat. "In the zipper pocket of my sweatpants. In the closet there." He opened his eyes, turning his head towards the closet. "There are some patches."

McParland waited.

After a moment, Lund continued. "Pain patches. A new thing to help. Supposed to use them one every six or eight hours. If I put a bunch of them on, like I kept trying to get rid of the pain and didn't know that they take a while to kick in, it would look like an accident. So there won't be a problem with the insurance." He paused. "She'll need the money."

"Bill, look, I—"

"I thought I was a tough guy. Not so tough. This—" his eyes swept the room—"is killing me." Something that probably was meant to be a chuckle passed his lips. "The doctor says another month or two, but I can't do it. Don't tell Rachel."

McParland sat very still. "Bill, it . . . it'll kill her too."

Lund closed his eyes. "You'll be here for them. I know you will." A tear ran down his temple. "Don't make me beg."

It was "The Veiled Lodger" all over again. McParland's least favorite Holmes story included a woman tempted by suicide. "Your life is not your own," Holmes admonishes her, sanctimoniously urging her to be an example of "patient suffering." He wasn't the one patiently suffering.

McParland got up and crossed to the closet, opened the door, found the sweatpants. He unzipped the pocket and found a packet of patches. Fentanyl, said the label. He brought them over to Lund and laid them on the bedside table, next to his water glass and straw.

Lund opened his eyes. "Now leave. And . . . take care of our girls."

Our girls, McParland thought. He stood and walked to the door. He turned to speak, but Lund waved a hand, dismissing him. "Go on. Go find Charlotte."

McParland left the room and walked over to the nurses' station. He waited, said a few meaningless words to one of the nurses. Then he turned and went down to the cafeteria, looking for his daughter.

That evening, Bill Lund was dead. Rachel's phone call had awakened McParland in his basket chair, where he'd fallen asleep drinking in front of his faux Sherlock Holmes mantel. Her hysteria cut through his grogginess. "He wasn't supposed to leave me—not yet!" she wailed.

After he'd calmed her down, he drove back to the hospital and met her in the visitors' lounge. There, he sat with her, holding her hand, while the doctor repeated over and over, "Respiratory failure from accidental overdose of morphine and Fentanyl." A hospital administrator was there too, a middle-aged woman in a rumpled suit, looking worried—probably afraid, thought McParland, that Rachel would sue the hospital. "The patient failed to turn in the medication," explained the administrator, "contrary to the rules set out clearly in his signed admission form." She read from a handwritten report, adjusting her glasses. "The patient evidently did not understand that the patch delivery system is not immediately effective. He repeatedly dosed himself with patches on the underside of his body, where the nurses could not be expected to discover them. Apparently, the patient also used the intravenous pump to the maximum extent permitted. The result was that the patient entered a drug-induced stupor resembling deep sleep and suffered respiratory failure."

"Jimmy?"

McParland realized that he'd been staring out the window, unseeing. He blinked against the dazzle in his eyes.

"Sorry," he said. "Not enough sleep on the plane last night. Let's get these papers done." He turned to look for Betty in the outer office, and waved her back in. Rachel rose to leave. He plucked at her sleeve. "Could you wait while I sign the papers? I want to talk with you for a second."

"Sure," she said. "I'll get some coffee." She left him in the conference room while he and Betty finished up.

When he came out, they stepped outside together.

"My car's over here," said Rachel. They walked toward it.

McParland opened the driver's door but didn't step aside for her to get in.

"Could I ask you something?"

"Okay," she said, hesitantly.

McParland took a deep breath. "Would you marry me? Again?"

Rachel looked confused. "You mean—now?"

McParland looked embarrassed. "It's been more than a year since Bill died."

Rachel looked him squarely in the face. "I know that. And I know how much it would mean to Charlotte if we did. But I can't. I can't lie to you or anyone else again. I can't pretend to the world that I love you . . . like that."

McParland nodded slowly. "You and your damned principles. Do you really think that all married couples are in love? Maybe some are together because they like each other? Or . . ." He shook his head. "Never mind."

"Jimmy . . ." Rachel said, reaching for his shoulder.

"No," he said. "I knew the deal." He stepped back and held the car door for her. "I'll let you know about the San Francisco trip."

Rachel got into the car and started it. She put down the window and looked up at him. "You're a good man, James McParland. Your friend Sherlock would be proud." McParland cringed inwardly, thinking of what Holmes would have said to Bill in those final moments. *Your life is not your own.* He leaned down and kissed Rachel softly on the cheek. She put the car in gear and drove off.

McParland watched her go, savoring her words. *If Holmes could come back from the Reichenbach Falls three years after he supposedly died,* he thought, *then maybe nothing is really over until it's over. He wouldn't wait that long, though—he'd call her next week.* "See you 'round, kiddo," he said to himself. "The game's afoot."

HOW I CAME TO MEET SHERLOCK HOLMES

by Gahan Wilson

I must confess I do not remember the precise date I first came to meet Sherlock Holmes but I know it was back in the brewing days of World War Two. Hitler and his Nazis had been building their extraordinarily powerful killing and crushing machine for some time and I was a very young lad living with my parents in a pleasant apartment building in Evanston, Illinois which had a very spacious backyard/parking lot to serve the tenants' needs.

The building was full of families with young people such as myself, and we children played games enthusiastically and generally got along quite well with one another. I grew to be particularly fond of young, blonde Helen Stumph who lived in a tiny cottage at a corner of the lot close to the tiny alley which divided the block we lived on. She was the daughter of Matt Stumph who was the building's janitor. He was a big, burly fellow with a thick German accent and, in spite of his rather threatening appearance and lack of higher education, he was a very intelligent man. He and I had long, thoughtful and very interesting conversations, which very often centered on Germany and the highly unfortunate happenings going on there, and which alerted my young mind to the solid reality of human lives going on in these foreign climes. This in turn led to my taking books concerning foreign folk and their countries from the nearby public library, with great enthusiasm.

I found my interest very much taking the lead in those volumes concerning England and—once I was fortunate enough to stumble upon them—the delicious ones written by Arthur Conan Doyle concerning none other than his glorious creation Sherlock Holmes!

Another grand Holmesian I adventure I always delight in recalling (I notice I still get an actual thrill from remembering it!) took place aboard an elevated train riding the rails back to Evanston from an late night evening's entertainment in Chicago, as a full grown adult. I had settled in my seat and after several stops going through the center of that toddling town my eyes lazily wandered over the passengers—and then my body froze, and my jaw did not drop only from an enormous effort of will, because, sitting a mere five feet away with his deerstalker hat, a Victorian rain coat, and a look of hugely profound thought working a startling series of different expressions across his lean face, was Basil Rathbone as Sherlock Holmes!

We rode all the way to Howard Street, which divides Chicago from suburban Evanston. His face continued, in a stately way, to move from one thoughtfully profound expression to another, until he rose and exited. He stood on the platform, looking thoughtfully (for Moriarity?), and then he made his way into the darkness of the night.

I am a very fortunate fellow.

"I'M DELIGHTED TO TELL YOU YOUR STORIES HAVE
WONDERFULLY INCREASED MY CLIENTELE, WATSON!"

"I HAVE NEVER SEEN A CLEARER TRAIL TO A MURDERER!"

"I SUSPECT THAT ONLY YOU, WATSON, COULD HAVE TURNED THE HOUND OF THE BASKERVILLES INTO A PERFECT PET!"

ABOUT THE CONTRIBUTORS

LAURA CALDWELL is a former civil trial attorney, now a professor at Loyola University Chicago School of Law where she founded Life After Innocence. A published author of 14 novels and one nonfiction book, she says she finally understands Sherlock mania.

Her website is: www.lauracaldwell.com.

MICHAEL CONNELLY is a former *Los Angeles Times* crime reporter, whose first novel *Black Echo*, published in 1992, won the Edgar® for Best First Novel. His 25th novel was published in 2015, and his books have sold nearly 60 million copies. Michael served as President of the Mystery Writers of America, and his writing has won virtually every award in existence for the mystery genre. He is currently producing and writing the television series *Bosch*, based on his books. He counts the Sherlock Holmes stories to be among the earliest mystery stories he has read.

JEFFERY DEAVER. A former journalist, folksinger and attorney, Jeffery Deaver is an international number-one bestselling author. His novels have appeared on bestseller lists around the world, including the *New York Times*, the *Times of London*, Italy's *Corriere della Sera*, the *Sydney Morning Herald* and the *Los Angeles Times*. His books are sold in 150 countries and translated into 25 languages.

The author of thirty-three novels, two collections of short stories and a nonfiction law book, he's received or been shortlisted for a number of awards. His *The Bodies Left Behind* was named Novel of the Year by the International Thriller Writers Association, and his stand-alone novel *Edge* and his Lincoln Rhyme thriller *The Broken Window* were also nominated for that prize. He has been awarded the Steel Dagger and the Short Story Dagger from the British Crime Writers' Association and the Nero Wolfe Award, and he is a three-time recipient of the Ellery Queen Reader's Award for Best Short Story of the Year and a winner of the British Thumping Good Read Award.

Deaver's character, Lincoln Rhyme, the quadriplegic forensic detective, introduced in *The Bone Collector*, was largely inspired by Sherlock Holmes, who, the author has said, is the essential model for cerebral crime-solving protagonists.

Readers can visit his website at www.jefferydeaver.com.

MICHAEL DIRDA was invested into The Baker Street Irregulars in 2002 as "Langdale Pike." A Pulitzer Prize-winning book columnist for the *Washington Post*, he is the author, most recently, of *On Conan Doyle*, which received a 2012 Edgar Award from the Mystery Writers of America. His next book, *Browsings: A Year of Reading, Collecting and Living with Books*, will be published by Pegasus in 2015. This will be followed by a reappraisal of popular fiction during the late 19th and early 20th century, tentatively titled *The Great Age of Storytelling*. Please note that the revelations in "By Any Other Name" are, despite their shocking nature, just as genuine and historically accurate as Watson's meticulous accounts of the many investigations undertaken by Sherlock Holmes.

At age 80, after 68 years as a writer, having won hundreds of awards, with almost 2,000 published stories, columns of opinion, essays, film & TV scripts, and 102 volumes of storytelling, HARLAN ELLISON® has only this to say of himself: "For a while I was here; and for a while I mattered."

CORNELIA FUNKE met Les Klinger at the L.A. Book Festival, where he was signing his annotated version of Sherlock Holmes. As he didn't mind her German accent at all and the fact that she prefers to write for children, they became friends and have been ever since. Cornelia didn't know that one day her daughter would live on the same street in London as Conan Doyle once did (she walks past the plaque quite regularly) or that one day she would stumble over his gravestone in an English village. Of course the next step had to be writing a story that honored one of the most impressive characters who ever escaped the pages of a book. Cornelia has published more than 60 titles in about 40 languages and 70 countries, but there has rarely been a greater and more thrilling honor in her writer's life than Les asking her to write this story. She bows her head in gratitude—and hopes it won't be her last encounter with the glorious Sherlock Holmes (and in her eyes equally glorious Doctor Watson).

Her website is at www.corneliafunke.com

ANDREW GRANT was born 118 miles north of 221B Baker Street in May 1968. He honed his deductive skills at St. Albans school, Hertfordshire and later progressed to the University of Sheffield where he studied English Literature and Drama. After graduation Andrew set up and ran a small independent theater company which showcased a range of original material to local, regional and national audiences. Following a critically successful but financially challenging appearance at the Edinburgh Fringe Festival Andrew moved into the telecommunications industry as a "temporary" solution to a short-term cash crisis. Fifteen years later, after carrying out a variety of roles—including a number which were covered by the U.K. Official Secrets Act—Andrew escaped from corporate life, and established himself as the author of the critically-acclaimed David Trevellyan series of novels—*Even*, *Die Twice*, and *More Harm Than Good*. His latest book, the standalone thriller *RUN*, was published in October 2014.

Andrew is married to novelist Tasha Alexander, and lives in Chicago, IL.

Further information is available on his website: www.andrewgrantbooks.com.

DENISE HAMILTON. As a child, Denise Hamilton was so terrified by *The Hound of the Baskervilles* that she swore never to visit a crumbling English manor house or traverse the moors. Luckily, she spent a college semester in London, saw the error of her ways and traveled widely throughout the U.K.

After years as an *L.A. Times* reporter, Denise turned to crime fiction. Her novels have been finalists for the Edgar and Willa Cather awards. She also edited the Edgar-awarding winning *Los Angeles Noir* anthology and *Los Angeles Noir 2: The Classics*. Her latest novel, *Damage Control*, was praised by James Ellroy as "A superb psychological thriller." When not pondering new and interesting ways to kill people, she writes about perfume for the *L.A. Times*.

Visit her at www.denisehamilton.com.

NANCY HOLDER is a *New York Times* bestselling author (the Wicked Saga, co-authored with Debbie Viguié). She has written many horror and young adult dark fantasy novels and over two hundred short stories. Her award-winning "tie-in" work for TV shows and iconic figures includes *Buffy the Vampire Slayer*, *Teen Wolf*, *The Rocketeer*, *Zorro*, *Nancy Drew*, and *Hellboy*. She has received five Bram Stoker Awards from the Horror Writers Association and her novels have appeared on recommended lists from the American Library

Association, the American Reading Association, and the New York Public Library's Books for the Teen Age.

Her first Holmes encounter was watching *Sherlock Holmes and the Secret Weapon*, one of the Universal movies set during WWII, as a very young girl. It was shown on *Science Fiction Theater*. For several years thereafter, she thought that Holmes and Watson were Victorian time-travelers or had possibly had been reanimated to save England from the Nazis.

Leslie Klinger cleared up her confusion during a book event in Los Angeles, and next thing she knew, she had been invited to the Baker Street Irregulars' Sherlock Holmes birthday weekend dinner in New York. Since then, she has enjoyed the company of BSI's who have shown her their art collections and taken her on private walking tours of Holmes's London. With the enthusiastic assistance of the Trust, she has discovered that she is related to the very Holder family whom Holmes assisted in "The Adventure of the Beryl Coronet." Even more astounding, she has come into possession of Mary Holder's diary. A second story based on this ignoble ancestress's true-life exploits will appear in *Sherlock Holmes and Dr. What?* Nancy's next book is *The Rules*, a teen thriller, from Penguin Random House. She lives in San Diego, California with her daughter, Belle.

Her website is www.nancyholder.com.

LAURIE R. KING, an award-winning, bestselling crime writer, is best known for her Mary Russell-Sherlock Holmes series that began in 1994 with *The Beekeeper's Apprentice* and continues with *Dreaming Spies*. She also writes mainstream crime novels, including a new series (*Touchstone; The Bones of Paris*) set in approximately the same time and place as the Russell & Holmes stories, although those characters have yet to meet. King figures that this series is a good fall-back for when the Sherlockians worldwide catch on and rise up in horror at her temerity. In the meantime, she is still an invested member of the Baker Street Irregulars, known there as "The Red Circle."

King and Les Klinger have bonded over the antics of the residents of 221B Baker Street, although by now it is hard to know who drags whom into their joint projects.

More can be found at her website: www.LaurieRKing.com.

LESLIE S. KLINGER is the Edgar-winning editor of *The New Annotated Sherlock Holmes* and more than 25 other books. Proud to have been called "the world's first consulting Sherlockian," he lectures and writes extensively on Holmes, Dracula, and the Victorian age, while squeezing in a full-time law practice. Having previously confined his writing to footnotes, he is honored to be in the company of the authors presented in this volume.

More on Les at: www.lesliesklinger.com.

JOHN LESCROART is a *New York Times* bestselling author whose books, translated in more than twenty languages, have sold over ten million copies. John initially honed his Sherlockian interests in a series of formal Martha Hudson Dinners that he hosted during his twenties. His first hardcover book, *Son of Holmes*, posited the theory that Nero Wolfe (with the original alias of Auguste Lupa) was the son of Sherlock Holmes and Irene Adler. The sequel, *Rasputin's Revenge*, explored the connections between Moriarty, Rasputin, Sherlock Holmes, and Lupa in the closing months of World War I. John's short story, "The Adventure of the Giant Rat of Sumatra," was selected for inclusion in *The Best American Mystery Stories 1998* (edited by Sue Grafton).

LEAH MOORE AND JOHN REPPION are a husband and wife writing team based in Liverpool, U.K. Working together since 2003, the duo have written two full-length comic book mysteries starring the Great Detective and the Good Doctor—*The Trial of Sherlock Holmes* (2009), and *Sherlock Holmes—The Liverpool Demon* (2013). Holmes aside, Moore & Reppion have worked on projects as varied as adapting Bram Stoker's Gothic masterpiece *Dracula* into a graphic novel, and creating the innovative Channel 4 Education (U.K.) web-series *The Thrill Electric*.

They can be found at: www.moorereppion.com.

("The Problem of the Empty Slipper" was written by Leah Moore and John Reppion, with pencils by Chris Doherty, inks and lettering by Adam Cadwell.)

ADAM CADWELL is a cartoonist and storyboard artist based in Manchester, U.K. He is best known for his darkly comic Northern vampire series *Blood Blokes* and his autobiographical web-comic *The Everyday*. He is also the co-founder of the publishing group Great Beast and in 2012 founded the British Comic Awards. The film *Young Sherlock Holmes* terrified him as a child and he has never solved a mystery in his life. See more on Adam at: www.adamcadwell.com.

CHRIS DOHERTY is an illustrator based in Manchester, U.K. He wrote and illustrated the graphic novel *Video Nasties* (2011), and has done illustration and comics work for *Mirage Studios, Electric Sheep Online Magazine* and *Cinema Sewer*. He's relatively new to Holmes and is catching up on his reading.

SARA PARETSKY's entire idea of London is based on having read the Sherlock Holmes stories at an early age. It was a great disappointment on her first visit not to find hansom cabs still tooling the streets. When fog rolls in from Lake Michigan, shrouding the Chicago streets, she knows that "as you value your life and your reason, keep away from the moor." Paretsky's own detective, V. I. Warshawski, created through some twenty novels and collections of short stories, is an anti-Holmes, relying on instinct and psychology more than forensic evidence to solve crimes. Holmes was perhaps the ultimate response to the Victorian believe in human perfectibility through reason, while V.I., growing up in the nuclear, post-Shoah world, believes there's always a psychopath lurking around a corner, prepared to kill us all because he thinks he's been dissed. What V.I. and Holmes share is a restlessness that leads them to plunge into action—in V.I.'s case, it's left her nearly dead in a swamp, trapped in a burning building, flung from the top of a high rise, and nearly drowned at sea. If she isn't as brilliant a deductive reasoner as Holmes, she's far more physically resilient.

For more about Paretsky or Warshawski, go to www.saraparetsky.com.

MICHAEL SIMS is the author of acclaimed nonfiction books such as *The Adventures of Henry Thoreau* and *The Story of Charlotte's Web*. He has written about Sherlock Holmes in his own books as well as in some of the numerous anthologies he has edited, especially *The Dead Witness* in his Connoisseur's Collection series for Bloomsbury. He has been the Distinguished Speaker at the annual meeting of the Baker Street Irregulars and is currently writing a book about the real people in the life of Arthur Conan Doyle who inspired the creation of Sherlock Holmes.

Michael's web site is: www.michaelsimsbooks.com.

GAHAN WILSON is an American author, cartoonist, and illustrator. His cartoons (usually featuring lovingly horrific monsters) and prose fiction have appeared regularly in *Playboy,* the *New Yorker,* and *Collier's* for over fifty years. He has drawn numerous cartoons depicting Holmes and Watson, and his 1998 novel *Everybody's Favorite Duck* featured the detective Enoch Bone and his companion John Weston. Gahan received Lifetime Achievement awards from the World Fantasy Convention and the National Cartoonists Association in 2005.

ACKNOWLEDGMENTS

Without the perseverance, skill, sound advice, and patience of our attorneys Jonathan Kirsch and Scott Gilbert and their colleagues, the book would have never been published. They were aided by some exceptional volunteers, Prof. Betsy Rosenblatt and Darlene Cypser, Esq., who added much to the legal arguments. Our friends and "expert witnesses" Peter Blau and Steve Rothman went out of their way to assist because they believed in our case. The estimable Zoë Elkaim put in an extraordinary effort keeping the www.free-sherlock.com website up to date, on holidays, birthdays, and while in labor. Les's wife Sharon never blinked at the time and cost of the endeavor, and cheered all along the way. And there were many others who donated money or enthusiasm or publicity to the effort—we're happy that we were able to bring it to fruition.

Thanks too are due to agent Don Maass, who helped us through some unusual dealings; our courageous publisher Claiborne Hancock, who believed in us even in the darkest times; and of course family, friends, and perhaps most of all, our very, very patient contributors—many of whom said "yes" back in 2012 when it all sounded so simple, created their little masterpieces, and then had to wait and wait!

Deepest thanks to all, without whom this book would not exist.

L & L

SUPPLEMENTAL COPYRIGHT PAGE